D1551746

MOLOKA'I NUI AHINA

Summers on the Lonely Isle

Also by Kirby Wright

Before the City

Punahou Blues

KIRBY WRIGHT

MOLOKA'I NUI AHINA

Summers on the Lonely Isle

LEMON SHARK
PRESS

Published by Lemon Shark Press
San Diego, California
www.lemonsharkpress.com

ISBN 978-0-9741067-2-4

Library of Congress Control Number: 2006939229

Copyright © 2007 by Kirby Wright
All Rights Reserved

Publisher's Note
This is a work of fiction. Names, characters, places, and incidents either
are the product of the author's imagination or are used fictitiously,
and any resemblance to actual persons, living or dead, events, or locales
is entirely coincidental.

Without limiting the rights under copyright reserved above, no part of
this publication may be reproduced, stored in or introduced into a
retrieval system, or transmitted, in any form or by any means (electronic,
mechanical, photocopying, recording or otherwise), without the prior
written permission of both the copyright owner and the above publisher
of this book.

Chapters have previously appeared in slightly different form in *Alsop
Review*, *The Arabesques Review*, *Chaminade Literary Review*, *Cortland Review*,
Hawai'i Review, *Liberty*, *Melic Review*, *River City*, *San Jose Studies*, *Three
Candles*, *To Be Read Aloud*, and *Trout Journal*.

Note to pidgin English aficionados: the characters Julia and Chipper
Daniels speak the pidgin English of Moloka'i paniolos. Jeff and Ben
Gill speak both English and pidgin English; they use pidgin English
whenever the mood strikes them.

Printed in the United States of America
Set in Palatino
First Edition

In Memory of my Grandmother

Contents

Prologue

*M*y Irish mother was blessed with optimism. She believed in fate, blind luck, and the idea you could achieve anything if you loved doing it. The cup was half full. She loved to sing and dance and was convinced she would someday star in a Broadway musical. This dream remained despite my father's chidings it would never happen. Her dream would never die because it had become a life preserver that buoyed her spirits whenever she felt she was drowning in the responsibilities of marriage and motherhood. When I was three, she took me out to our driveway in Honolulu and pointed at the rising sun. "That's where I'm going," she said and tap-danced on the blacktop. I did my best to keep up. I was sure we were helping the sun break over the coconut trees on Aukai Avenue. Passing cars honked. My hapa haole father ran out and told us to get the hell back inside before he phoned the pupule house in Kaneohe.

My mother was the first postwar Miss Massachusetts, a statuesque blonde who wowed the Faneuil Hall judges with her

song and tap interpretation of Cole Porter's "Begin the Beguine."
I grew up believing she was touched by magic, having witnessed
her win every contest on our first and only cruise to Disneyland,
from Best Muumuu to Best Hat & Gown to first place in the Talent
Show for her rendition of Al Jolson's "California, Here I Come."
Admirers sent champagne to our cabin. We had hors d'oeuvres
with the heirs to the Clorox fortune and dined at the captain's
table. When the first mate suggested my mother accompany
him to a matinee of *Splendor in the Grass*, my father told him to
back off before he got a fat lip. A black steward called Ben and
me "The Last of the Mohicans" upon discovering we'd used the
bathroom sink for number two. Even though our cabin was not
equipped with a latrine, my mother used the comment to gain
her freedom.

"That steward had a point, Dear," my mother said upon
our return from Disneyland.

"Point about what, Mary?" asked my father.

"The boys are Mohicans."

"They wouldn't be Mohicans if you disciplined them once
in a while."

"Discipline or not, they're wearing me down."

"I'll fix their wagons," he said.

Ben and I were banished to Moloka'i, where we spent
the rest of that summer with my father's mother, a no-nonsense
woman from Honolulu who'd adapted to the rigors of country
life. My father knew if anyone could tame his kolohe sons it
would be her. One of his earliest memories was watching his
mother rope cows on the beach at Puko'o Harbor. She'd drag
the cows out one by one until the horse beneath her was

swimming and pulling a tethered cow. A ship anchored in the harbor dropped its winch. Two Hawaiian men treading water secured a girth around the cow's belly while she returned to shore to rope another. Sharks came from the deep water. Most lost interest after the cows were hoisted into the air but a tiger shark went for her horse.

That's when she pulled her rifle.

Book One
Tsunami

Gramma

Moloka'i's rugged hump looms east of Oahu. No beaches or hotels are visible. Splotches of red earth seem like wounds on the island. There are few lights on Moloka'i at night and it makes you think only a few live there and that they don't want visitors. Captain James Cook of the *HMS Discovery* avoided Moloka'i because of the fortress-like sea cliffs along its northern shore and a barrier reef protecting its southern coast. There were stories of cannibals and rumors the waters were infested with leviathans that could crack a ship's hull like a coconut.

Julia Daniels, my grandmother, settled on Moloka'i with her third lover and first try at marriage. She told me about crossing the channel in a steamer from Honolulu. Chipper Daniels stood next to her wearing his buckskin jacket and cowboy hat. They had matching gold bands. She liked placing her hand over his to make the rings touch. She was superstitious and looked for signs of their future—she saw sharks attacking a whale marooned on a lava pinnacle. "Dey havin' one big kine luau," the Portuguese skipper said. Despite this bad omen, Julia was determined to make her marriage work. She'd lost at love twice already and didn't want to lose again. Her love affairs had produced two keiki manuahi: my father and his half-brother. Chipper hated her boys but he didn't want to risk losing Julia. He compromised by letting them spend summers at his ranch on the east end.

*   *   *

My father perpetuated the cycle of summer visits by sending Ben and me over every June. He figured that, since he hadn't been raised by his mother, the least she could do was tolerate her grandsons three months of the year. As a four-year-old, I sat in the window seat of a Hawaiian Airlines twin-prop. Ben sat beside me. I admired the Lego-like construction of Waikiki. Then came the deep blues of the channel separating Oahu from Moloka'i. It was the first summer of the Sixties and, although I already missed my parents, my adventurous heart kept any homesick feelings at bay. We flew over miles of red dirt and landed on a desolate strip. A man pushed a staircase on wheels to our plane and it was time to disembark. I was eager to meet my grandmother. Her last visit to Oahu was before I was born but I had seen a picture of her sitting on a blond man's lap. She wore a dress and he had on a white suit.

I crossed the tarmac with Ben. A lady stood behind a cyclone fence—she wore a lauhala hat, a palaka blouse, and jeans. Her face was a road map of wrinkles. Her thin lips and stern expression reminded me of the witch in *Hanzel and Gretel*.

"Mistah Ben and Jeffrey," the lady called, "come see yo'

Gramma."

We made our way through the gate. Gramma struck a match against a tiny wooden box and lit up a cigarette. "You keeds are right on time," she said. Her face was white and her dark eyes slanted. The wrinkles in her cheeks went deep—I was certain they hurt. She wasn't the girl in the picture. She sucked at her cigarette and blew smoke through her nose.

"Are you sure you're my grandmother?" I asked.

" 'Course I'm shuah. Who the hell else would I be?"

"The bogeyman's wife," Ben said.

She dropped her cigarette. "Fo' the luva Pete," she said grinding out the cigarette with the heel of her boot.

We claimed our suitcases and she led the way to the parking lot. Ben and I shared the passenger seat of an olive green jeep with a canvas top. Gramma drove a road skirting the pineapple fields. She held the steering wheel between her knees, lit another cigarette, and said we didn't look like brothers. Ben had our mother's blond hair and green eyes. I had the brown hair and eyes of our father.

"Can you keeds tie yo' shoes?" she asked.

I looked at Ben and we nodded.

"Can you shovel?"

We shook our heads.

"You'll learn," she promised.

*   *   *

The beach house was a dark gray home perched on stilts at the edge of the channel. Its sloping roof reminded me of a Chinaman's hat. Gramma said it had survived a tsunami. "Full of sand, limu, and fish," she told us, "but still standin'." It had one bedroom, one bath, a kitchen, and a big room that doubled as a living and dining room. The big room's picture window framed the pasture, the mountain, and a sliver of sky. The walls were painted creamy white. A screen door led to a lanai with forest green walls and rafters.

The beach house was decorated with a mix of Asian art and gifts from the ocean, everything from Chinese brush paintings to green glass balls that had broken free of their nets in the Sea of Japan. Deer heads were mounted on the walls of the lanai and a cane table displayed conch shells, poi pounders, and ulu maikas. Wooden storm windows on the lanai could be swung open and suspended on hooks attached to the ceiling. When the windows were open, the trades flooded the house with the clean salty smell of the channel.

Gramma served corned beef hash over rice our first night. We ate off chipped plates at a table with one side wedged against the picture window. After dinner, we watched *Hawaiian Eye*. "Time to hit the bunk," she said when the show ended. Ben and I put on our pajamas. She had pjs too. We slept in the big room on a pune'e. Gramma had the outside and Ben had the wall. I was in the middle. My brother talked in his sleep while my grandmother snored. I heard footsteps outside and saw a hand crawling the window above the pune'e.

"Brownie," a big head said as the hand banged the glass. The head had a skinny body. The moonlight struck its face—it was a man with deep-set eyes and a jaw like Captain Hook. "Ran off da bridge at Puko'o, Brownie," he said. "You gotta tow me out."

"Go home, Uncle Chipper, go home!" Gramma had us

say. Fear turned Ben and me into a pleading chorus. He finally stumbled off, his form absorbed in a sea of shadows.

She pulled on her jeans in the moonlight.

"Whacha doing?" Ben asked.

She slid a bolt, opened a wooden door, and then a screen door. She held a coil of rope. "Don't let a soul in," she said. "Goin' to help yo' Uncle Chippah."

The doors closed. The jeep roared to life and beams of light sliced through the darkness. Ben and I knelt on the pune'e and watched the lights cut deep paths into the flatlands.

"Who's Uncle Chipper?" I asked.

"Her old husband," he said.

"Where does he live?"

"In the swamp."

"Where's the man in the white suit?"

"On the moon," he answered.

We went back to bed and he fell asleep. I tossed and turned on the pune'e until the wooden door swung open and Gramma got into bed. I fidgeted between her and Ben.

"Quit kickin'," she told me.

"I can't sleep."

"Count some bloody sheep."

I reached for my pillow and accidentally smacked her face. She switched on a standing lamp and popped out her teeth. I was amazed that this old woman had the power to unlock body parts. Ben woke up and we started crying. She said the teeth had a mind of their own and they'd chew us up if we didn't "get some shut eye."

*   *   *

The cries of roosters woke me. Ben slept through the racket until Gramma said, "Rise and shine!" My brother said he wasn't finished sleeping and she told him to get up before she whacked his okole with her bamboo stick. He used the bathroom first and then it was my turn. We pulled T-shirts and jeans off big fishhooks attached to the wall. The sharp points and barbs had been filed off and we each had our own hook. I didn't want my grandmother to know I couldn't tie my Keds so I promised Ben a penny a day to tie them. He held out his hand.

"I'll pay up in Honolulu," I said.

"Okay," he replied, "but I want interest."

"What's that?"

"Extra money for not paying up on time."

"Can you tie them now?"

"After breakfast," he said.

Ben was the Thief of Wishes. On Oahu, he would leave our table at Pat's at Punalu'u to go wading for coins in their wishing well. He returned to the table stinking of algae but with a bulge in his pocket and a smile on his face. I wondered what happened to the wishes when the money wished on was stolen.

"Hui," Gramma called from the kitchen, "you keeds get in hea."

We walked across mustard-colored linoleum into a narrow kitchen. The walls were pale yellow. Gramma was hunched over a skillet frying bacon. The paint was shiny behind the stove where grease had splattered it. There was a screen window above the sink but I was too short to look out. She cracked an egg on the skillet's side and dropped it in the hot grease. It popped and crackled. The smell made me sick to my stomach.

"Sit down," she said nodding at a stainless steel counter.

Ben sat on a chair beside the wall and I pulled out the stool attached to the counter. Termite droppings looked like black sand on the steel. Forks rested on paper napkins. A bottle of Kikoman Soy Sauce, a jar of Hawaiian rock salt, and a bowl of red chili peppers sat in a tray. A black phone hung off the wall. An Ancient Hawaiian Moon Calendar tacked next to the phone noted the best days to fish and plant.

"Sunny side up or down?" she asked.

"Sunny side what?" asked Ben.

She frowned. "Doesn't yo' muthah cook you eggs?"

We shook our heads.

"Wot you eat fo' breakfast?"

"Frosted Flakes," he said.

I raised my fork. "Sugar Pops!"

"Yo' not gettin' that up hea."

"You can buy it anywhere," he told her.

"I'm not feedin' you sissy crap," she said. "When you come to Molokaʻi, you eat wot men eat." She lifted the eggs with a spatula, plopped them on blue plastic plates, and slid a plate in front of each of us. Bacon and buttered toast followed. The fat on the bacon sizzled and the toast was burnt. "This is a paniolo breakfast," she said.

"Any jam?" Ben asked.

"Buttah's planny. Yo' damn lucky to get buttah."

"Guava jelly?" I pressed.

She winced. "Go on," she said, "feed yo' faces."

I picked up my fork and poked the yellow. It oozed and

spread to the crusty edges of the white.

"When I get back," she said, "those eggs bettah be gone."
She left the kitchen—her cowboy boots clippity-clopped away.

"Smells like kukae," Ben decided. He slipped his egg in
the pocket of his jeans. "Yummy," he said and nibbled a strip of
bacon.

I picked up my egg and stuffed it in my pocket. "Can
you tie my shoes?" I asked.

He patted his thigh. I swung my feet up and rested my
Keds on his lap. He started tying. Boots clippity-clopped toward
us.

"Hurry," I said.

He finished and I swung my legs down.

Gramma walked into the kitchen, put her hands on her
hips, and examined our plates. "Pau?"

We nodded.

"Wot about that toast? You keeds don't eat toast?"

"No," he said.

"Want Gramma fix you mo' eggs? Got planny grease."

Ben rubbed his belly. "I'm stuffed."

"Me too," I said.

She plopped on her lauhala hat. "Hana hana time."

We followed her out the front door. A poi dog was lying
under a hala tree. Gramma told us his name was Skippy and
that he had German Shepherd blood. I was scared he might bite
so I didn't pat him. We walked down a knoll to a blue
wheelbarrow with a red-handled shovel resting in its bucket.

"I need one strong boy," she said.

Ben gripped the handles and pushed the wheelbarrow.

She led us to a tree with branches reaching into the clouds. It was as tall as the tree in *Jack and the Beanstalk*.

"Wot kind of tree is this?" she asked.

"A Christmas tree," Ben said.

"It's a Norfolk. Planted it thirty years ago."

"A giant lives at the top," I said.

"Ridiculous," she replied.

We reached a dirt road fenced in on its mauka side. She swung open a wooden gate and shut it behind us. The pasture was covered with pili grass and kuku weeds. There were lemon and lime trees and a bathtub with a dripping faucet.

"This way," she said pointing at five horses nibbling grass. They flicked their tails as they ate. A brown horse with watery eyes ambled over. "This is Ol' Sissy," she said holding out her hand. Sissy sniffed it and she patted her forehead. "Good girl."

"Which one's a boy horse?" I asked her.

"Don't got any. They're all mares."

"How come?"

"Stallions are nothin' but trouble."

We continued on through the pasture. Gramma had Ben park the wheelbarrow beside a pile of horse manure. "Each boy fill one wheelbarrow," she said.

"Stinks," Ben said.

"Pee-U," I added.

"It's only grass," she said, "you damn sissies."

Ben pulled out the shovel and sunk in the blade. He lifted the manure and flies buzzed around it. He dropped the load in the wheelbarrow and went for another.

"When that's full," she said, "wheel it to the gate." She walked to the tub and turned the faucet on full blast.

Ben finished the pile in three scoops. He pushed the wheelbarrow to the next pile and dug the shovel in. Gramma turned the water off and headed to the fence. She ducked through the wires and walked the dirt road to a garden beside the Norfolk. Ben kept shoveling. He was dripping sweat when he handed me the shovel. He wheeled his load to the gate and she opened it. He followed her to the garden, tipped the wheelbarrow, and the load spilled out. He pushed the wheelbarrow to the pasture and set it down in front of me.

"Weakling's turn," he said.

"I'm not weak."

He picked up a rock and threw it at Old Sissy—it flew over her head and she trotted off.

"I'll tell," I warned.

"Tattle tale," Ben said and ran across the pasture.

I searched for manure. The fresh piles were greenish-brown and fluffy. The old piles were dark brown and flat as pancakes. I found a fresh one near the mares. I dug the blade in, lifted, and dropped the shovel. The manure went flying. I swept the manure into a pile and shoveled it in. I returned to the pile, stabbed it with the blade, and lifted. I held the handle tight and flipped the load in. A vanilla mare trotted by and stopped to drink from the tub. I found fresh piles and kept going until the wheelbarrow was full. Sweat poured down my cheeks. The wheelbarrow was heavy and it nearly tipped when the wheel hit a root. Ben opened the gate and I pushed my load through. Gramma was watering her garden. The plot was long and narrow and it ran from the Norfolk to a patch of wild ginger. There were green onions, bok choy, tomatoes, and rows of lettuce.

"Dump it in mah flowah garden," she said.

"Where?" I asked.

"Beside the beach house," she explained. "Ben, help yo' li'l bruthah."

I pushed the wheelbarrow past the Norfolk and up the incline. Ben grabbed the front and pulled the wheelbarrow toward the flowers. We tipped it over beside a bed of white tuberoses and purple orchids.

Gramma finished weeding and made her way up the knoll. Her boots were caked with mud. "Good boys," she said. She told Ben to go to the lanai and get her tackle box, scoop net, and two bamboo poles. He scampered around the beach house.

"Where do we fish?" I asked her.

"Down by Chippah's."

"The bogeyman?"

"Chippah's no bogeyman. Now show me you can tie yo' shoes."

I looked down at my Keds. The knots had come loose and kuku burrs stuck to the laces. "I'll tie 'em later," I said.

"Tie 'um now."

I knelt down and plucked off the kukus. I made loops with the laces and secured them with a pretend knot.

She frowned. "Yo' bruthah's been tyin' 'um fo' you, hasn't he."

"No."

"Don't lie to me."

Ben returned with the poles, a red scoop net, and a green

tackle box. "Let's go!" he said.

"Hold yo' horses," she replied. She showed me the starting knot. She showed me how to make a loop with one end, wrap the other end around it, and pull the loop through. She had me untie it and do it again on my own. I tied my Keds and she said, "Let's go fishin'."

We walked the dirt road. The road ended at an ironwood tree. A yellow house appeared and Gramma said Uncle Chipper lived there. Undershirts and BVDs hung on a clothesline. A mangrove forest behind the house blotted out the sun. She led us through the mangrove to a swamp and said our bait was hiding in the long blades of swamp grass growing underwater. Ben dragged the scoop net through the swamp grass and caught 'opae. She dropped them in a Folgers Coffee can full of water. She pulled 'opae from the can and handed us each one.

"Run yo' hook between the head and body," she told us.

My 'opae kicked with its tail trying to get away—I missed with the hook and stabbed my finger. Ben climbed the bank. He held his pole over the murky water while I threaded my hook through the 'opae. The barb set and I dropped the bait in the swamp. My line had two lead weights the size of peas. Silver flashed in the water. I felt nibbles moving through the pole.

"What's in the water?" I asked.

"Aholehole," Gramma said.

I had blisters from shoveling and my fingers hurt holding the pole. I moved closer to the edge.

"Not too far," she warned, "aholehole won't strike if they see you."

I couldn't tell if the swamp was deep. The mangrove

had roots that grew above ground and reached into the water. The branches of the mangrove were filled with glistening webs. Spiders with yellow bodies and black legs waited for bugs.

"Those spiders are fat," I said.

"Shuah fat," she said, "they eat anythin' that flies."

"Even birds?"

"Silly business," she replied and lit a cigarette.

A mosquito landed on my arm. Swatting it might disturb my bait so I let it suck my blood. Ben caught his first aholehole and a second. I dangled my bait closer to his spot and pretended I was a fish. My body was made of silver and I circled the 'opae with my silvery friends. It was an underwater luau.

The tip of my pole jerked. I pulled hard—an aholehole flew over my head, broke free of the hook, and landed in the mangrove. I heard it flapping so I crawled through the dead leaves and roots.

Gramma puffed her cigarette. "Don't be diggin' around in those god damn roots," she said with a smoky mouth.

"Why not?"

"Centipedes live theah."

I gave up finding the fish. I figured it had flapped itself down the rooted bank into the water. I imagined it warning all the swamp creatures about the two boys with the poles and the old smoking woman.

*   *   *

Gramma made us eggs every morning. We stuffed them in our pockets the second she left the kitchen. When it was my turn to shovel, I picked shiny black beetles out of the manure and stuck them in with the eggs. But, when the time came to wash my jeans, I'd forgotten to unload everything.

"Fo' chrissakes," Gramma said from the wash room while I pushed the wheelbarrow.

Ben and I flipped the wheelbarrow in the flower garden and out tumbled the manure.

"Damn these keeds!"

We ran to the wash room and peeked through the space between the double doors—Gramma was emptying my pockets. The linings were yellow and beetles fell out with the eggs. She squashed them against the cement floor with her boots. The squashing sounded like tap-dancing. "They're gettin' it, believe me, Al!"

"Uh, oh, Spaghetti-Os," Ben said.

"Let's go fishing," I said.

We scampered to the lanai, snatched our bamboo poles, and high-tailed it for the swamp.

                    *   *   *

Gramma wasn't always getting mad at us. There were times we enjoyed each other's company, especially when we gossiped about our parents. She loved hearing about their fights in Honolulu. She brewed tea and asked for "the latest." Ben and I did our best to describe the battles. I told her our father yelled at our mother for spilling his milk and that she found a hammer and chased him around the dining room table. Gramma laughed so hard that it triggered a coughing fit. She said that my father, as a boy, would tell everyone about her fights with Chipper and now he was getting a taste of his own medicine. "Serves 'um right," she told us. Ben said our mother had locked our father out on Halloween night and that he acted like a

Frankenstein monster busting louvers trying to get in. Gramma rewarded us with cups of cocoa. She made the cocoa extra special by dropping in a marshmallow. She played old time music on a black transistor radio and danced across the room with an imaginary partner. We took turns dancing with her. She was light on her feet and had a great sense of rhythm. She taught us the fox trot, the waltz, and even the Charleston. She told us she'd danced with Alan Ladd in the ballroom of the Young Hotel in Honolulu. I didn't know who Alan Ladd was until she told me he'd played the lead in *Shane*.

"Why didn't you marry Shane?" I asked.

"He was already married," she replied.

"Why'd you marry the bogeyman?" Ben asked.

" 'Cause I loved 'um," she said.

My brother got so good at the Charleston that Gramma told him he should enter a contest. She told us our great grandmother had been a hula dancer in the court of King Kalakaua and that we had dancing in our blood.

"My mother says I've got Saint Vitus' dance," Ben said.

She frowned. "Wot the hell's that?"

He herky jerked across the floor and shook his body as though being shocked.

"Fo' chrissakes, that's not dancin'."

"It's Irish," I piped up.

"Irish, Irish, Irish," she said, "why don't they all go back to Ireland?"

Ben quit shaking and took a swig of cocoa.

"What was our grandfather like?" I asked her.

"Wot you know about 'um?"

"He was from England and his name was Norman Wilkins."

"Who told you?"

"My mother."

"Yo' muthah's gotta big mouth."

"Was he nice?" Ben asked.

Gramma said she was fourteen and dancing a Zeigfield Follies act with her sister Sue at Ala Park the day his ship steamed in and docked at Aloha Tower. He disembarked and wandered over to the park in his white linen suit and clapped as she high kicked in her can-can petticoat. He wasn't alone. His big brother Fergus was with him. The song ended and he complimented her and asked where he might find a glass of coconut milk. She had never heard an English accent. He was tall and thin and his blond hair reminded her of the manes of the prized Palamino stallions she'd seen at the polo matches on the North Shore. He smelled like lilacs, sweet lilacs from fields overseas where days were cool and birds sang enchanting songs. He was a pretty boy but there was nothing vain in his manner. He was a perfect gentleman and he told her she put the London girls to shame. She listened to his melodic voice while his brother flirted with Sue.

*   *   *

My mother rarely visited us on Moloka'i. If she did, it was just for a weekend. She was a city girl who found country life crude and uncivilized. She also resented Gramma for never remembering her birthday. That slight, combined with the rural setting, made Moloka'i unbearable for my mother. She stayed in the bedroom with my father while Gramma slept on the pune'e with Ben and me. My mother complained about my father's snoring, chirping geckos, and crowing roosters. She hated hiking, fishing, and swimming. She said the sun was too strong and that the smell of manure gave her a headache. Her idea of roughing it was eating egg salad sandwiches on park benches while swan boats glided by on the Charles River. Moloka'i brought out the worst in her. She told me the island was full of dark, uneducated people. "No wonder they put a leper colony there," she said.

Ben hated it whenever our mother came up. He didn't mind so much that she disliked the island—what got him mad was how she pretended to like the ranch. He punished her by throwing bufos at her whenever our father wasn't nearby. She always screamed and threatened to tell.

"Yo' muthah's red as a bloody lobstah," Gramma said watching my parents stroll along the beach.

"She orders lobster at Fisherman's Wharf," Ben said.

Gramma winced. "I'll bet."

"She loves buying dresses," I added.

"Shuah," she said, "spendin' all yo' pua fathah's money."

"She calls you 'that ignorant woman,' " Ben told her.

"Yo' muthah's a big lazy horse," she replied.

Gramma knew there was nothing special about her son's marriage. She figured my mother only liked him because he was a good provider. His melancholy eyes and thin jaw reminded her of Wilkins. Wahines had always thought he was handsome but there was so much hurt in him from being raised hanai that they sometimes misinterpreted his brooding nature as a sign he wasn't interested.

*   *   *

My mother tested Gramma's stamina by sending Ben and me over for an Easter vacation. We arrived at Hoolehua Airport wearing matching pink suits and swinging Easter baskets.

Ben raced me across the tarmac. "Gramma, Gramma," he said, "look what the Easter Bunny brought me!"

"No such thing as the damn Easta Bunny," she said.

"Is so," he replied, "he lives at Ala Moana."

"And if you're nice like us," I told her, "he brings you chocolate and marshmallow eggs."

"Oh, he does, does he?"

"Yes, but only if you're nice."

She shook her head. "Who in hell dressed you keeds?"

"Mummy!" we said.

"Buncha god damn sissies."

Ben swung his basket defiantly. "I'm telling Mummy you swore."

"Tell, nothin'," she said, "yo' damn Mummy's across the bloody channel."

We got in the jeep and Gramma sped through the pineapple fields. She braked suddenly and made us get out. We picked pineapple after pineapple, until our pink suits were stained with red dirt. The jagged leaves of the plants cut my hands. Before we left, she flung our Easter baskets into the opposite field. When we got to the ranch she had us shovel manure and wheelbarrow in those same suits until the seams split. She told us to stuff all our pockets with dung beetles. She never washed the suits. Instead, she packed them in a box that she sealed with duct tape. Ben presented my mother with the box upon our return to Honolulu. She opened it and the smell nearly knocked her over. A note read "Dear Mary, if you know what's good for you, quit dressing your sons up like girls."

Horses

*T*hat was the first and last Easter we spent on Moloka'i. My mother called the Boxed Suits Incident "a dirty trick" but she wasn't about to confront her mother-in-law. Summer was fast approaching and, although we'd already spent three summers under Gramma's supervision, she thought complaining might revoke our visiting privileges. But my grandmother was anxious to have us return—she considered my mother a spoiled, lazy girl who'd turn her sons into spoiled, lazy boys.

*   *   *

My father started visiting without my mother. He'd grown tired of her complaining that the ranch was his "mistress" and she was "just along for the ride." He flew over on the Fourth of July weekend and hired a stallion for Fizz, a thin gray mare with a nervous disposition. He'd decided to breed her after she bucked him off and caused him to pinch a nerve in his neck. My father hated it when people and animals didn't do what he

26

wanted. He was a trial attorney who'd lost only one case and nothing disturbed him more than anyone or anything that did not obey his rules. Fizz wasn't productive in one way so he vowed to make her productive in another.

Fizz had been a loner in the big pasture bordering Kam Highway. She'd never made friends with the other mares and survived on a patch of centipede grass growing near the mauka fence. She was new to the ranch and Old Sissy kicked her whenever she came close. Fizz's exile from the herd upset Gramma. She put her in the lot next to the beach house and kept an eye on her from the kitchen window.

*　　*　　*

I stood at the gate to Fizz's lot watching a blue horse trailer back up on the dirt road. The morning was hot and humid. Blood flies swarmed.

My father walked the fence line in a moth-eaten undershirt, khaki shorts, and a lauhala cowboy hat too big for his head. He had thin lips, a broad nose, and a ruddy complexion. His cheeks were dark with stubble. He never shaved on Moloka'i and my mother called this behavior "going native." His horn-rimmed glasses made him look like he was plotting his next move. He had furrows on his forehead and worry lines above the bridge of his glasses. He'd joined the Army the day after the Japanese bombed Pearl Harbor and got stabbed in combat during the Marshalls Campaign. He'd said the only good thing to come from the war was going to Harvard on the GI Bill. He swung the gate open and stepped in a pile of manure. "Cheesus Christ," he said and took off his leather sandal.

The trailer entered the lot. The stallion's black nostrils

flared against a breathing hole.

"Let 'im loose, Mendoza," my father said.

Mendoza, a stocky Portuguese man, pulled down a ramp and unhitched the trailer door. A gold stallion charged out—he had a huge head and muscular flanks. He sniffed the grass and kicked at it with a hoof. His mane was cropped and braided.

My father studied his watch. "Give 'em 'til dusk," he said.

Mendoza spat. "Ten dollah mo'."

"Paid you planny," my father groused.

He climbed into his red truck and the trailer moved out.

My father secured the gate and told me to get behind the fence with him. He scraped the manure off his sandal with a stick. "You should be with Ben," he said.

"I wanna be with you."

"Suit yourself."

"Daddy?"

"What."

"Will Gramma ever marry again?"

"She's too old for that."

"Can't old people get married and have fun?"

"Your grandmother's had more than her share of fun," he answered.

Fizz was grazing and the stallion galloped over. He sniffed her tail, mounted her from behind, and clawed her with his front hooves. The stallion's flanks sweated as he balanced.

"What are they doing, Daddy?"

"Fighting," he said. He untied and retied the two ends of laundry cord holding on his hat.

Fizz whinnied and tried bucking the stallion off. She bucked so hard that she farted.

"He's hurting her!" I said.

"Let 'em fight."

Ben marched toward us in his T-shirt and trunks. A BB rifle rested against his shoulder. The gun had been a birthday gift from our father. Our mother said there should be a law against a boy in the third grade having such a dangerous weapon. He was bored shooting coconuts and was on the prowl for moving targets. He loved it when things ran or flew away from him and he had a chance to end their lives. Two poi pups tagged after him. The pups were males and they'd wandered onto the ranch skeleton thin on Christmas day. Leo was rust colored; Spotty was black with white spots. Gramma pulled ticks off them every Sunday and dropped the ticks into a pickle jar filled with kerosene.

"See any doves?" Ben asked me.

"Only storm birds."

"They're too big to kill," he said and aimed his rifle at the horses.

"Put that gun down," our father said.

He lowered the rifle and cradled it in his arms.

"You boys leave Fizz alone."

Ben made the "Kiss My Ass" sign behind our father's back. "They're not really fighting," he whispered.

"Duh," I replied.

Leo whined for attention. Ben put his gun in the wheelbarrow and knelt down. He gripped Leo's snout, blew into his nose, and Leo wagged his tail. "You're a cute li'l honay," he said.

A mare in the big pasture neighed and the others joined in. There was a chorus of whinnies. The stallion climbed off Fizz and galloped for the fence. My father pulled off his hat and tried shooing him back but the stallion flew over the top wire.

"God damn that Mendoza!" he said and ran to the beach house.

Ben grabbed his rifle and we chased after the stallion. We watched him trot over to the garden and munch orchids. Ribbons of saliva hung from his mouth. The poi pups barked. Skippy crawled out from under the house and snarled. The stallion galloped off.

My grandmother opened the screen door wearing a green blouse, jeans, and her lauhala hat. She hustled over to her jeep.

"The stallion's loose!" Ben said waving his rifle.

She eased into the driver's seat and unwrapped a fresh pack of Chesterfields. The tobacco smelled good. "Get rid of that damn gun," she said, "and get in the jeep."

"How come?" he asked.

"So you won't get trampled, that's how come."

The screen door slammed and my father raced over the lawn.

"Where's Daddy going?" I asked her.

"The saddle room."

"What for?" Ben pestered.

"The lasso," she said. "Now get in and pa'a the waha."

I climbed into the back of the jeep. The cushions had rotted away so I had to sit on rusty springs. Ben leaned his rifle against the trunk of a hala tree and hopped into the passenger seat. We watched the stallion run through the oleanders. Blossoms fell like snow. He jumped the fence to the pasture and it became a circus, with the stallion chasing the mares and the mares galloping and Skippy chasing the stallion. The stallion grew tired of being chased and kicked—Skippy whimpered and limped home. My father and Valdez, the Filipino ranch hand, flapped their arms like madmen. The stallion sniffed Old Sissy's rump.

"Shoo, shoo, shoo!" my father said.

A blood fly landed on my arm. I slapped it and examined its crushed body and the blood on my skin. "Didn't the stallion like Fizz?" I asked.

Gramma stuck a Chesterfield in her mouth. "Finished with her."

"That stallion sure loves to screw," Ben said stretching his right leg out of the jeep.

She struck a match against its box and lit her cigarette. "Good way to lose yo' leg, Mistah Ben," she said, "with that damn stallion loose."

"Look," he said, "he's after Sandy!"

The stallion chased my father's Arabian into the corral. Sandy quit running and backed into the fence posts. My father twirled the lasso—he released and it grazed the stallion's neck. The stallion reared up and the lasso fell in the dirt. My father ran. So did Valdez. My father's cowboy hat flew off and rolled on its brim.

"You keeds shouldn't be watchin'," Gramma said.

Ben chuckled. "We've got front row seats."

She tossed her cigarette and it smoldered in the grass.

The stallion forced Sandy against the wire. Her legs got caught in the bottom strands and he mounted her. Sandy tried bucking but his weight kept her pinned down.

"We have to help Sandy!" I said.

She tucked the pack of Chesterfields into the pocket of her blouse. "Not a damn thing we can do."

"I'll shoot 'im," Ben offered.

"Botha a stallion, he's liable to kill you."

The stallion finished with Sandy and left the corral. The mares neighed. My father and Valdez lifted Sandy's hooves out of the wire.

Gramma climbed out of the jeep. "Fo' chrissakes," she said, "hea comes that damn Mendoza."

The red truck with the blue trailer pulled up alongside the pasture. Mendoza opened the gate and drove until he reached his horse. He eased out of his truck and put a rope around the stallion's neck. He tied a slipknot in the rope and dropped it over a water pipe sticking out of the ground.

We followed Gramma up the road. Her boots clumped across the red dirt. "Hui," she called, "yo' bloody horse jumped mah fence!"

Mendoza pulled down the trailer's ramp and slipped the rope off the pipe. He led his horse over to the ramp.

"Damn puhi'u," she said as we closed in.

Mendoza cleared his throat and spat. "Quit belly achin', Brownie." He coaxed his stallion up the ramp and into the trailer.

My father jogged over. His face was flushed and he had on his mean face. His cowboy hat was still in the corral and his hair was mussed. "I want my kala back," he said.

He secured the trailer door. "I get da foal?"

My father took off his glasses. "Now listen, you."

Mendoza opened the door of his truck. He reached into the cab and pulled out a machete. The blade was black except for its silver edge. He tapped the blade against his palm. "Wot," he told my father, "like one close shave?"

"I'm gettin' mah gun," Gramma said.

Mendoza winked at her and climbed into his truck. His trailer kicked up a swirl of dust as it rolled off our ranch.

                    *   *   *

The visit by the stallion did nothing for Fizz. If anything, it made her more of a loner. Whenever a truck rumbled down the road, she hid in the coconut grove as if expecting the stallion to reappear.

"Good for nothing mare," my father said. He couldn't ride her and he couldn't get her pregnant. He told us to stop feeding her barley. But it wasn't long before Sandy's opu swelled.

"No more barley," my father ordered. "I won't ride a fat horse."

"I think yo' Sandy's hapai," Gramma said.

Dr. Lucky confirmed her suspicions so we doubled Sandy's feed. She polished off every grain and wanted more. Her belly got as big as a barrel.

"She's going to explode," Ben said balancing her bucket on the top strand of wire. Old Sissy and the other mares took turns trying to nudge their mouths into her bucket but he shooed them away.

I reached up and patted Sandy's head while she ate her

barley—she took her head out of the bucket and looked nervously from side to side.

"She hates you," he told me.

*   *   *

My father phoned Dr. Lucky the morning he found Sandy belly up in the corral. A yellow Toyota truck pulled into the pasture and Ben and I ran through the wet grass to flag it down. The truck pulled over and the driver's door swung open—a husky man with short red hair sat behind the wheel. He wore a white short sleeve shirt, jeans, and sneakers. He plucked a black bag off the passenger seat and said, "Hello, boys."

"Hi, Dr. Lucky," we said.

Dr. Lucky was from Los Angeles. He'd moved to Moloka'i to escape the rat race and lived in a bungalow overlooking the leper colony at Kalaupapa. "Is Sandy in the corral?" he asked.

"Yes," Ben said, "she's with my father."

"Can you help her, Dr. Lucky?" I asked.

"Don't worry, son," he said, "the cavalry's here."

He hustled through the pasture and we followed him to the corral. Sandy's head was in my father's lap and she was shivering. Blood flies buzzed her eyes.

"How's our patient doing?" Dr. Lucky asked.

"She's in shock," my father replied.

Dr. Lucky crouched and ran his hands over Sandy's opu. He poked and prodded her rib cage. Sandy neighed. She shook her head free of my father and tried getting up but Dr. Lucky put all of his weight on her chest and held her down.

"There's something rotten in the state of Denmark," Dr.

Lucky said.

"You boys get back to the house," my father said.

"What for?" Ben asked.

"Don't lemmee tell you again."

Ben shrugged his shoulders and we walked through the grass and weeds. Our sneakers were soaked and our jeans covered with kuku burrs. He went as far as the fence line.

"What?" I asked.

"Don't follow me, Jeff."

"Why not?"

"This is a one-man mission."

Ben snuck over to the corral using the hala trees for cover. He crawled through the pili grass, climbed a breadfruit tree, and perched on a limb.

I continued on to the house and saw Gramma behind the picture window in the big room. I got closer and she stood at the screen door. She had a look that tightened her face.

"Wheah's Ben?" she asked.

"Watching Sandy."

"Worried about her foal," she said. She told me the mares would gallop when Sandy gave birth so it was best to keep her and the foal in the corral. "Yo' bruthah's comin'," she said.

I saw Ben running. He ran so fast that he had to jam a shoulder against the top wire of the fence to slow himself down. He slipped through and headed for the house. "Twins," he said when he reached the lawn, "Siamese twins!"

I thought about human babies joined at their bellies and hips. I wondered where foals might get joined and imagined a horse with two heads galloping on eight hooves.

Gramma squinted at the corral. "She's not built fo' twins."

"Is too. Dr. Lucky's cutting 'em free."

The door creaked and Gramma walked out. Leo and Spotty ran around from the lanai and whined for attention. Ben patted them and we followed her to the edge of the pasture.

"Wait hea," she said.

"I'm old enough," Ben replied.

"Wait with the dogs."

Ben held Leo and I held Spotty. Gramma slipped through the fence and took off for the corral. Spotty yelped. She held out her hand when Old Sissy approached. Old Sissy sniffed her hand. She joined Dr. Lucky, my father, and Valdez in the corral. She knelt next to Dr. Lucky. My father cradled Sandy's head in his lap.

"One of those foals is mine," Ben told me.

"Can I have the twin?"

"No," he replied.

My father took Sandy's head off his lap and walked with Valdez to a spot in the pasture near the corral. Valdez had a shovel. My father pointed at a patch of dirt and Valdez stabbed the ground with the shovel's blade.

Ben released Leo and ducked between the wires of the fence.

I grabbed Leo's collar. "What about the pups?"

"Let 'em go."

I did and they scampered to the corral.

Ben and I used the trees for cover. It felt as though we were soldiers advancing toward the front line. Dr. Lucky was doing something between Sandy's legs. Gramma stroked Sandy's head. My father returned to the corral and stood with his hands on his hips. I heard what sounded like a woman's cry. The mares mumbled. Dr. Lucky and my father dragged something to the side of the corral. Spotty licked the dirt. The air smelled like metal.

"Let's get closer," Ben said.

We crawled through the grass and hid behind a breadfruit tree.

"Deeper," my father told Valdez.

"Already hittin' waddah, Mistah Gill."

"Then go wider." My father returned to the corral. He knelt and examined the thing he'd dragged with Dr. Lucky through the dirt.

"The babies," Ben said. "My foal."

The three men dragged the bodies to the hole. They didn't look like foals—there was no hair and I saw right through their skin all the way to their insides. They were a tangle of glassy flesh and heads. Dr. Lucky said something and they shoved the bodies over the edge. There was a splash and a blast of sand shot from the hole. Valdez picked up his shovel.

*   *   *

The next day, Gramma drove her jeep up the mountain. Ben and I went with her and helped pick ferns and gardenias in the high country. We returned and she made a gardenia wreath and placed it on the grave. She told Ben her foal at Pu'u O Hoku Ranch had been trampled to death by a herd of cattle the morning of its birth. "Makes the world seem funny and cold," she said.

"Maybe Sandy can have another foal," I suggested.

My brother started crying. "I don't want another one."
She put her arms around Ben and held him close.

*   *   *

My father didn't ride Sandy that summer. He never
talked about hiring another stallion for Fizz. Despite not getting
barley, Fizz gained weight eating the pili grass in the lot. I snuck
her apples and cubes of sugar. She got fat and my father said
he'd never known such a worthless animal.

*   *   *

Gramma planted a mango tree over the foals' grave. The
first fruit appeared the following summer. That tree provided
shade for the mares and, every summer, they waited for the fruit
to fall. I climbed the tree and picked mangoes. I gave the best
ones to Sandy. She always held her head low and spooked easy.

"Give the horses some?" Gramma asked when I returned.

I pressed the fruit to my chest. "The soft ones."

"Good boy."

I handed her a mango. She sat on her doorstep and
skinned it with her paring knife. Her gnarled fingers guided
the blade. She watched the pasture as the skin fell away.

Tsunami

My grandmother seemed more like a mother after we'd spent four summers on Moloka'i. She made sure we got three meals a day and always had her refrigerator stocked with milk and ice cream. We weren't allowed to open the fridge without her permission. Ben respected her because she ran the ranch all by herself. Animals respected her too. Whenever she rode a horse, it raised its head and pranced.

Gramma and Uncle Chipper were the only adults at the ranch. Chipper scared me. I'd seen him drink himself drunk and demand that she sleep with him. The more time I spent on Moloka'i, the more I realized it was not an island for the meek at heart. I would soon discover there were things that terrified my grandmother, traumas from her past that made her run to her gun for comfort.

*   *   *

Gramma said we were too big to be sleeping together on the pune'e so she bought two twin beds and put us out on

39

the lanai. We kept the storm windows open and slept under mosquito nets.

Gramma slept in her bedroom. We all got up at dawn to search for glass balls on the beach. Eggs weren't on the breakfast menu. She cooked oatmeal and we managed to choke down spoonfuls with heavy doses of milk and sugar.

I was certain I was the favorite simply because I took after my father. Ben tried everything to tip the scales in his favor—he picked papayas, vacuumed the big room's Oriental rug, and cooked teriyaki venison on the hibachi. "Good boy, Ben," Gramma would say. Her praise was genuine and he kept thinking up new ways to butter her up.

"Gramma likes me best," he said when we fished the swamp.

"How come?" I asked.

" 'Cause I'm the hardest worker."

"I shovel manure."

"That's nothing," he replied.

*   *   *

At midnight, the tsunami sirens started to wail. Ben and I were sitting in the back of the jeep. The jeep was parked behind Uncle Chipper's Impala on the mauka side of Kam Highway. Our grandmother was somewhere out in the darkness. There was no moon and the air was still and heavy. Kona weather. The scent of lilikoi drifted down from the mountain. Gramma had made us put on jeans—she didn't want us cutting our legs on lantana running up the first hill.

The Impala's rear lights came on and turned the jeep's insides red. Chipper was slouched down in the driver's seat.

His Impala was a two-door hardtop with blossoms of rust on its chrome bumpers. The green paint had faded from years of neglect and, in the light of day, the color reminded me of lima beans.

The sirens quit and dogs howled in the kuleanas to the east. Across the road, Sandy hung her head over the top strand of wire. I saw the tip of a cigarette glowing. It looked like a firefly. The firefly got brighter when the smoker puffed. Boots clippity-clopped and Gramma appeared. A lit cigarette hung out of the side of her mouth. "The minute I give you keeds the signal," she said, "run up this mountain and don't look back. Undastand?"

We nodded. The way she said it made me think if I looked back I'd be turned into a pillar of salt.

"Aren't you coming?" Ben asked her.

"Gotta turn mah mares loose."

"What if they get lost?" I asked.

"Bettah lost than dead, Peanut." She handed us each a flashlight. "Don't play with 'um," she warned and walked to the Impala.

I was small for my age so Gramma called me "Peanut." She called Ben "Juicy" because of his fondness for juices. She'd make pitchers of canned grape and orange concentrates and sometimes mixed the two. Ben guzzled like a man dying of thirst.

The sirens roared and shut down. The Maui news played on the Impala's radio. The reporter's voice faded and then got stronger. I pieced together the critical words—earthquake, Aleutian Islands, forty-foot waves.

Ben flicked on his flashlight and lit up the roadside brush.

"Cut it out, Juicy," I said.

"What for?"

"You'll wear out the batteries."

"I'm testing them."

"Retard."

Ben stuck the light under his chin and growled like Wolfman. "You're going to drown, Peanut." His two front teeth were missing and his hair and eyebrows had turned white blond from the sun. Girls made goo-goo eyes at him when we shopped in Kaunakakai. The sun had turned his skin the color of honey. My skin was the reddish-brown of Moloka'i's dirt roads. He switched off his flashlight and hummed the theme song to *The Rifleman*.

Headlights came from the direction of Halawa Valley. Leo and Spotty trotted behind Skippy on the side of the road. Our poi dogs weren't pups anymore but they still followed Skippy everywhere as if they were ducklings and he was their duck mother.

A truck pulled up and Gramma greeted the passengers.

"Hope not like in '46," a local woman said.

Gramma poured coffee from a thermos into a mug and handed it to the woman. A black Fairlane stopped next to the truck and kept its lights on. Children jounced in the Fairlane's back seat. The adults smoked, drank coffee, and talked story.

Gramma had told me about April Fool's Day in 1946. That was before the civil defense sirens were installed, when news of danger came by way of Maui radio. "This is the real McCoy," the newsman reported as waves swept through Hilo. The water in our harbor receded—it was as if God pulled a plug out of the bottom of the ocean. The reef appeared and the channel between Moloka'i and Maui became a valley of sand. "Squid and fish floppin'," she said, "and fullas runnin' out to get 'um." Gramma and Chipper had the beach house and a cottage. Chipper freed the horses while she drove her truck east to warn her friend Sarah Naki. She stopped to free a white stallion roped to a stake and spotted a blue mountain rolling off the ocean. A boat was caught on the reef at Honouliwai Bay and a man pushed his oar against the coral. The blue mountain picked up the boat like a toy and carried it to its crest. The man disappeared. She jumped in her truck, floored it, and sped to the bridge. She made it to the bridge first but the blue mountain was upon her—it engulfed the bridge and water slammed down on the roof of the truck. The compartment flooded. She cranked the starter but the engine wouldn't turn. She gazed into the open ocean—a second blue mountain was on its way. The driver's door opened and Sarah pulled her out. They ran up a ridge as the wave buckled the bridge and flung the truck into a gully. Three more blue mountains rolled in before the water receded. She found the stallion she'd set free and rode him back to the ranch. The tsunami had knocked her cottage off its foundation and carried the lumber into the gulch. But the beach house was still there.

*   *   *

Gramma stomped out her cigarette and approached the jeep. "You keeds eat sushi?" she asked.

"Sushi's ono," Ben said.

She handed us each a cone sushi wrapped in a paper napkin. "Sarah Naki made these," she said. "Wot you say?"

"Thank-you," we answered.

"I don't want you keeds sleepin'. We'll know when Maui's hit."

"Then what?" Ben asked.

"Run fo' yo' bloody lives."

She returned to the Impala and leaned against its hood. The truck and the Fairlane pulled away. Headlights approached from the west. A white Falcon parked beside the Impala—a man rolled down the passenger window and spoke to Chipper.

Ben gobbled up his sushi.

I took a bite. The sushi tasted bitter from the vinegar on the cone part. But inside, the rice and carrot shavings were sweet. "Why don't we call Chipper 'grandpa?' " I asked.

Ben licked his fingers. "He's not married to Gramma anymore."

"What if she marries him again?"

"She wouldn't marry him if he was the last man on earth."

I wondered if Uncle Chipper would live with us if the waves destroyed his house. The waves were supposed to follow the rivers and streams up into the mountains, reversing them. Chipper's house was built beside Kainalu Stream and it was the worst place to be during a tsunami.

The sirens wailed again, followed by a series of short blasts. The Falcon left. Chipper's headlights came on and Gramma fired up the jeep. I smelled the exhaust through the holes in the metal floor.

"What happened?" Ben asked her.

"That's the 'All Cleah' signal."

"Maui's okay?" I asked.

"Maui's no ka oi."

We drove home behind the Impala. I felt cheated. It felt like a waste of time waiting for danger and not having danger show up. I wanted to run up the hill and feel the cool air burning my lungs. I wanted to aim my flashlight at the tsunami as it devoured the flatlands.

The Impala turned left off Kam Highway and we followed it down the row of white oleanders beside the pasture. Our dogs jogged alongside the jeep. Gramma tooted goodbye and we took the driveway home. Uncle Chipper kept going—his lights trailed off toward Kainalu Stream. He must have felt good talking story with old friends. He must have liked being with Gramma. I couldn't understand how they could live apart after loving one another for so long. Uncle Chipper scared me but I felt bad for him too. I hoped he'd be safe driving the dark stretch of road.

Kahuna Lady

*T*he morning after the sirens, Gramma drove us to Kam Highway and headed east. Ben sat in the jeep's passenger seat and I was in back. We wore Boston Red Sox T-shirts, jeans, and rubber slippers. The tires shook the wooden slats of the bridge at Kainalu Stream. There were no churches east of the ranch and locals were reading the *Holy Bible* handwritten in the Hawaiian language. Kiawe and kukui nut trees grew on the mauka side of the road. Telephone poles were smothered by vines. Our tires squashed guavas and lilikoi that had rolled down from the mountain. The air smelled tangy. Red and yellow torch ginger flashed in the underbrush. I spotted purple orchids and the snowcaps of "Chinese" pikake.

On the makai side, kuleanas were fenced in by rusty posts and barbed wire. Dirt roads led to plywood shacks with tar paper roofs. Men drank beer on doorsteps. A woman stood in a loi cutting taro leaves with a sickle. Children chased one other through a gauntlet of coops, pigpens, and mounds of tires. Poi

dogs barked. Families on the east end were so large that, when
they ran out of Christian names, the parents named boys after
cars. I'd met Mercury and Dodge when I was catching pollywogs
in Kainalu Stream and we watched their brother Plymouth spear
a Samoan crab.

We passed the last big fishpond on the east end. Peace
Corps tents squatted on the land beside the pond. Volunteers
had been sent from California and Oregon to cut trails from
Kaunakakai to Wailau Valley. The volunteers were supposed to
educate islanders about planting and survival but the locals were
the ones bringing them food and teaching them how to fish.

Gramma pointed at the encampment. "Monkeyin' in
those tents," she said and launched into the benefits of abstinence.
She said sagging breasts signaled low morals. A girl was letting
boys "monkey" with her if she sagged.

"You monkeyed with Wilkins," Ben said.

"Kulikuli," she scolded.

We reached a sandy cove. A Hawaiian man named Jesse
Duva stood behind a cardboard table combing his silver hair.
He wore a SUCK 'UM UP tee and his opu protruded over the
table. A painted shingle on the table read "East End Treasure."
The table was crammed with glass balls, balloon fish lamps,
lacquered turtle shells, coconuts carved into ashtrays, and black
sand in plastic bags. Pink clumps of coral dangled off a line of
barbed wire behind him. White was the coral's natural color
after being bleached by the sun but I figured pink gave tourists
a reason to stop. Gramma tooted and Jesse waved.

"Guess what he wanted for that coral," Ben said.

"A dollar?" I asked.

"Five bucks."

We reached a cottage overlooking Sandy Beach. This was where Auntie Esther lived, a hapa haole who'd been a man before going to Sweden for a sex change. Sandy Beach was where she sunbathed in the latest fashions from Frederick's of Hollywood. There was a shortage of women on Moloka'i and Esther had a reputation for seducing any man she wanted. Rumor had it she was going steady with the Chief of Police. Esther had driven to the ranch in her pink Dodge to style Gramma's wig and she gave her the phone numbers of the island's hardest working transsexuals. They'd come to clean house and do odd jobs. Sometimes my grandmother gave a transsexual a bra or silk panties as a bonus. She felt sorry for women trapped in men's bodies but was hopeful they'd all find nice boyfriends and lead happy lives.

We headed along the lip of a bay and eased past a tower of black lava. Locals spoke in whispers when discussing it. They called it "Pohakumake," the Death Rock. It was thirty feet tall and wider than the jeep. The county had tried bulldozing it into the sea but the bulldozer operator died. They tried dynamite and two county workers were crushed by falling lava. Pele, the fire goddess, had stood on the tower on her way to Haleakala. Pele's visit meant Pohakumake was immortal.

We rolled over the rickety slats of Honouliwai Bridge, a reconstructed version of the bridge Gramma'd tried crossing the day of the tsunami. A small house stood on the eastern edge of the bay.

"You keeds mind yo' Ps and Qs around Sarah," Gramma said.

"Why?" Ben asked.

"She's a kahuna."

Kahunas had the power to throw spells. The spell attacked the weakest person in the family first. The weakest was usually the youngest. A faceless ghost strangled the youngest in a dream. The spell worked its way up the ladder of strength until it invaded the dreams of the mother and father. If a kahuna was particularly strong, the spell spread like a disease, jumping from the cursed family to aunts, uncles, second and third cousins, and even pets. If the person throwing the spell was a relative, the curse might come back and kill, returning like a deadly boomerang.

We pulled over beside a trellis of orange bougainvillea and got out. A breadfruit tree balanced its fruit in the front yard. Other trees were loaded with fruit—lichi, banana, mountain apple, and mango. A garden boasted rows of taro, Swiss chard, and green onion. The big green leaves of the taro fanned out. There was a narrow plot of purple dirt where magic things grew underground—awa, uhaloa, and secret roots used for healing and spells.

The front door was open and I saw the ocean through it.

"Hui," Gramma called.

Sarah Naki appeared at the doorway. She was a dark woman with a shock of white hair. She wore a blue muumuu and a mokihana lei. "Pehea 'oe i ke ea la kakahiaka?" she asked.

"Maika'i," Gramma answered.

Sarah looked down at Ben and me. "Mo'opunas from Honolulu?"

"Ae," Gramma said. She placed one hand on my head

and the other on Ben's.

Sarah was the first Hawaiian woman I'd seen with green eyes. She stared at me as though looking into my heart. "Hemo da slippah," she said.

We took off our slippers. Gramma stepped out of her cowboy boots and we stacked everything beside the door. I stood barefoot with Ben on a lauhala mat and Sarah pulled out a whisk broom made of coconut fronds and dusted our feet. The dusting made my feet itch.

"Pakalaki spirits," she explained, "from Hahnahlulu."

We walked a floor of dark brown koa. On either side of the door were stones stacked one on top of the other, nine stones per stack. These were Sarah's aumakua, stone fetishes protecting her family. She said the stones were male and female and they mated during the night to give birth to smaller stones by morning. Tapa cloth with printed designs hung on the walls. There were no chairs so we sat on the floor. The only hint she lived in modern times was a Frigidaire moaning in the corner.

Sarah served Ben and me kulolo, a light green pudding, in monkey pod bowls. She sprinkled on poha berries from a breadfruit-leaf bag. "Fo' flavah," she told us.

"Gimmee a spoon," Ben said.

"A'ole," she answered. "Eat like poi."

I looked at Ben. I waited until he dipped a finger into the kulolo and stuck it in his mouth. "Ono," he said and dipped again. I copied him. The kulolo was sweet and creamy and tasted like coconut.

Sarah and Gramma sat on a lauhala mat. Sarah warned us to never take kalua pig from a luau. She spoke of demons crawling out of the lava to take the forms of sharks and killer whales. A beautiful girl who'd been turned into a dolphin protected surfers when the big waves came. A tornado filled with water and eels had been born in Pailolo Channel—it entered the calm confines of Halawa and followed the river into the gulch. Her mo'opuna Kaui had been netting prawns when the tornado tried swallowing him up. The more she spoke, the more her eyes grew in intensity. A fire kindled inside of her.

"Are you Madam Pele?" I blurted.

Gramma glared at me.

Sarah said a giant squid living near the tip of the lava attacked the small boats. She was convinced the squid was the reincarnation of Great Uncle Kamake'aina, a giant who dug up the dead for the gold in their teeth. He'd been ransacking Father Damien's graveyard at Kalaupapa when a scorpion bit his foot. A leper girl had come from Saint Philomena Church to lomilomi his foot and he died falling from a cliff on his way down to marry her. She spoke of islands appearing at sunset and disappearing by sunrise. And there were the 'O'io Marchers, ghosts who walked single file from the mountains to the shore on moonlit nights. "When blue halo stay around da moon," Sarah said. She told us dogs howl when they see the ghosts.

"I wanna see 'em!" my brother said.

Sarah shook her head. "Haole no can see." But she said if we took the maka piapia from a howling dog's eye and put it in our own we might see the ghosts.

Gramma and Sarah started speaking in Hawaiian so we checked out the stones to see if any new ones had been born. I saw wet pictures on a ledge drying in the sun. There was a black and white picture of a tall, thin man wearing a Panama hat who could have been a young Uncle Chipper. He stood at the stern of a boat and used a pole to push off the bottom. A Hawaiian girl sat at the bow.

Ben snuck into the kitchen to get more kulolo and I walked out to the backyard through an open door. Suji gill nets were piled beside a rusted anchor. Tiki gods grimaced on totem poles and flies buzzed a stack of fish heads. The ground was black lava, wet from the surf. The poisonous spines of wana stuck out of crevices. A wave sprayed me. I shivered looking into the ocean—there was no reef, only deep blue.

A fishpond had been built at the edge of the lava. A wave crashed over a stone wall and spilled into the pond. Mullet swam to the surface and swallowed the foam.

"Peanut," Gramma called, "time to hele."

We stepped into our slippers and Gramma pulled on her cowboy boots. Sarah stood at the doorway with her arms crossed. She seemed happy we'd come but glad we were leaving. We said our alohas and she pointed to her breadfruit tree. "Ulu," she said, "take."

Ben climbed the tree. He wanted a big one high up. The trunk and branches were sturdy and the tree didn't sway as he climbed. Gramma would cut a breadfruit in half, bake it for an hour, and smother both sides with butter. It tasted somewhere between a banana and a potato.

"Mai nani i ka ulu i waho, a'ole nau ia ulu," Sarah said.

Gramma laughed. "No look so high," she translated.

"Nano no i ka ulu i ke alo, nau ia ulu," Sarah continued.

"Look right in front."

He looked to his left and a breadfruit the size of a basketball was next to the trunk. Its green skin was sticky with sap and he twisted it back and forth. "Catch!" he said and tossed it down. I caught it against my chest. The breadfruit was warm from the sun and the sap stuck to my shirt.

We returned to the jeep, waved goodbye to Sarah, and headed home across the bridge. I had wanted to stay longer and explore the fishpond. Legend said if you ate a mullet from a kahuna's fishpond you would live a long life.

"Sarah taught you keeds a lesson," Gramma said as she drove.

"What lesson?" Ben asked.

"Open yo' makas."

I asked her what happened if the stones kept multiplying and she said Sarah used the newborn stones to reinforce the fishpond wall. She told us Sarah's place was the only beach house besides hers that had survived the tsunami.

"It's good she's gotta fridge," I said.

She lit a cigarette. "That's not fo' kaukau."

"What's it for?" Ben asked.

"The Kua'aina Bag."

"What's that?"

She blew a puff of smoke. "Sarah freezes pictuahs of bad people."

"She was drying a man in the sun," I said.

"Musta learned his lesson."

"Bet he's dead," said Ben.

"Did Uncle Chipper ever wear a hat?" I asked.

"Wot's this about Chippah?"

"Nothing."

She gazed at the bay. "I don't 'membah any hat."

I never told her about the picture of Chipper. I figured she was drying him out because he'd suffered enough. I would find out later Uncle Chipper had proposed to Sarah's teenage daughter when he was still married to Gramma.

Book Two
Hale Kia

Uncle Chipper

Chipper Daniels was my grandmother's first try at marriage. He came in the Indian Summer of her romantic life, a month after her affair with Alan Ladd in Honolulu. By that time she had one boy from Wilkins and a second from Danford, a Portuguese longshoreman. She met Chipper at Kapiolani Park during her brother Sharkey's bootleg fight. "I bet on yo' bruddah," Chipper told her. Sharkey knocked out his Australian opponent and Chipper invited her to dinner at the Royal Hawaiian. He'd never married but came close a few times with girls from missionary families. Their fathers had wanted him to run their sugar mills and pineapple plantations but he didn't want the life of a businessman.

*   *   *

I called Chipper "uncle" because he wasn't my real grandfather. But even today, whenever I imagine a grandfather, he always comes to mind. My memory of him is a mosaic of fragments, pieces gathered like beach-smoothed glass along the

57

coast of Moloka'i.

Gramma liked telling me about her history with Chipper. She showed me pictures of them riding horses along the beach, dropping net near the barrier reef, and holding hands at a campfire in Halawa Valley. They were lovers living in paradise. She pulled out photos of them drinking in front of the beach house—they stood apart and you could tell something bad was on the way.

At first, the ranch belonged to Chipper. His parents gave it to him when he returned a hero from the Great War. He called it Hale Kia, Hawaiian for "Home of the Deer." Hale Kia was an ahupua'a—it started at the beach, stretched through the pasture, and extended up to the skyline. The property recognized the same boundaries King Kamehameha had devised when granting crown land to his ali'i. The sacred elements of water, earth, and sky defined the ahupua'a.

Chipper's depression began when the Japanese bombed Pearl Harbor. He realized this was going to be a war with big stakes and new heroes would emerge. His bravery in the Great War was diminished by American victories in Europe and the South Pacific. My father returned with a Purple Heart and a pair of Battle Stars—Chipper had to eat his words for telling him he wasn't "military material."

Chipper embraced the bottle while Gramma learned how to ride, round up cows, and mend fences. She got a job at Pu'u O Hoku Ranch after proving she could drive fifty head of cattle down to Puko'o Harbor. Men on the west end of Moloka'i, fascinated by stories of a beautiful wahine who worked as a paniolo, traveled thirty miles on horseback just to catch a glimpse of her. Vladimir, a Russian luna ten years her junior, asked her to get a divorce and marry him. Chipper found Vladimir at the Midnite Inn in Kaunakakai—the fight started in the bar and spilled onto Main Street. Vladimir pulled a knife and cut him. On the second lunge, he grabbed Vladimir's wrist and the knife fell in the dirt. Vladimir was so badly beaten he had to be ferried to Queen's Hospital in Honolulu.

Chipper started throwing parties and his friends showed up wearing button-down shirts, slacks, and cowboy boots. My grandmother was a goddess to them, a thin brunette wearing a kimono with her hair up like a geisha. Her face was painted— mascara, rouge, pink lipstick dragged over her thin lips. She wanted to show Chipper she could be beautiful and act submissive. "All dolled up," she muttered as she carried a white wicker chair over the lawn. She sat down. The men stood around her drinking okolehao from pickle jars. At first they were straight as fence posts but the okolehao made them lean. Chipper handed her a jar. She watched the ocean between men as her mind filled with thoughts of her lovers. The lows and highs flashed like images on a newsreel, from Wilkins to Danford and finally, to Chipper. She had chosen to be on Moloka'i with him and that was that. "I've made mah bed," she mumbled and raised the pickle jar. The okolehao burned her heart. She wanted to smash the jar against the cinder block retaining wall on the makai side of the beach house. She finished her drink and he poured another. She had forgotten where she'd hidden her Wild Turkey and then remembered the bottle was in the sour grass behind the Norfolk. She thought about Norman and Bobby living with her mother in Kaimuki. She loved her boys but Chipper refused to raise them. She couldn't leave him. Moloka'i was her island now and she would make the best of it. She hated how he ignored her boys during their summer visits and she cussed herself for allowing them to be raised hanai. She was worried about Norman. She had lied to him about marrying his English father and divorcing. There was no marriage so there was no divorce. Norman had told her he'd been beaten by her mother's gentleman boarder and she'd seen him following Chipper around the ranch like a pup starved for attention. She watched her husband gulp from his jar. He was five years older. It seemed more like ten. She was glad the men lived far away on other ranches so they could not hear the fights in the days and nights between parties.

Chipper was not dressed like the other men. He wore rolled-up Levi's and his bare chest was red from the sun. He crouched next to her chair. His expression was a mix of guilt and defiance, as though she should forgive past indiscretions since he owned everything north of the beach up to the clouds. She'd caught him kissing Anika, Sarah's daughter, that morning in the ironwoods. "I own this ranch," he'd said, "I can do any god damn thing I want."

"Kua'aina!" she'd answered and busted the bottom off an Old Grandad bottle and chased him through the forest with the jagged neck.

*   *   *

After a decade of hard drinking, Chipper couldn't pay his property taxes. He signed over Hale Kia to Gramma in exchange for a life estate between the dump and the mangrove swamp. The swamp marked the southeastern edge of the property, the border where Kainalu Stream pooled and nourished the roots of the mangrove. In the early days on Moloka'i, the days before garbage was hauled to the highway for collection, landowners reserved their less desirable acres for things they lacked the heart or the ability to destroy. If something once held value in my grandmother's world, it found a final resting place near the banks of Kainalu Stream.

Chipper built a small house beside the stream. His luaus were frequented by teenage wahines and paniolos from Pu'u O Hoku Ranch. The house was his outpost and he saw himself as the leader of a defiant tribe on the ranch he once owned. He could stay on the land as long as he lived and he planned on living it up. The rowdier his guests were the happier he got—he knew Julia would hear it from the beach house. He was sure she was drinking. Drinking alone. At least he had friends and plenty of wahines. He loved the imu and the aroma of steamed pig. Men cheered as girls danced around his bonfire. His luaus were marked by gambling, brawls, and wild sex. Sometimes he woke up with three wahines in his bed not knowing whether he'd made love to any or all. He got two girls hapai and paid off their parents. Then Anika got crazy drunk and drowned in the swamp. The wahines quit coming and the luaus petered out.

But he still had the bottle.

*   *   *

Ben and I attended Star of the Sea Elementary in Honolulu. I was heading into sixth grade and Ben was starting seventh. My brother had never outgrown his desire to steal from wishing wells and, before we left for Moloka'i that summer, he went on a rampage that would warm Blackbeard's heart. When he ran out of wishing wells he plundered coins from public koi ponds and park fountains. "Boys will be boys," my mother said. His favorite fountain was at Kapiolani Park—he dragged a scoop net over its bottom whenever our parents took us to the Elks Club.

"Can't you quit stealing people's wishes?" I asked.

"That's what they get for throwing their money away," he answered.

Moloka'i didn't have wishing wells, koi ponds, or fountains so Ben combed the beach and pasture for treasure. He found glass balls, wooden floats, and cowrie shells along the coast and unearthed an ancient poi pounder in Fizz's lot. I helped him scour the shore in search of fuel for our first bonfire. We gathered kamani logs, kiawe branches, shingles, old coconuts, planks full of rusty nails, and lumber with Japanese symbols. I even collected string and rope. We kept our stockpile on the shore in front of the beach house. Our parents were across the channel in Ka'anapali and, when our father phoned, Ben asked him if he wanted to see a bonfire from his hotel room. Our father said he'd like that since he couldn't see a single light on Moloka'i.

Gramma wasn't thrilled about our bonfire, especially after she caught me playing with matches. She walked to the beach and circled our mound of wood.

"Wheah'd you keeds find all this?" she asked.

"Down the beach," Ben said.

"And past the point," I added.

She stuck her hands in the pockets of her denims. "Yo' too damn young fo' fiahs."

"Ben's twelve," I argued, "and I'll be eleven."

"And Daddy wants it," Ben said.

She gave us the stink eye. "If one spark hits, you'll burn me down."

"Nothing'll happen," I replied.

"Drag it down by Chippah's."

We dragged our stockpile east and piled it on the shore next to Kainalu Stream. I wasn't worried about Chipper. A forest was between us and his house. He rarely came down to the beach. A wooden boat had been turned upside down next to his garage and I took that as a sign he'd abandoned the ocean.

Ben and I found a stretch of dry sand above the high tide mark. We stood up the planks and leaned them into one another. Soon we had the skeleton for our bonfire. We stacked lumber, shingles, and logs against the planks. He tossed in coconuts and I threw in my string and rope.

Uncle Chipper walked out of the forest and picked his way through the naupaka. He was a tall thin man with pale skin. His arms reminded me of snakes. He wore a green cap, an undershirt, shorts, and sandals. Toes were missing on each foot and he smelled like wine.

"Wot's this ruckus?" he asked.

"This is our bonfire," Ben said.

"Wot the hell fo'?"

"So our parents can see us."

"They're goofing around on Maui," I explained.

Chipper smirked. He still had his front teeth, but his mouth was full of gaps. According to Gramma, he'd guzzle okolehao and have his friend Moki yank bad teeth with pliers. He hobbled over and picked up a shingle. This's still good."

"Help yourself," Ben offered.

"Gotta 'nough junk."

"Gramma said burn it here," I said.

"Brownie said that?"

"Yeah," Ben said.

"How come you call her 'Brownie?' " I asked.

Chipper told us a boy named Billy Duva noticed her resemblance to a cartoon character on the box of his Brownie camera. He called her Brownie and the name stuck.

"Was she the prettiest woman on Moloka'i?" I asked.

He dropped the shingle. "Nearly killed a man ovah her."

"Then why'd you get divorced?" Ben asked.

"I was a damn fool."

"Gramma says there's no fool like an old fool," I said.

Chipper scowled. "When it's time," he said, "come get me." He turned and hobbled through the naupaka. He didn't seem like a bad man. But Gramma had said he put a litter of kittens in a burlap bag with a brick and tossed the bag into the harbor. He'd been mad at Gramma for bringing a hapai cat onto the ranch and got even by drowning the babies.

"Did you see his feet?" I asked.

"Yeah," Ben said.

"How'd he lose his toes?"

"Mowing his lawn without shoes."

"Why'd he do that?"

"The old fut was drunk on okolehao."

*   *   *

That night, Ben and I waited on the lanai for the phone to ring twice. That would be our father's signal to start the fire.

We were to call him after the bonfire was lit. The storm windows were open and I looked across the channel. The moon was full and the water between islands was a silver meadow. Ka'anapali twinkled. My mother loved Maui's hotels, restaurants, and piano bars. At times I felt she didn't miss us at all and only had Ben and me to satisfy some motherly image she'd concocted for herself. She spent her summers shopping at Ala Moana, cooking dinners for two on her push button stove, and visiting all the islands except Moloka'i. She never picked up the phone to call Ben and me on her own and always sent postcards saying how much fun she was having. I could never understand how she could be having fun if she really loved us.

The phone rang two times and quit.

"Shoot yo' pickles!" Gramma said from the big room.

Ben and I ran down the beach. He had newspaper and a box of matches. We reached the wood and he shoved in a wad of paper and struck a match. The wind blew out the flame. He lit a second match and it died too. "We need help," he said and headed into the forest.

I imagined my father watching from his balcony. He was an impatient man so I figured he was ready to give up. Branches snapped and shadows moved through the trees. Ben had brought Uncle Chipper. He still had on his cap and he spilled gas from a can over the wood. He lit a match, cupped it with his palm, and carried a blue flame to the mound. The logs ignited with a rush. Every piece we'd gathered, even the wet wood, flared to life. My coils of string and rope burned in the guts of the bonfire. The wind fanned it—we watched flames leap for the stars.

"They'll see you tonight," Chipper said. I saw the scar

on his arm from Vladimir's knife. He walked off with his can
and disappeared in the ironwoods.

I danced near the flames. "Righteous!" I cheered.

"Call Maui," Ben said.

"You're not coming?"

"Promised I'd stay with the fire."

I ran along the shore. The beach was wet from the rising
tide and my Keds went deep in the sand. I ran the incline to the
beach house. Gramma was on the lanai.

"That damn fiah's huge," she said.

I climbed over the sill of an open window. "Uncle
Chipper used gas to help us light it."

"Fo' the luva Pete."

I followed her into the kitchen. She called the hotel and
put me on the line.

"Can you see us?" I asked.

My father laughed. "Moloka'i's on fire!"

That made me feel great. It struck me that my father was
a good man. For the first time in a long time, I felt close to him.
Ben and I had finally done something right. My mother got on
the phone and said she'd performed "Beyond The Reef" at the
Hyatt piano bar and that a man had come up and asked if she
was a professional. She said our fire was beautiful. I was glad
she saw the flames but she might as well have been a million
miles away. I wanted her to be with us on Moloka'i. I wanted to
show her the hills I'd hiked and the places I'd fished. I wanted
to show her a different son than the one she knew in Honolulu.

"Are you having fun?" I asked her.

"I'm getting a good rest," she said and turned the phone

over to my father.

"Keep an eye on that fire," he said.

I told him I would and charged out of the beach house. I sprinted along the shore and saw sparks flying over the forest. A coconut exploded. The night had a rich, exotic smell. My brother picked up a palm frond and dragged it across the sand.

"Wha'd Daddy say?" he asked.

"Moloka'i's on fire."

He tossed the frond in. "Bitchin."

Our father saw us across seven miles of ocean. The fire was our flag on this dark coast and it felt as though the island belonged to us. We were a victorious tribe of two. But I felt funny Chipper wasn't celebrating with us. He was in his house rolling cigarettes, drinking, and watching TV.

I watched the flames destroy everything we'd gathered.

The British War Medal

I don't remember when I stopped fearing Uncle Chipper. Maybe it had something to do with me fishing the swamp and seeing him stumble around his yard. I suppose knowing he was once married to my grandmother made him less threatening. I wondered how he felt being alone. He was living off memories the way certain plants live off air but I doubted the past could sustain him without someone's affection or caring.

*   *   *

Gramma kept her gold wedding band in a jewelry box tucked in the bottom drawer of her bedroom bureau. She brought it out only after I'd begged her all summer to see it.

"Fo' chrissakes," she said handing the ring over, "quit pesterin' me."

The band was thin but heavy. She'd told me Chipper had one that matched. Her ring had the initials "JD" engraved in it. "Julia Daniels?" I asked her.

"That's right."

I tried slipping the band on my index finger but it was too small. Every finger was too big except my pinkie.

"Bad luck tryin' on otha people's rings," she said.

I handed it back. "Where does Chipper keep his ring?"

"On a chain around his neck."

"Why there?"

"Who the hell knows," she snapped.

Gramma said it was fine if Uncle Chipper flirted with wahines but if she so much as looked at another man he would have a fit. He threatened her with a skinning knife the night she danced with a handsome lieutenant at a USO party in Kaunakakai. When Chipper moved out of the beach house, men rode over on horseback at night and begged her to come out for a drink. One man plucked a ukulele and sang "Moloka'i Nui Ahina" as she waited inside with her rifle to see what would happen. He got tired of singing and hurled a bottle at her bedroom wall. She fired a round through the screen window and he galloped off.

"Sang like a dyin' cat," Gramma said.

"Do men still come around?" I asked.

She nodded. "Keep yo' eyes peeled."

*   *   *

Ben and I were shooting crabs on the beach with his BB rifle when Gramma waved at us from a storm window. "Boys," she called, "come inside!"

Ben lowered his gun. "What for?"

"Yo' Uncle Chippah's on television!"

We raced to the big room and watched soldiers charging off a boat into the surf. They carried long rifles with fixed bayonets. The only sound was the voice of the narrator.

"Is that Waikiki?" Ben asked.

"Waikiki, mah foot," she said, "that's Gallipoli."

"Where's Uncle Chipper?" I asked as the last man entered the water.

"Christ, Peanut, Chippah was the third fulla off. Didn't you see 'um?"

I looked over at Ben for help. He shrugged his shoulders. I had expected an old man in the ranks of the young.

I have always felt bad for not recognizing Uncle Chipper in that clip. Now, whenever I see soldiers assaulting a beach, Chipper is always the third man off the boat, even if the footage is in color and the helmets are from another war.

Gramma said Chipper didn't have to fight. He wasn't drafted. The great Duke Kahanamoku didn't fight and nobody held that against him. He volunteered because he thought the Allies could use his help. The English were so impressed with his bravery that they awarded him the British War Medal.

"Did Chipper fight with Daddy?" I asked her.

"That was a diff'rent war."

"But who killed the most men?"

"Chippah."

The British War Medal was round and silver. It dangled from a ribbon on Chipper's living room wall and the light from his bay window ignited the silver. The side facing out showed Saint George riding a prancing stallion. The stallion's hoof was crushing a German shield.

                    *   *   *

Chipper's house caught fire a month after I saw the

medal. He waded into Kainalu Stream, the cinders raining on his shoulders and head. Only the coconut trees surrounding the house and a rectangle of ash remained. The British War Medal melted into a silver tear that dripped through the ashes.

"Damn fool smokin' in bed," Gramma mumbled as we stood in what had been his living room.

I knelt and dug through the ashes. My wrists and forearms turned gray as I scooped away ashes like sand.

"Wot you lookin' fo', Peanut?"

"The British War Medal."

"Christ," she replied, "it's long gone."

I stood up and kicked the charred remains of a table. The ash heaps seemed a sad grave for so much courage. I felt as though the part of the war that had meaning for Moloka'i died in the flames.

*   *   *

Moki was a carpenter and he helped Chipper build a shack over the ashes. I supervised their progress while fishing the swamp—Moki carried a scorched water heater over his head and tossed it in the water. The heater floated to the mangrove and got lodged in its roots. We offered Chipper our lanai but he refused. He camped in his Impala and celebrated the end of every day with a bottle of okolehao. Moki drank with him. The walls of the shack were a hodgepodge of plywood, irregular lumber, and driftwood. The roof was made of overlapping sheets of corrugated steel. Chipper said steel was better than wood since falling coconuts would bounce and roll off. The coconut trees around the shack seemed liked victims of some undeclared war—a circle of charcoal trunks crowned with black fronds.

"Wish I had that lumba from yo' bonfiah," Chipper said the day Gramma had me bring a plate stacked with ham sandwiches. Chipper and Moki stood beside a pile of burnt coconuts smoking hand-rolled cigarettes. Moki was a husky man wearing red overalls and sneakers—he snatched a sandwich and took a bite.

Chipper wasn't interested in sandwiches. He didn't have on a shirt and his chest was sunburned. He wore his cap, Levi's, and rubber Tobbies.

"I can find more wood," I told him.

"Damn tide's no good."

Moki nodded solemnly. "Da kine kai make tide."

The currents that carried the usual gifts of glass balls, floats, and driftwood couldn't breach the exposed reef at low tide. Almost everything, including Clorox bottles and light bulbs, bypassed our coast. Only stinging Portuguese man-of-wars were getting in.

*   *   *

After the shack was built, I ducked under a clothesline strung between two papaya trees to reach the swamp. Underwear waved like white flags in the trades. The same laundry stayed up for weeks. Chipper rarely came out. It was as though he'd surrendered something vital inside and all he could do was maintain a ghostlike existence behind the patchwork walls of his shack. While his first house had been bright yellow and challenged the dreary landscape, the shack blended in. The yellow house had been full of windows. The shack had pale green walls with a single window facing west. He would sit at that window smoking a cigarette, staring at the beach house.

*   *   *

Gramma thought Chipper should have some company
so she gave him a gray kitten she'd found wandering the foothills
of Hale Kia. The kitten was a long hair with white boots and
white markings on her face.

"She's one of these Persians," Gramma said.

He didn't want the kitten. He said he was no good with
dogs or cats and that sooner or later they'd leave to find a better
home. He took the kitten on a trial basis and warmed up to her
right away. She liked climbing the rope he used to hang food on
and loved catching mice. He called her Abigail after his mother.
He fed her Little Friskies and asked me to drop off any extra
fish. He pampered Abigail day and night and took her to see Dr.
Lucky to get all her shots. One time I heard him singing "Skip to
My Lou" on his porch with her perched on his shoulder grooming
his head.

*   *   *

I liked fishing the swamp. But I wasn't there just to catch
fish. Ben had said a girl named Alice swam naked on the Duva
side of the swamp. I had yet to see her. One morning when I
had my eyes peeled, Chipper came over and handed me a silver
half-dollar.

"It's not much," he said.

The coin sparkled in my hand. I remembered the British
War Medal and the power from his courage in the war entered
that coin, from the British War Medal to the shimmering half-
dollar, silver to silver. Strange how the date on the half-dollar
was 1918. That was the year the Great War ended, the year my

father was born.

*   *   *

I see the dirt road cutting through the trees along the coast. The islands of Lanai and Maui float like whales on the horizon. The Impala moves west to Kaunakakai and Uncle Chipper drives with his windows rolled up. He must be the slowest driver on Moloka'i. Gramma honked and I waved as we passed but he didn't wave back. He never did. Sometimes we'd find the Impala with the engine running, the transmission stuck in DRIVE, and the front bumper pressed against the trunk of an ironwood. He would be either slumped over the steering wheel or lying on the front seat. He depended on the forest to keep him from heading into the ocean. I was glad he hadn't traded in his big American car for a compact. With a smaller car, he might have been able to squeeze through the ironwoods and end up at the bottom of Pailolo Channel. One time Ben found him with his feet sticking out of the passenger window.

"What should we do?" Ben asked Gramma.

"Not a damn thing," she replied.

"I think he's dead," I said.

"Dead, mah foot. The ol' fool's sleepin' it off."

"But Gramma," Ben pleaded, "shouldn't we at least shut off his engine?"

"Leave well enough alone, Mistah Ben," she said. "Be good fo' 'um to run outta gas and walk home fo' a change."

After the Impala idled for what seemed like hours, Gramma got Chipper to pull his feet back inside. She reached in, killed the engine, and opened the door. The car door seemed to be opening too wide, straining at its hinges, revealing the long

pale legs of my uncle. Before, nothing seemed tragic. But
something about her holding him under the ironwoods touched
me. I never thought a grown-up could be that helpless, that
vulnerable. For the first time I realized adults could back
themselves into corners so remote that love, or its memory, could
no longer reach them.

The East End Rodeo

The first ever East End Rodeo was scheduled for July Fourth at a working ranch in Kamalo. Posters in Kaunakakai advertised paniolos riding bucking broncos and Brahman bulls. The posters also promised clowns, popcorn, and candy apples. Nothing like this had ever happened on our end of the island. Gramma thought the rodeo was a waste of time and money until she received a flyer in the mail saying there'd be a Greased Pig Contest for children.

"You keeds are fast," she said, "yo' fast, aren't you?"

"I think so," I said.

"You think so?" she asked.

"I'm faster than the Flash," Ben announced.

"Fast enough to catch a greased pig?"

"I could catch a greased rabbit," he replied.

She said it would make her proud if one of us would catch the pig. I was heading into junior high at Punahou and the thought of chasing a pig wasn't very appealing. But I wanted to please my grandmother.

"If Ben doesn't catch that pig," I said, "I will."

"Easier than picking pineapples," Ben said.

"Like taking candy from a baby," I continued.

"Good boys."

*   *   *

We drove west the day of the rodeo. Ben and I wore T-shirts, trunks, and Keds. I was full of anticipation and dread, the same way I felt before Little League games in Honolulu. I played outfield for the Kahala Angels and my team was on a twenty-game losing streak. We didn't talk much on the drive. It felt as though we were going to the dentist to have our teeth pulled. Gramma wore her lauhala hat, palaka blouse, and blue jeans. She was so intent on getting to the rodeo that she'd forgotten to light up.

We reached the outskirts of Kamalo. Ben spotted a sign on a bamboo stick advertising "East End Rodeo." Gramma turned onto a gravel driveway. We drove between rows of sturdy posts and glistening wire. The ranch was "working" because cows and pigs were raised on it and slaughtered. The Seven Sisters, a mountain range to the north, rolled up to the sky. Gulches joined the mountains. Four of the Seven Sisters were part of the ranch and cows grazed in a green meadow halfway up the nearest Sister. Clouds clung to the peaks but it was sunny down below.

"Wot a spread," said Gramma.

The pastures were blanketed with Kentucky blue grass, not common pili grass like ours. Their horses were lean, not fat with barley bellies. Their fence posts were redwood, not cheap kiawe. Their wire was tight, not loose from mares itching their rumps.

We parked between a horse trailer and a red barn. I climbed out behind Ben. Paniolos on horseback whistled as they herded cows inside.

My brother stretched and pointed at the barn. "Bet I know what goes on in there."

"What?" I asked.

He dragged a finger across his throat.

Families filed through the main gate. Twin popcorn machines popped away and a clown with green hair, purple cheeks, and blue lips rode by on a hobbyhorse. "Whoa, Nelly!" he said yanking on the plastic bridle straps. We got in line. Gramma paid the dollar admission and smiled without showing her teeth. I knew she considered this an investment that would reap great rewards. Grandstands were set up on one side of the corral and we found seats in the middle.

"How you keeds feel?" Gramma asked.

"Like a million bucks," Ben said.

"How's li'l Peanut?"

"Fine," I said.

"I'm countin' on you boys to bring home the bacon."

"We'll bring it," Ben promised.

A man wearing an Aloha shirt carried something black with white markings from the barn into the corral. It was the size of a small dog.

"I want that piglet," she said.

Ben frowned. "You wanna eat that?"

"We'll have a big luau."

The man opened a can of oil. A paniolo held the pig while the man poured. The pig squealed and struggled so the paniolo pinned it against the ground. "Rope 'um, cowboy!" a lady called from the grandstands and everyone laughed. The paniolo let the pig go—it ran to the far corner of the corral and tried shaking off the oil the way a dog shakes off water. The man in the Aloha shirt wiped his hands on his pants. He had a microphone and welcomed us to the First Annual East End Rodeo, an event he said they'd have every Independence Day. He introduced himself as George Wilcox and boasted the ranch was modeled after the Parker Ranch on the Big Island. He invited the children to come down for the Greased Pig Contest. "Doesn't cost a thing," he said.

"Shoot yo' pickles!" Gramma told us.

Ben led the way to the corral. Parents tried coaxing their children to enter. "No be shy," a father told his daughter. "Brave girl," said her mother.

We waited outside the corral with the other contestants. A paniolo with yellow teeth told everyone to duck under the wire and all the children gathered in front of the gates for the bucking broncos. We were probably the oldest, except for the Ciaccis. The Ciaccis were a brother team like us. They were altar boys and we saw them every Sunday at Our Lady of Sorrows Church. "The Holy Mahus," Ben called them.

"Huddle," Ben said and placed his hands on my shoulders. He said he'd trip the Holy Mahus to give me a clear shot at the pig.

"Don't do it," I said.

"Why not?"

" 'Cause we'll start fighting and forget all about the pig."

He stuck his hands in his pockets. "All right," he said. "Let's spread out. We have a better chance winning if we spread out."

"How do you catch a greased pig?" I asked.

"Pretend it's a wet football." He walked to the fence, hunched down, and took a sprinter's stance.

Gramma was in the stands talking to Mr. Ah Pong, the man who owned the only store on the east end. She saw me looking and waved. She pointed us out and he stroked his jaw.

One of the paniolos carried the pig over and crouched down in front of the children. The pig squealed and the paniolo put both hands on its throat. George Wilcox patted a Hawaiian girl on the head and welcomed the children to the East End Rodeo. Parents came down for a closer look. "No sked 'um!" they said and "Go fo' broke!" Fathers fought for views along the fence. Mothers balanced on the bottom strand of wire.

"We're nearly ready," Wilcox said over the microphone.

The paniolo who'd helped oil the pig entered the corral with a revolver. He pointed the gun at the sky and fired.

"Go!" Wilcox said.

The pig charged toward the far side of the corral. Ben sprinted down the fence line and took the lead. The older Ciacci was right behind him. The younger Ciacci ran near me. I tried sprinting but my legs resisted. It seemed the harder I tried, the slower I ran. I looked for my grandmother in the stands but everything was a blur. Ben caught up to the pig, jumped, and landed with his arms around its legs. The pig squealed and kicked free. The crowd roared. The older Ciacci had his chance but a Filipino boy ran into him and they both fell. The pig veered and ran toward the wooden gates. The children converged but the pig reversed directions. The slower runners tried catching it. A blonde girl held the pig by its ear and it squealed as if it were being murdered. It got away from the girl and a Chinese boy chased it to the center of the corral. The pig finally collapsed and spurted out a stream of pee. I ran over but the younger Ciacci had already picked it up. The pig kept peeing. Ciacci's shirt was drenched and his arms glistened.

"We have a winner!" Wilcox said over the microphone. The pig was awarded to the Ciacci boy. The paniolo who'd fired the gun wiped the oil off with a rag. The boy peeled off his wet shirt and waved it at the crowd. Everyone clapped. He raised the boy's hand like he'd won a fight.

The riding and roping that followed was fun, but Gramma was in a foul mood. She chain-smoked and criticized the riders. "Call themselves paniolos?" she asked. She never laughed once at the clowns and frowned at one coasting by with his head on the seat of a unicycle. "Silly business," she said. The vendors walked through the stands and she refused to buy popcorn or candy apples. "I'm not payin' fo' that crap," she said.

Ah Pong was eating a bag of peanuts behind us. "Dis Ciacci keed not fast," he decided, "but planny akamai." He tapped a finger against his temple.

"Fasta than mah mo'opunas," she said.

*   *   *

Gramma doubled the speed limit on the ride home. She was all over the road. She flew through dips and the jeep bounced. A lady at Puko'o waved but she didn't return the greeting. She acted as though she'd bet on a sure thing and the sure thing lost.

"Those Ciaccis put you keeds to shame," she said when we got home.

"Ben did good," I said.

"Call that good?"

"He had the pig," I said, "for a second."

"At least yo' bruthah tried."

"Who wants that poor little pig anyway?"

"I do, that's who."

"It was just for fun," said Ben.

She shook her head. "Fun, nothin'."

*   *   *

The day after the rodeo, Gramma bought wire pullers from Alvin's Hardware & Feed so Valdez could tighten the fence lines. She said the mares were too fat and to quit feeding them barley. She phoned the Chamber of Commerce in Louisville, Kentucky to find out where she could buy blue grass seed.

We received a luau invitation by mail from the Ciaccis. Gramma examined that invitation for days trying to make a decision. Finally, she asked Ben and me to escort her to the luau.

"No way," Ben said.

"Not in a jillion years," I said.

"Why not?" she asked. "Half the island'll be theah."

"Because," Ben said.

"Because yo' pua losahs," she replied.

"Why don't you ask Chipper?" I suggested.

"He's a kua'aina."

"Then why'd you marry him?"

"Who the hell knows," she barked.

*   *   *

Gramma spent days deciding what to wear. She took out her suitcases and tried on her "Honolulu clothes," outfits she wore to weddings and funerals in the big city. She posed in her bedroom mirror wearing different dresses and hats. She made a special trip to Moloka'i Drugs to buy Oil of Olay. She even had Esther drop by to style her wig.

"Shuah you keeds don't wanna go?" she asked the day of the luau. She wore a black dress, a pearl necklace, heels, and her salt-and-pepper wig. Her face was caked with rouge and she had on pink lipstick and mascara. She smelled like a beauty salon.

"How does Gramma look?" she asked.

"Like the bogeyman's wife," I said.

"Like who!"

Ben laughed. "Feed your face," he told her.

"You puhi'us can fend fo' yo' bloody selves." She climbed into her jeep and pulled out of the garage. We watched her speed off and hang a left at the Norfolk.

"Thank god she's gone," Ben said.

"Now what?" I asked.

"Let's check the fridge."

We went into the kitchen and he swung open the refrigerator door. Wax paper tented a paper plate. He lifted the wax paper—the plate was stacked with tuna sandwiches. A pitcher of grape juice cooled beside it.

"This beats kalua pig," he said and grabbed a sandwich.

I poured juice from the pitcher into two glasses and handed one to him. I took a sandwich and sunk my teeth into it. I was glad Hale Kia wasn't a working ranch. I washed down my sandwich with grape juice and wondered how the luau meat would taste to the Ciacci boy who'd caught the pig.

We finished lunch. Ben went outside to put new line on his reel. It was funny without our grandmother there. I felt guilty for not going with her.

"Wanna go fishing?" he asked from the lanai.

"No," I said.

"Whacha wanna do?"

"Read some *Huckleberry Finn.*"

"Doofus," he replied. He walked out the back door with his pole.

I wandered into the big room, flopped in Gramma's cushioned chair, and rested my elbows on the arms. Her corner of the table was packed with smoking paraphernalia: a carton of Chesterfields, Lancer's matches, and a tin can full of ashes and butts. A pencil was wedged between the pages of *TV Guide* and the *Holy Bible* was perched on the sill of the picture window. A brass vase glowed the middle of the table; it was surrounded by a transistor radio, a pair of binoculars, an abalone shell, and a paper cup crammed with pencils and pens.

I heard a car chugging and spotted the Impala on the dirt road. Chipper parked and got out. Skippy was sprawled on the grass near the Norfolk and he wagged his tail.

I opened the door and walked down the slope. He held a hunk of raw meat in one hand and a choke chain in the other. The chain was attached to a nylon rope. "C'mon, boy," he called waving the meat, "gotcha some venison." Skippy trotted over. He sniffed the venison and Chipper slipped the chain over his head. He dropped the venison on the grass and Skippy wolfed it down. He tied the end of the rope to his rear bumper.

"Hi, Uncle Chipper," I said.

"Wot you want?"

"Nothing."

He scowled at Skippy. "Damn killah."

"Killer?"

"Skippy killed my Abigail."

"Abigail's dead?"

He climbed in the Impala and fired it up. He inched forward until there was no slack in the rope and the loop in the chain shrunk. He gave it some gas—Skippy's head jerked violently.

"Stop!" I said.

The Impala moved down the dirt road with Skippy in tow. I jogged barefoot behind it. The exhaust pipe rattled and spewed soot. Skippy tried pulling himself free but the choke chain tightened like a noose. He kept pace with the Impala so he wouldn't get dragged. The Impala stopped outside the shack. He got out and slammed the door.

I ran to Uncle Chipper. "Don't hurt him!"

He untied the rope on his bumper. "Look inside that box," he said, "undah the hangin' tree."

I walked to the hanging tree, the big ironwood on the corner of the property. This was the tree hunters used to butcher their kills. A cardboard box was beneath it with its flaps closed. I opened the flaps—Abigail was curled inside. I thought she was napping but I noticed splotches of red in her coat. Her tongue was out and her eyes had glazed over white.

"Oh, Abby," I said.

Chipper dragged Skippy. He whined pulling against the chain. Chipper tugged and Skippy yelped. He kept tugging and they disappeared behind a mound of garbage bags. I darted over. Mangrove surrounded the dump's mauka side so no one could see in from the highway. He pulled Skippy to a kiawe stump. He tied the end of the rope to the stump and took a path through the pickleweed to his shack. I headed in. The dirt was covered with glass shards, cigarette butts, and rusted cans. I squeezed through trash bags, old mattresses, and busted chairs. Maggots spilled from a tear in a bag. A mongoose scurried through the trash. I kept going and reached Skippy. He circled the stump trying to get loose and the rope wound around it.

"Everything's cool, Skip," I said holding out my hand.

Skippy growled.

"Outta da way," came Chipper's voice.

I turned. He had a shotgun and he worked the pump action. He aimed down at Skippy.

"Don't do it!" I said.

"Scram."

Skippy hunched on the dirt. I knelt down and patted him.

"Gunfunnit," he said, "leave us be."

"No."

"I'm warnin' you, get back to the beach house."

"I'm not leaving."

He pointed the barrel up at the sky and fired a blast that

made my ears ring. Dogs barked in neighboring kuleanas. Chipper hobbled away. I slipped off the choke chain and Skippy ran through the trash to the dirt road. I found a path to the lawn and saw him running to the beach house. Chipper tossed the shotgun in his trunk and slammed the lid. He walked to the ironwood, picked up the box, and disappeared inside his shack. I waited on the porch and he finally came out.

"Can I trust you?" he asked.

"Yes," I said.

"Tell nobody this happened."

"I won't tell. Scout's honor."

"Take it to yo' grave."

*   *   *

The Skippy Incident was a secret Uncle Chipper and I shared from one summer to the next. I never told Gramma what he'd done because it could have severed their fragile bond. Secrets are like lies when they hide the truth. But sometimes the truth needs to be hidden when nothing good comes from it.

Gramma didn't punish Skippy when she found out he'd killed Abigail. She said he had the killer instinct and that hitting him would just make him mean. Chipper buried Abigail in the forest. I found her burial mound in a patch of sunlight between two ironwoods. I made a cross from driftwood and said three Hail Marys and two Our Fathers before sinking it in the ground. Chipper watched from his porch. It didn't seem fair that Abigail was in the earth and life went on as usual.

*   *   *

Skippy acted funny two weeks after Abigail was buried. He ate only half his dinner and growled at Leo and Spotty

whenever they came close. He yelped one night and Ben found
him quivering in the pasture. Gramma had Dr. Lucky come the
next morning. Dr. Lucky said he had heartworms and put him
out of his misery with a shot. Chipper told Gramma she could
bury him beside Abigail so she wrapped his body in his winter
blanket and I wheelbarrowed him over. Ben dug the hole. I
mumbled an Our Father as we buried him. I marked his grave
with a bamboo cross.

Gramma was between Ben and me when we headed back
to the beach house. She didn't talk. I listened to the doves coo
in the ironwoods and the crunch of fallen needles.

Puanani

Gramma smelled liquor a week after Chipper moved out of the beach house. She went to bed thinking the smell was from a bottle Chipper had tossed in her garden. Her vicious dog Bozo was outside so she wasn't worried about trespassers. The springs on her bed creaked and she opened her eyes. Someone was sitting on the corner of the bed. A hand reached under the covers and stroked her leg. "Chippah?" she asked. She turned on the lamp—there sat Billy Duva holding a bottle of Jim Beam. He was only sixteen but big for his age.

"Hungry?" she asked.

"Pololi," said Billy.

She walked to the kitchen. She wanted to grab her butcher knife but instead, returned with an apple banana. He sat on her bed eating the banana and swilling Jim Beam while she pulled on her jeans. She told him his mother was a nice woman and praised his father for helping her string wire. He finished the banana and put his bottle on her bureau. "Gettin' late," she told him. She picked up her rifle and followed him through the big room. She heard voices on the lanai. He walked out the screen door and she stood in the doorway holding her rifle. "Hele on now," she said loading the chamber, "befoa somethin' bad happens." Billy and four boys scrambled over the ledge of an open storm window. The next morning, she found her dog Bozo in the pasture with his throat slit.

* * *

Gramma armed my father and Bobby with rifles every summer and assigned them guard duty at night. She stationed Bobby in the Norfolk and my father in the hala tree next to the beach house. "Shoot first," she said, "ask questions laytah." My father took it seriously until he figured out the sounds his mother was hearing were caused by the wind blowing things over and rain on the roof. After the third night of guard duty, Bobby fell asleep in the Norfolk and my father climbed out of the hala tree and went to bed.

* * *

We were never assigned guard duty but I knew my grandmother's mind was freewheeling. Her paranoia introduced us to high drama—hunters were shining lights on Hale Kia after midnight and trespassers were stealing gas. She said someone had replaced her jeep's American engine with a Japanese one. I asked her why thieves would bother exchanging engines and she answered, " 'Cause they don't want me knowin'." I told her she would have heard something if her engine was being removed but she said the ring leader snuck into her room, pressed his thumb against her carotid artery, and knocked her out. She showed me a "bluey mark" on her neck the size of a thumb print.

*   *   *

Gramma called Ben and me into her bedroom after *The Lawrence Welk Show*. The window overlooking her garden was open and a breeze blew through the screen.

"You keeds smell somethin' funny?" she asked.

"Fish?" Ben asked.

I sniffed the air. "Manure?"

"Whiskey on the wind," she said. "Heah that?"

Ben wrinkled his brow. "Hear what?"

"Some puhi'u up on mah roof." She slid a rifle out from under her bed and worked the bolt action. A bullet jumped into the chamber and she fired at the ceiling. The brass casing spun like a top on her bureau. "That'll fix 'um," she said.

*   *   *

I attributed Gramma's odd behavior to living alone and being in constant fear of Billy. Whether it was a psychosis or a neurosis I didn't know. My father told her to quit eating sweets late at night to avoid "moments of pure fantasy." She sucked on Coffee Nips candies during *Hollywood Palace* but I doubted that triggered mental instability. I thought love would rescue her mind so I wanted her to reunite with Chipper. But whenever I asked if she'd try again she always said she was better off without him.

*   *   *

Gramma needed a cash crop to help with expenses after she got the deed to Hale Kia. Her pay as a paniolo wasn't enough. On Moloka'i, you had to find ways to make money because classified ads didn't exist. It was a man's island. Even the most industrious of women had failed. She planted hala trees in the pasture, along the coast, and near the beach house. When the leaves turned brown, she plucked them and stripped off their thorns. She rolled the leaves into bales and sold them to weavers in Kaunakakai. In the old days, she wove mats. Now her arthritis made it too painful.

We helped Gramma pick the long lauhala leaves. The trees were tall and bushy, with roots growing above ground like mangrove. Ben was a fearless climber. He tested the strength of narrow branches and balanced on one foot.

I stood beside Gramma and watched him climb.

"Fo' the luva Christ, Ben," she scolded, "that's high enough."

He touched the end of a leaf. "Almost there."

"Watch for centipedes," I warned.

He jerked the leaf and it fell to the ground.

She turned it over. "No ka oi."

The lauhala was perfect—a rich brown without a blemish. It was shiny and pliable, which meant it hadn't lost its natural oils and wouldn't crack when woven.

The lauhala thorns cut me whenever we harvested. When it came to climbing, my left foot was bigger than my right and I had trouble balancing. I picked the leaves lower down, the ones with water stains and holes. I felt bad for the leaves that wouldn't get woven into mats.

"Look," I said holding up a leaf with a red stain.

"Toss it," Gramma said.

"But this part's good."

"Hundreds of bettah leaves, Peanut."

Ben finished pulling leaves and we tied the ends together

and stacked them in bundles next to the garage. Gramma stripped off the thorns with a knife and the rolling process made her hands blister and bleed. The lauhala was streaked with blood but she refused gloves—they made it hard to grip the handle of the knife. She wiped the blood off with a rag when she finished a bale.

"Let me help," Ben said.

She continued stripping thorns. "Only I can do this."

*   *   *

We drove to town in the jeep with lauhala bales stacked in a trailer. The bales resembled skinny brown tires. We pulled up beside Ku'u Ipo Dance Hall on the outskirts of Kaunakakai. A woman named Becky Lima told us to bring in the harvest. We carried the bales inside and put them on a table. Women sat in circles. One circle wove mats. A second did a finer weave for hats and baskets. The floor was scuffed and it bowed in the middle. Gramma had been the USO's social director during the war and she used the hall for dances and shows. Fletcher, a handsome lieutenant on R & R from the Marianas Campaign, had danced with her. They snuck off into a taro patch outside the dance hall and he held her close in the twilight. He knew she was married but he still kissed her under the stars.

I pretended a band was playing Benny Goodman's "In the Mood." I did an impromptu fox trot and imagined my grandmother as a young woman dancing with Fletcher. They moved gracefully across the dance floor. He was great at spinning her while the flutes and saxophones wailed. I tried spinning my partner and tripped over my feet.

"Quit actin' silly," Gramma told me.

A woman looked up from her weaving. "Auntie Brownie!" she said and hustled over.

"Hello, Kitty," Gramma said and they hugged.

"Dese mus' be yo' mo'opunas."

"Ben and Jeff," she said. "Norman's boys."

Kitty hugged us. She was hapa haole and her short hair was brown and streaked orange. Her hands were thick with calluses.

"How is Norman?" Kitty asked. "Long time, no?"

"Long time is right."

Kitty studied Ben. "Dis one look like Norman."

"A'ole. Spittin' image of the muthah."

"Am not," he said.

They talked about how Honolulu was a magnet for crime, a snarl of traffic, and a town run by crooks. Kitty said she'd heard the governor was smuggling in diamonds from Japan and the mayor was laundering Hong Kong money. Gramma said Oahu was sinking from all the concrete. Kitty said limu kohu was getting hard to find.

"Gotta go way outside da reef," she said, "stay in da purple waddah."

"Next time yo' neah Hale Kia," Gramma said, "drop by."

Kitty promised to visit and returned to her circle of weavers. Becky measured our bales from the center to the edge with a koa stick. She stamped a book, Gramma signed, and Becky gave us cash and a handful of coins.

A girl wearing a shark tooth necklace sat in Kitty's circle. Her skin was like polished koa and her muumuu hugged the curves of her body.

"That chick's a fox," I told Ben.

He saw her and blushed. She looked up and smiled.

Kitty scolded the girl for not keeping up and looked over at us. Ben took his eyes off the girl.

The weavers waved goodbye as we headed for the door. The girl gave Ben one last smile. He hid his hands in his pockets and walked to the jeep. He hardly talked as we drove east past the onion fields. He contemplated the mountains to the north.

"Meow," I said on the ride home, "meow."

"You sound like a dyin' cat," Gramma said.

"I'm Kitty."

Ben turned around and punched me in the leg.

"Owie!" I said. "Gramma, Ben just hit me."

"That's wot you get fo' makin' fun."

I rubbed my leg. "But her name's funny."

"Kitty used to be yo' fathah's girl."

"Really?" Ben asked.

"When yo' fathah was a boy," she explained. "They met at Ku'u Ipo Dance Hall one summa. He thought Kitty was the cat's meow." She told us how Kitty had walked to Hale Kia from Kamalo on a pitch black night to see him.

"Who was that girl with Kitty?" Ben asked her.

"Puanani."

"Is she her granddaughter?" I asked.

"Ae."

"I wanna ask Puanani out," he said.

She shifted gears and slowed for a dip. "I don't want you mixin' with any kanaka girls."

"We've got kanaka blood," I said.

"Three drops." She shifted after the dip and floored it.

"What's wrong with Hawaiian girls?" Ben asked.

"Get one hapai and that'll be that."

"That'll be what?"

"Yo' life'll be ruined, that's wot."

"Was Daddy's life ruined when he mixed with Kitty?" Ben asked.

"Pa'a the waha."

Ben waved at the cars and trucks heading west. We sped past the sign marking the Smith Bronte crash landing of 1927. He whistled the theme song to *Gilligan's Island*. Gramma told him he was calling the devil by whistling. He didn't stop. She said his puckered lips reminded her of "a horse's okole."

He whistled the rest of the way home.

Kaka Lines

Gramma said the time had come to fish the ocean. She searched her wash room and returned with three bales of one hundred-pound cord. One bale was wound around a bamboo stick and the other two were secured to pieces of driftwood. At the end of each cord was a steel leader, lead weights shaped like tiny balloons, and a huge fishhook.

Ben fingered a hook. "This could catch a shark," he said.
"Shahk, nothin'," she said. "These are kaka lines."
"What are they for?" I asked.
"Ulua," she replied.

*   *   *

I held a baited hook in my left hand and a steel leader in my right makai of the beach house. The bait was an octopus leg full of purple veins and it swayed on its big steel hook.

Gramma sat behind an open storm window and let her line unravel off the bamboo stick. "Spit on mah bait, Peanut," she said, "fo' good luck."

"Now?" I asked.

"Just befoa you throw it in."

I pulled the steel leader and hook down the incline. The stick that held the cord spanked the floor of the lanai. Gramma controlled the kaka line by letting it slip between her legs. It was late afternoon and the tide was rising. I entered the water with bare feet. The waves broke at the reef and rolled in white. "Landing at Normandy," my father had said in similar conditions. I stumbled over a chunk of coral. The tide chart said the ocean would keep rising until midnight—that's when ulua swam through the harbor to hunt in the shallows. Gramma wanted our bait to be fresh so we dropped the kaka lines at sunset. It was almost impossible to catch ulua during the day— they saw the cord and steered clear of the bait. Ulua was the best-eating fish in our waters but tough to net. I'd skin dive and see their silvery blue bodies hover in place a few seconds before zooming off.

The water reached my waist. White caps rolled through the harbor and over the reef. A black fin surfaced twenty feet out but I knew by the curve of the fin that it was a manta ray. I kept going until the water lapped at my chest. I felt a tug on the line—that was her signal to stop. I spat on the bait. "Lotsa luck," I said and tossed it in. The lead weights carried the baited hook to the sandy bottom.

I returned to the beach house to put out my line. Gramma held the driftwood while I headed toward Mokuhooniki, an atoll to the east. The sun dropped behind Kahoolawe and shadows swept over the ocean like whales. I felt a tug so I spat on the bait and threw it in. I saw Ben wading west toward Lanai. Gramma's line was between ours, straight at Maui. My brother hated his spot because eels swam out of the coral to swallow his bait. He usually hooked morays, yellowish-brown eels with nasty dispositions. The morays twirled their bodies around the line so you couldn't unhook them without risking a bite. In the early days, Chipper would find them in his deep water traps. He'd gutted a twenty-footer on his boat to recover a bounty of octopi and lobster.

Ben pulled in a moray the next morning and Gramma phoned Chipper. He came over, picked up a coconut, and smashed the moray's head.

"Please, Uncle Chipper, please," I begged, "let the poor eel go."

He crushed the moray's skull and its mouth gushed blood. It was hard watching the eel die.

"Why kill him?" I asked.

"Eel makes good bait," Gramma said.

Chipper reached down the moray's throat and yanked out the hook.

"But what eats eel?" I pressed.

"Ulua," he replied.

*   *   *

We tied the ends of our kaka lines to the posts between storm windows. Gramma liked watching TV while the lines were out. She said you had to clear your mind of catching fish so you wouldn't jinx the bait. She turned off the TV after *The Lawrence Welk Show* and asked Ben to demonstrate the latest dance steps. He switched on the radio and spun the dial to KKUA. He performed everything from the Swim to the Monkey, and even did some acid rock improv to "L.A. Woman." She said it was my turn and I did the cha'-cha'-cha' to "Incense and Peppermints" by Strawberry Alarm Clock. She clapped and reminded us we had dancing in our blood. Ben showed her how to do the Frug to "Winchester Cathedral" and she threw in a little Charleston for good measure. She let Spotty in and he stood up on his hind legs—she held his front paws and danced with him across the room. Spotty whined when he'd had enough and she slipped him a hunk of roast beef.

*   *   *

Ben grew frustrated catching eels. Part of the fun was catching fish we could eat. He thought hooking an ulua would make our grandmother respect him as a keiki o ka aina. He asked her to switch spots with him. "It's not fair," he said, "you're catching all the ulua."

"Ulua knows no home," she replied.

"So let's switch places."

"Be happy with wot you got."

I always caught balloon fish. They were so exhausted trying to stay alive all night that by morning they couldn't puff up. I wanted to let them go but they'd suck the bait so deep that the hook wouldn't come out without tearing up their insides.

Gramma phoned Johnny Crystobal the morning I pulled in a twenty-pound balloon fish. Johnny was a small, wiry Filipino who did odd jobs. He bicycled over on a rusty Schwinn and cut out the poison glands.

"One drop an' pau," he said as green jelly that smelled like iodine oozed from the glands. He dug a hole and buried them. Leo and Spotty sniffed the sand and he shooed them away.

Gramma walked over and watched Johnny cover the hole. "How's that fish look?"

"Maika'i." He wrapped the balloon fish in a ti leaf, placed it in the basket on his bicycle, and pedaled away.

*   *   *

Ben wanted to catch ulua so he pretended to head for Lanai with his kaka line and made a run at Maui. The next morning, we tugged on our lines at the storm windows.

"I caught somethin'," Gramma said.

"Me too," said my brother.

They raced to the beach. They pulled and pulled at the shoreline—a ball of tangled cord surfaced.

"You caught Ben," I told Gramma.

She spent all morning separating them. "Why you droppin' yo' kaka line so close to mine, Mistah Ben?"

He shrugged his shoulders. "Currents musta pushed them together."

"Currents, mah foot. From now on, stay in yo' own damn spot."

"You're always trying to control things," he said.

"Ridiculous."

"I can't call Puanani, right?"

"Right."

"See," he mumbled.

*   *   *

My brother's bed was on the mauka side of the lanai. I slept on the makai side. The kaka lines were tethered to the beach house. The moon made the lines glow as they moved up and down with the tide. These were our umbilical cords, linking

us to all the mystery in the ocean. I took my foot out of the
covers, slipped it past the mosquito net, and rested it on my line.
I felt the ocean's pulse through the cord.

"What's going on, Peanut?" Ben asked from the dark.

"I'm feeling the tide."

"You're lolo."

"Am not."

"Don't put your momona foot on my line."

"Go to sleep, Juicy."

"Think Daddy really killed that hammerhead?"

"Sure," I said. "Why not?"

"Gramma's full of kukae."

I wondered why the tsunami had taken the cottage but
spared the beach house. Maybe it had been built on sacred land.
That night, I dreamt I could breath underwater. I walked my
kaka line like a tightrope down to the ocean floor as canoes slid
over the surface. My parents were in an outrigger and my mother
waved at me. A canoe of warriors wearing feathered capes
pursued them. The warriors dug their paddles deep while my
father paddled furiously with his briefcase. "Don't hurt them!"
I cried. The lead warrior quit paddling. He dropped a poi
pounder with a line attached and I pulled myself up until I was
treading water beside the canoe. The warrior extended his hand,
I took it, and he pulled me in. My mother waved from beyond
the reef and I picked up a paddle. I slipped on a feathered cape
and paddled until we caught my parents. The waves battered
their outrigger. A briefcase floated by. My father was on the
stern in a fetal position while my mother tap-danced on the bow
of their capsizing boat. The lead warrior pulled out a spear and

I tried pulling it away but he was too strong. The warrior hurled the spear. I flinched and my eyes opened—I'd fallen asleep with my foot on the line.

*   *   *

Gramma tied pink string from a pastry box to the end of her kaka line and used the string to suspend the line from an eave. The string would break if something big hit.   She had Narakiro, her handyman and taxidermist, install a socket on the lanai. She screwed in a floodlight so she could see her line at night. The string snapped during *The Ed Sullivan Show* and the kaka line went out to sea. She examined the frayed cord.

"What was it?" I asked.

"A damn big ulua."

Ben looked at what was left of her line. "It was a shark."

"Shahks can't make it ovah the reef," she said.

"Saw a fin yesterday," he said, "past the point."

She crossed her arms. "Black fin?"

"Yeah."

"That's a damn ray."

A week later Ben caught a tiger shark with his kaka line. It was three feet long and its teeth were like razors. We watched it flail on the sand as the dogs barked and ran circles around it.

"Thought you said no sharks?" he asked Gramma.

"This ocean's changin'," she said.

I sensed a growing antagonism between my grandmother and brother. He didn't believe her when she said our father had killed his first buck when he was twelve and that he'd roped and tamed wild horses in the high country. According to her, our father had located the source of Kainalu Stream after running two days up Hale Kia's mountain and, when he returned to the flatlands suffering from appendicitis, he withstood the pain for a week so he could drop sea traps with Chipper. He'd killed the hammerhead with a single thrust of a spear he'd made from a steel fence post. Ben wanted to establish himself as our father's equal by proving Gramma's stories false.

Our father's adventures as a boy could never be disputed. He would always be a keiki o ka aina in his mother's eyes, a child of the land and the sea. It was during her watch he had done great things. His triumphs on Moloka'i were her triumphs too because they reminded her she'd been there for him.

Keoni

We weren't allowed to invite friends to Hale Kia because my father didn't want to push Gramma over the edge. But one summer he needed permission to build a sea wall in front of the beach house. My father found out Red Applegate granted ocean easements for the State of Hawaii. He knew Keoni was Red's son and my friend at Star of the Sea so he phoned Red and insisted Keoni visit us on Moloka'i.

My father's concern for the ranch was fueled by his desire to own it. He didn't want Bobby inheriting anything since he never sent their mother any money. He hated Bobby's selfish nature. He told me when they were boys he got stuck cleaning the house and the yard while Bobby was "standing on Waialae Avenue watching all the girls go by."

*   *   *

Keoni didn't look like his parents. His mother was so white she'd blister hanging out the wash. His father's face was as red as a tomato. Keoni was a husky kid with a baby face and an olive complexion. If he spent time in the sun, he just got darker. He could polish off a dozen malasadas in five minutes— Ben said that proved he had Portuguese blood. Keoni seemed more sophisticated than my other classmates. He discovered a secret path through the kuku weeds from the rectory over to the convent.

"The nuns and priests do it," he said.

"Do what?" I asked.

"The birds and the bees."

The nuns had flunked him twice for failing math. He'd started out one grade ahead of my brother and now was one grade back. He was close to flunking a third time when I left Star of the Sea for Punahou School.

"Keoni's a birdbrain," Ben had said, but this was before he found out he'd have to repeat seventh grade in order to attend Punahou.

Mr. Applegate bought Keoni a blackboard and put it in his bedroom. He told him to write his math problems and answers on the board so he could check them. I chalked out problems for Keoni. "Bo-ring," he said. He produced a mahogany box and showed me his collection of brass knickknacks from Indian Imports and a jade ring a widow gave him for massaging her okole with plumeria oil.

"Why doesn't Keoni look like his parents?" I asked my mother.

"He's adopted," she said.

"How come?"

"Poor Mrs. Applegate couldn't have children."

"Are adopted kids dumber than regular kids?"

"Keoni was a heroin baby," she whispered.

My mother and Keoni gossiped about everyone in Kahala. Her favorite topics were who'd divorced, who'd died, and who was cheating.

"Mrs. Rosewood's doing the birds and the bees with Mr. McCormack," he said.

"Oh, Keoni," my mother said, "tell me you're kidding."

"His car's in her driveway the second Mr. Rosewood leaves for work."

"Well," she said, "imagine that."

Sometimes I felt that Keoni was more her friend than mine, especially after he became a regular at the Kahala Hilton and reported on the stars who'd checked in. "Try and be nice," my mother told Ben when Keoni was over. I figured a boy could never beat up someone older than himself, but Ben proved that wrong when he beefed him in our driveway for squirting him with a hose. Keoni was big but soft—he could throw a punch but he couldn't take one.

Despite his troubles at school, Keoni had a quality that made me think he'd become a great businessman. He opened a mango stand and earned two hundred dollars every summer.

"Keoni's very enterprising," my mother said.

The curb in front of the Applegate house had cars coming and going. Haoles arrived in station wagons. Tour buses double-parked. Samoans pulled over in trucks. Keoni gave locals the Kama'aina Discount—ten percent off. He saved the best mangoes for the bus drivers. "Gotta grease 'em," he explained. The bus drivers stayed as long as it took the tourists to make their purchases. He figured prices in his head and gave correct change.

I couldn't understand how someone so good with money could be so lousy at math. He sold rotten mangoes when he ran out of ripe ones. If he was busy selling and I was over, he'd have me scoop mangoes off the dirt.

"How can you tell if a mango's ripe?" a lady from Chicago asked.

"The softer," Keoni said, "the better." He pushed his thumb through the skin of a mango. "This one's perfect."

She paid fifty cents for that rotten mango. I hoped her first bite wouldn't be full of worms.

*   *   *

My father was driving home from work when he saw Keoni standing in the middle of Aukai Avenue waving weeds like pompoms at all the cars. "Hooray," he said, "hooray, for Beef-a-Roni!"

"Is that kid retarded?" my father asked when my mother greeted him at the door.

"His mother took heroin," my mother whispered.

"Sharon Applegate's on heroin?"

"No, Dear. His real mother."

My father didn't think twice about inviting Keoni to Moloka'i even though he knew he'd qualify as "a damn hellion" in Gramma's book. He'd seen him throw a vase through a porthole just before the Applegates cruised to San Francisco aboard the SS Lurline. Local boys were diving for coins thrown by passengers and the vase nearly hit one. Keoni stuck his head out the porthole.

"Punk," a boy called up, "geev you dirty lickings when you get off!"

"Dirty lickings your mother," he called down, "I'm cruising to Frisco!"

My father was willing to sacrifice a little of Gramma's sanity to get on Red's good side. He was more concerned with beachfront erosion than the potential erosion of his mother's mind. Besides, he'd bought her a gold International Scout with leather seats to ease her conscience about signing over Hale Kia.

*　　　*　　　*

We picked Keoni up at Hoolehua Airport on Father's Day. He wore a yellow Outrigger Canoe Club T-shirt, pineapple pants, and loafers. He'd put on weight and sported a faint moustache.

"Aloha, Mrs. Daniels," he said to Gramma in the airport lobby.

"Hello," Gramma replied.

Keoni pulled a ten-dollar bill from an eelskin wallet and flashed it at Ben and me.

"That's big money," she said.

"It's for emergencies."

Ben smirked. "No emergencies on Moloka'i."

"I'll save it then," he said, "for Harvard."

We claimed his suitcase and headed outside. The Scout was the shiniest truck in the lot. Ben tossed the suitcase over the tailgate and I stepped up on the bumper and climbed in. Keoni followed. We sprawled on the metal bench seats built in the bed.

Gramma started the Scout and Ben got in the cab. He was wearing horn-rimmed glasses to correct his vision. He also had braces on his teeth to anchor what Dr. Doe Fang called "drifting bicuspids." He wasn't wearing his prescription black shoes to correct his pigeon-toed stride. He'd convinced Gramma that cowboy boots worked just as well.

On our ride east, Keoni quizzed me about my new school. He wanted to know what fashions were in at Punahou, whether anyone smoked pakalolo, and if the girls were going all the way. I told him Mr. Dresman had been caught in the music room with an eighth grade girl. I said Punahou had three big fields, Olympic-size pools, and tennis courts.

"You're a snob now," he said.

"Am not."

"Buncha spoiled haoles go there."

"You're just jealous 'cause you can't get in."

"Wouldn't go if you paid me," he replied.

I pointed out heiaus, the foothills where King Kamehameha had camped, and Kaunakakai Wharf. "Bo-ring," he said. He spotted the island's only fast food restaurant next to the power plant and talked about cheeseburgers, golden fries, and swirl cones dipped in chocolate. He seemed worried when we reached the pastures of Kamalo—he said his money was worthless if stores didn't exist.

"Keoni wants Dairy Queen," I told Gramma when we arrived at Hale Kia.

"Dairy who?" she asked.

"The burger place," he said, "in that wild west town."

"Fo' the luva Pete," she said, "we-ah miles from Kaunakakai."

"I'll pay for gas, Mrs. Daniels."

"Gas, mah foot."

Gramma cooked Hawaiian stew for dinner and served

guava cake for dessert. She let Keoni have her bedroom while she slept on the pune'e. She gave him his own hook in the bathroom to hang up his clothes. But that didn't make him like Hale Kia. He hated going to bed early and getting up at dawn. He hated hiking and fishing. He hated it when we shoveled manure. "You're slaves on a kukae farm," he said slapping at a blue fly. He mentioned child labor laws and how Gramma was duping us.

"You're just a lazy okole," Ben said.

"Does she pay you?"

My brother leaned on his shovel. "No."

"See? You're slave labor, metal mouth."

I extended the handle of my shovel toward Keoni. "Wanna help?" I asked, thinking if he tried shoveling he might enjoy it.

"I'm on vacation."

Keoni couldn't believe Gramma wouldn't drive us anywhere fun. Mrs. Applegate called the second night and he said he wanted to come home. Gramma knew my father needed that favor so she volunteered to take him the next day to the only store on the east end.

"Do they have candy?" he asked.

"Enough to rot yo' bloody teeth," she said.

*   *   *

On the drive the next morning, Keoni and I stood up on the Scout's bed and hung our arms over the cab's roof. Ben rode in the cab with Gramma. The road was narrow in places so she drove in the middle.

"Road hog," Keoni said.

"Quiet," I told him.

He pounded on the roof. "Road hog!"

The Scout swerved and we nearly flew out. I sat down but Keoni clung to the rain gutters and beat his fists on the roof. "Sunday driver!" It became a duel, with Gramma swerving trying to force him down while he shouted and banged the roof like a drum.

He was still standing when we pulled alongside a beige house with AH PONG'S painted in red over the entrance. A gas pump was out front. Everything Mr. Ah Pong sold was more expensive than stores in Kaunakakai. "Planny ovah-head," I'd heard him say. Gramma kept her purchases to a minimum. But she always topped off her tank in case there was a run on gas. She rolled up to the pump.

"Charge!" Keoni said and we jumped out.

A Filipino man stuck a nozzle in the tank. Yellow seed pods were scattered over the dirt and asphalt. The dirt was darker where motor oil had soaked in. I smelled the sweet gas being pumped. The man popped the hood, pulled the dipstick, and wiped it with a swatch of lauhala.

"You keeds make it fast," Gramma said.

"Why the bum's rush?" Keoni asked.

"You've gotta smart mouth, Mistah Keoni."

He led the way over a sidewalk flanked by red hibiscus. Ben followed us up the creaky wooden steps. The screen door was open and we walked inside. The store was deserted. Bees buzzed a rack of empty soda bottles. Mr. Ah Pong was on a stool behind the counter stroking his jaw. He had his glasses on and was checking out pictures in *Playboy*.

"Summer reading?" Keoni asked.

Ah Pong looked up. "Ah," he said, "welcome, boys."

I was suspicious of his candy and snacks. I'd barfed after eating a bag of Cheetos and had found worms in a Hershey bar. Even the canned and bottled goods were suspect. Gramma had once bought a jar of Best Foods mayonnaise loaded with black spores.

A red dispenser crammed with bottled pop was just inside the doorway. I lifted the wooden lid, plunged my hand in the icy water, and pulled out a bottle of strawberry soda.

"I'll buy you guys something," Keoni said.

"Got my own money," Ben replied.

"Yeah," I said. "Gramma gave us each a quarter."

Keoni laughed. "She's so generous."

Ben and I paid for our sodas while Keoni walked the aisles checking items and prices.

"What a momona," Ben said. He popped the cap on his root beer and gulped. Foam shot up the bottle's neck.

Keoni ignored my warnings about rotten food. He snatched packs of Yick Lung's cracked plum seed, mango seed, dried abalone, Maui potato chips, Ding Dongs, gum, and an assortment of candy bars. He stacked everything on the counter.

"Chee," Ah Pong said, "hungry boy!" He closed his magazine, rang up the items, and took the ten-dollar bill. The register slid open and Ah Pong tucked the bill under the money tray. He placed a dollar and a dime on the counter. "Honolulu boy?" he asked.

"Yeah," Keoni answered, "I'm a millionaire."

He smiled as he bagged.

Keoni saw us holding drinks. "How much are sody pops?"

Ah Pong stroked his jaw. "Quarta."

"I'll take three." He fished around in the water and stuck two creme sodas in his bag. He grabbed a Coke and waved it in the air. "One for the road!"

Ben finished his root beer and placed his empty in the rack. Keoni and I popped our caps.

"No forget change, millionaire," Ah Pong said.

"That's a tip for the east end playboy," Keoni answered.

Ben went down the steps first. Keoni burped guzzling his Coke. Gramma was signing a receipt when we returned. The man took the receipt, gave her a carbon copy, and rolled up the air hose.

"Wot's in that damn bag?" Gramma asked.

"Candy and junk," Ben said opening the passenger door.

Keoni waved his Coke bottle. "Wanna sody pop, Mrs. Daniels?"

"No. And don't eat any of that crap befoa lunch."

Keoni sat next to me in the Scout's bed on the ride home. He broke open the bag of chips and waved it in front of my face. "Betcha can't eat just one."

"We're not supposed to," I said.

"Dare you."

"No."

"Double dare."

I shook my head.

"Why are you such a goody goody on Moloka'i?"

I reached in and took a handful just as Gramma looked.

She said something to Ben. He saw me chewing and puffed out his cheeks. Keoni and I chugged our sodas. We crossed the first bridge and he threw his empty—it broke on the river stones below. I hurried to finish my strawberry soda and, on the next bridge, I hurled my bottle over the kukui nut trees. It sounded like a gunshot when it shattered.

Gramma slammed on the brakes and got out with the engine running. "Who threw that god damn bottle?"

We didn't answer.

"Go on," she said. "Tell the bloody truth."

"I threw it," Keoni said.

"Well, get down theah and pick up that glass."

"But I'm the guest."

"Do as I say, or I'm shippin' you home."

He jumped out with his bag of goodies. I followed him and we hiked down. Glass glittered on the banks of a stream. Mosquitoes came out of the woods and swarmed us.

Gramma watched from the road as we gathered up the shards. "Last of the bloody Mohicans," she said.

"Where should we put the glass?" I asked her.

"Bury it."

"Hillbilly," Keoni mumbled.

"Wha'd you say, Mistah Keoni?"

"You don't wanna know."

" 'Course I do."

"Really?"

"Really."

"Hillbilly, hillbilly, hillbilly," he said, "you're a triple scoop hillbilly with a macadamia nut on top."

She stood there with her hands on her hips. "You two puhi'us can walk home," she said and returned to the Scout.

Ben put his thumb to his nose and made the "Kiss My Ass" sign at us as they drove off.

Keoni slapped at a mosquito. "Just for that," he said, "I'm not picking up any more glass." He dropped his shards in the stream.

I dug a hole beside the thick trunk of a kukui nut tree and buried my pieces. "Let's start walking," I said.

He shook his head. "I'm not walking."

"So how do we get home?"

"Don't you watch the movies?"

I followed him up the embankment and we crossed the bridge. We reached the road and he stuck out his thumb.

"Why'd you take the blame?" I asked.

"I get to leave on Friday."

A truck approached and sped by.

"Thought this was the Friendly Isle," he said.

"My mother calls it 'The God Forsaken Isle.' "

"She's right."

A pink Buick motored through the forest. The hubcaps were chrome and the pink paint freshly waxed. Its brakes squealed before the bridge. "Aloha, Jeffrey," said the driver. It was Auntie Esther.

Keoni walked over to the Buick. "How do you know my friend Jeff?"

"I work fo' Auntie Brownie."

The passenger door swung open—Raynette the Transvestite rode shotgun. Her fat cheeks were bright with rouge and she wore a silver sequined top that glittered like fish scales. She got out and we climbed in the rear seat. The Buick smelled like strawberries.

"To Brownie's house?" Esther asked. She was thin and wore a slinky green dress.

"Yes, please," I said.

Raynette slid into the passenger seat and closed the door. "Li'l red ridin' hoods," she giggled.

Esther floored it over the bridge. "Who's yo' friend, Jeffrey?"

"Keoni."

Raynette turned around and flicked out her tongue. "Cute enough to eat."

"Eh, Keoni," Esther said, "know wot is 'sex?' "

"Sure. That's when my parents tell me to get to bed during *Ed Sullivan*. They swill a bottle of Lancer's Rose and lock the bedroom door."

"Wot kine sounds dey make?"

"The bed squeaks five minutes tops, my father farts, and on comes the vibrator."

Esther and Raynette started laughing. They laughed so hard that they cried. Esther had to slow down to keep the car from veering off the road. They finally calmed down and passed a bottle of Boone's Farm Strawberry Hill back and forth. Raynette told us they were going to a luau thrown by Marines in Kainalu. They wanted to drop us off beside the pasture but Keoni pretended he'd sprained his ankle and talked her into taking the driveway. Esther drove us to the beach house.

Keoni reached into his bag and pulled out the Ding

Dongs. "Thanks for the ride," he said handing them to Esther.

"Oh, mahalo," she said, "I jus' love dose Ding Dongs."

"Don't I know it," he replied.

*   *   *

Gramma told Keoni to "get the hell out" of her bedroom. Ben gave up his bed on the lanai and moved to the big room.

Keoni opened the screen door to the lanai, walked down the cement steps, and plopped his suitcase on a cane table between the two beds. The lanai was decorated with paintings of seascapes and fishponds. Gramma had painted them the first year she lived on Moloka'i. Green glass balls in cord nets hung down from the ceiling. The biggest ball was painted with underwater scenes—there was a mermaid with red hair and a sea turtle was chasing a school of pink fish. Keoni examined the walls, the ceiling, and the floor. Narakiro had glued red vinyl tiles to the cement floor on King Kamehameha Day. "This place is neato," he decided. He spotted a buck's head with a huge sixteen-point rack. The buck's chest was mounted to a koa plaque and the plaque had been nailed to the wall. "Who shot that?" he asked me.

"Gramma. She calls him 'Charlie.' "

"She's a murderer."

*   *   *

Keoni and I kept the storm windows open at night so we could hear the ocean. We crawled under mosquito nets and swapped stories. I told one about Charlie coming to life and freeing himself to search for his body. He said that would be pretty hard seeing Charlie had no legs. He told me a nun at Star of the Sea was really a man.

"People would know," I said.

"Oh, no. He has boobs and everything."

"How could he fool Mother Superior?"

"He really doesn't need to," Keoni replied. "He is Mother Superior."

"Centipede!" Ben cried from the big room.

We darted to the screen door and peered in. The standing lamp was on. Ben pulled up his pillow and yanked the sheets off the pune'e. He told us a centipede had been crawling on his face.

I saw a huge centipede running over the Oriental rug. "By your foot!" I said.

He jumped up on the pune'e.

Gramma walked in. She wore a bathrobe full of holes from smoking. "Wot the hell now?" she asked.

"Centipede," Ben said, "under the table!"

My grandmother got her butcher knife and moved two chairs. The centipede scurried away. She moved another and cornered it against the wall with the blade. She hacked at the centipede but it outran the blade and took a detour around a wooden tiki. She swung and chopped the centipede in half. Two sets of legs ran in different directions. She found the head and squashed it with the side of the blade. "Theah," she said, "that'll fix 'um."

"Glad I'm on the lanai," Keoni said.

"Don't be too glad," Ben replied.

"How come?"

"That's where the scorpions live."

*   *   *

Early the next morning, Valdez was raking the lawn makai of the beach house. He was the only Filipino I'd seen with light skin and freckles. "Spanish blood," Gramma had said. She'd met him when he was throwing net at Puko'o Fishpond and asked if he needed work. He was a quiet man who lived alone in the foothills above the fishpond. Gramma said he'd knifed Quanto, a Japanese muscleman, for flirting with his girlfriend.

"Who's this manong?" Keoni asked me from his bed.

"Valdez."

"Bet he eats dog."

"You're lolo."

"Well," he said, "if someday you can't find your poi dogs, you'll know where they went." He pulled up his mosquito net and walked to an open window. "Quiet," he told Valdez.

Valdez stopped raking and he returned to bed.

"Now he knows who's boss," Keoni said.

Valdez resumed his raking.

"Hush, Valdez, or I'll fire you."

"Cut it out," I told Keoni.

Valdez spat. A few minutes went by and he was raking again.

"You're fired!"

He dropped his rake. I was sure he wanted to beef Keoni. He walked to the hala tree next to the beach house, picked up his black lunch box, and headed for the road.

"Uh, oh," I said.

Ten minutes later, Gramma swung open the screen door. "Have you keeds seen Valdez?"

"I fired him," Keoni replied.

"You wot?"

"He wouldn't quit raking," he explained. "I need my beauty sleep."

Gramma clenched her hands and gave him the stink eye. I knew she wanted to whack him with her bamboo stick. Instead, she slammed the door. She wandered over to the table, stuck a cigarette in her mouth, and flipped open the *Holy Bible*.

*   *   *

Keoni asked if deer ever came near the beach house and Gramma told him she'd killed a buck with a shotgun from the back door. The buck had been grazing on awa roots at the fence line when she fired. "Just peppered his hide," she said, "but he dropped."

"Doubt it," Ben muttered. He said we should go fishing so we put on our trunks and tees. Ben led the way down the dirt road carrying three bamboo poles and a scoop net. The dogs tagged along. Keoni said Moloka'i was the most boring place in the world. Ben told him he hadn't seen all of it so he couldn't judge it. We reached the swamp. Ben dragged the scoop net along the water's edge and caught 'opae. He handed me one and we baited our hooks. He dangled his line in the water beside the mangrove. Keoni didn't want to fish. Ben asked how just peppering a deer's hide could kill it. He said the distance from the door to the fence line was over one hundred feet.

"How do you know it's a hundred?" I asked.

"I walked it."

"Who cares about a dumb deer," Keoni said.

But it wasn't just the deer that bothered my brother. He

was struggling to sort fact from fiction so he could figure out just how far he had to go to become a man. If our grandmother was telling the truth, his competitive heart demanded he kill a bigger buck the same way.

I suspended my bamboo pole over the water and a fish nibbled the bait. The trades rustled through the mangrove. Locals believed Anika's spirit shook the branches whenever she spotted a handsome boy. The shaking was Anika's invitation to join her. Dodge had told me he'd seen the branches move and, after wading into the swamp, the water turned ice cold. Arms embraced him and pulled him into the deep water. Mercury heard the cries—he floated out a tethered inner tube and pulled Dodge to safety.

Keoni dipped the scoop net in the swamp grass. He'd found a jar on the bank and filled it with water—hundreds of 'opae swam around inside.

"Gramma's lying about that buck," Ben said.

"A shotgun can blow your head off," I said.

"Not from a hundred feet."

"Who's the weirdo?" Keoni asked.

I turned and saw Uncle Chipper hanging clothes on the line between his papaya trees. He wore a white undershirt, BVDs, and his green cap. He glanced over at us but didn't wave. He liked it best when you pretended he wasn't there.

"That's Uncle Chipper," I said.

Keoni put down his net. "We should give him some fish."

"Chipper just drinks okolehao and eats pills," Ben said.

He finished hanging out his clothes and hobbled to the shack.

"What a sourpuss," said Keoni.

"He was married to Gramma," I said.

"He's your grandpa?"

"No. My grandpa ran away."

"Don't blame him." He pulled an 'opae from his jar and tossed it on the web of a yellow-bellied spider. The 'opae kicked and that alerted the spider. We watched the spider wrap up the 'opae.

"Shrimp roll," Keoni said.

*   *   *

We returned from fishing and I gave Rudy, Gramma's new orange tabby, two of the smaller aholehole I'd caught. Ben tried giving Spotty a fish but he just sniffed it and whined for Ben to pat him. Gramma put the rest of the aholehole in her freezer. We would use the fish for our kaka lines when we ran out of octopus and eel. She didn't want to put the lines out with Keoni around because she said he brought bad luck. We drank grape juice in the kitchen and Gramma lifted the cover off her pot. The aroma of cooked flank steak, soy sauce, and sherry wafted through the kitchen.

She poured a colander full of bean sprouts into the pot. "You eat chop suey?" she asked Keoni.

"Yes, Mrs. Daniels," he answered, "but I prefer lemon chicken and kung pao shrimp."

"Fo' the luva Pete."

Ben mentioned the limited range of shotguns. He said he heard on *American Sportsman* that a shotgun was the wrong choice for animals bigger than birds. He challenged Gramma's story about the buck.

"You say I'm lyin'?" she asked.

"Tall tales," Keoni said, "like Paul Bunyan."

Her face turned red. She looked over at me but I didn't say a word.

"Let's go ask Uncle Chipper," Ben suggested.

"Let's go," she said.

We headed to Chipper's. Gramma carried a pot of Hawaiian stew leftovers. She always brought something on her visits and she'd have to wait weeks to get her pots and pans back. She let him keep a pot after he'd admitted using it as a bedpan.

We walked by the hanging tree and scooted past a cluster of jasmine flanking the dump. The sweet jasmine was no match for the stench. Ben reached Uncle Chipper's porch first but Gramma was right behind him. Keoni and I followed. I looked in through the screen door and saw clothes, pill bottles, and cigarette butts scattered over the cement floor. The bed was a mess of newspapers and crumpled yellow sheets. A rope hung down from the ceiling.

"What's the rope for?" Keoni asked.

"To hang stuff on," Ben said.

"Why's he do that?"

"So rats don't get it."

"Chippah," Gramma called. "Oh, Chip."

Uncle Chipper slow-stepped to the screen. He wore khaki pants and an undershirt. He was bald, except for gray stubble around the crown of his head. He smelled like cigarettes. "Fixin' chowda," he said.

Gramma raised the pot. "Brought you a li'l somethin'."

The door opened and she passed him the pot.

"Lemmee get mah cap," he said. He set the pot down in his sink and pulled the cap off a pair of antlers nailed to his plywood wall. He came out barefoot. We sat in dilapidated lounge chairs and listened to his stories about hunting rams on the Big Island. He pulled out rolling papers, a pouch of tobacco, and a box of matches. He creased a rolling paper with his finger and sprinkled on tobacco. As I sat there watching Chipper and Gramma, I tried imagining what their lives would have been like had they stayed together. They were together in a way, separated only by a big rolling lawn and a forest of ironwoods. But they remained isolated and lonely because of the half-mile between them.

Ben fidgeted in his chair. "Uncle Chipper," he said, "did Gramma ever kill a buck with a shotgun?"

He licked the edge of the rolling paper and sealed the cigarette. "Seems I 'membah somethin'," he said striking a match.

Gramma spent the next fifteen minutes trying to convince Chipper he remembered while Ben insisted it had never happened.

He puffed his cigarette and winked at Ben. "If Brownie says it happened," he said, "then it probably did."

"What about that hammerhead?" I blurted.

He blew out a cloud of smoke. "Wot hamma head?"

"Yeah," Ben said. "Did my father really spear a shark?"

A trap sprung. A mongoose squealed as it struggled in the jasmine. The mongoose twisted and shook the trap free—it scampered off into the dump.

"Damn things always get loose," Chipper said. "Wish

that cat of yours'd catch a few, Brownie."

"I can kill all your mongoose next summer," Ben offered.

"How's that?" he asked.

"My father's buying me a .22."

"Ridiculous," Gramma said, "Chippah doesn't want bullets whizzin' by."

Keoni stared at Chipper's feet. "Excuse me, sir," he said, "what happened to your toes?"

He wiggled the stumps. "Had a li'l accident." Chipper said it was time for chowder and we said our goodbyes.

"Told you I shot that buck," Gramma said on our walk home.

"He didn't say for sure," Ben said.

" 'Course he did."

"Keoni," Ben said, "did he say for sure?"

"Not for sure," said Keoni.

"See?"

"See, nothin'," she said. "You heard 'um say so, plain as day."

"No," he said. "Not even plain as night."

She pursed her lips. I knew by her wrinkled brow she was hunting for the right words. But the words never came.

"Don't make your grandsons shovel horse poop," Keoni told her.

"Why the hell not?"

"They're not manongs."

Gramma headed for the beach house.

We stood beside an ironwood and watched her scurry across the lawn. Leo and Spotty greeted her with wagging tails.

She didn't pat them. She opened the front door and slammed it shut.

*   *   *

I knew our relationship with Gramma had changed when we returned to the Scout after watching Keoni's plane taxi down the runway. Ben refused to ride in the cab on the way home. I rode in the bed with him. Gramma never looked back to see how we were doing. She didn't pull over to let Ben and me steal pineapples. She drove right through Kaunakakai without stopping for milk and ice cream. She took every turn hard, never slowed for dips, and doubled the speed limit. I saw her lips move and figured she was cussing.

"She's mad as a hatter," I said.

Ben stared up at the mountains. "Big deal."

"Think she'll still cook us dinner?"

"Are you kidding?" he asked. "Be ready to eat limu and coconuts."

*   *   *

Keoni told his parents Gramma could outswear "the saltiest of sailors." My father got Red's approval to build the sea wall and my grandmother became the main topic of conversation between my mother and the Applegates.

My father asked for the deed to Hale Kia and Gramma said she wanted to keep it in her name. He barraged her with phone calls about rising property taxes, inflation, and the outrageous cost of maintaining the ranch. He told her that without his help the ocean would erode the coast and take the beach house with it. He said he was thinking of sending Ben and me to military camp the following summer. She caved in and signed the paperwork that gave my father title in exchange for a life estate and a small monthly income.

It seemed as though she had given up too easily, as if she owed her first born for being raised hanai and was paying him back by signing over the land. Now everything Gramma had struggled a lifetime to keep belonged to my father.

Johnny

Gramma changed the summer after Keoni's visit. She said we didn't have to shovel manure any more and she let us open the fridge without her permission. We weren't allowed to touch anything on the middle shelf, especially her Cool Whip and Sara Lee Pound Cake. She gave us the freedom to roam the entire expanse of Hale Kia. Part of that freedom meant bringing along a pole or a gun to put food on the table. I enjoyed spin-casting for barracuda and papio along the coast. My brother gravitated toward the mountain. Gramma let him borrow her .219 rifle and a single bullet. She felt that if a hunter couldn't hit his mark with one shot the animal deserved to live.

Ben took off at dawn. I hated hiking early so he went by himself. Gramma kept the dogs indoors so they wouldn't follow him. He wanted to shoot a buck and have the head mounted. He was more interested in proving his skills as a hunter than providing us with venison. Killing a buck and packing it down was his rite of passage—he wanted to enshrine himself in the pantheon of hunters who'd hiked the mountain and returned with a buck. His goal was to shoot one with antlers bigger than Charlie's.

* * *

When Gramma found out Johnny Crystobal had a car, she phoned and offered him twenty dollars and an 'o'io for driving to Hadulco Ranch on the west end to pick up two hundred pounds of chicken manure. She'd have gone herself but she was busy transplanting fan palms from buckets into the ground. He said he had a bad back and that he couldn't go alone. She put her hand over the receiver and asked me if I'd help. Ben wasn't there because he was off hunting.

"I'll go with Johnny," I said.

* * *

I opened the padlock on the garage door and swung the gate open. The gate's wooden slats were reinforced with sheets of corrugated aluminum. Gramma had added the aluminum to prevent thieves from sticking their hands between the slats. She backed out her Scout and I climbed in the passenger seat.

She handed me an 'o'io wrapped in foil. "Give this to Johnny."

I placed the fish on my lap. We zipped past the Norfolk and drove along the pasture. Valdez was pulling a fan palm out of its bucket and Gramma tooted. He waved. He'd returned after I apologized for Keoni's bad behavior.

We reached Kam Highway and headed west. Gramma said she knew Johnny from the old days. The pineapple workers had pooled their money to buy a Model T and Johnny showed up at the beach house with six men. Johnny had placed a photo of a picture bride on the table; she read his fortune first.

The smell of fish made me nauseous. I took the 'o'io off my lap and dropped it on the steel floor. We sped by Puko'o Fishpond. I stuck my head out and smelled the sweet mangoes of Queenie's Mango Grove. We passed Our Lady of Sorrows Church and Ah Pong's. Gramma had a determined look that tightened her face. She said she needed the manure for her palm trees. She wanted to sell mature palms for "big money" to developers.

"Can I count on you, Peanut?" she asked.

"Yes."

"Good boy."

Getting a "good boy" in advance made me determined to earn it. The idea of going west to pick up chicken manure was hardly exciting, but I decided to make it an adventure. Gramma talked about her two sons and their Moloka'i summers. She said Chipper never warmed up to my father and that they got along "like two strange dogs."

"Do you still love him?" I asked her.

"Love who?"

"Chipper."

She braked for a dip and floored it over a straight stretch. "A li'l part does," she admitted.

"Would you ever marry again?"

"You mean, Chippah?"

"Yes."

"Fo' the luva Pete."

Just beyond Lili'uokalani Elementary, she had me hold the wheel while she lit a cigarette. I kept the Scout in the right lane. She took the wheel back, skidded off the highway, and followed a dirt road through a kiawe forest. There was a clearing with a house and a big lawn with lime trees. We parked in the forest.

"Is that Johnny's house?" I asked.

"No."

"Where does he live?"

She got out and left the door open. "Bring the 'o'io, Peanut."

I grabbed the fish and followed her through the forest. Kiawe seed pods and tiny brown leaves carpeted the ground. I smelled something rotting and saw a screen box hanging off a tree—an octopus was drying inside. The legs looked like red licorice and blue flies crawled the screen.

A root beer-colored Valiant was parked next to a cardboard shack. Rust had eaten holes in the Valiant's roof. Luckily, the rust was the same color as the paint.

Gramma stood in front of a plywood door wedged between walls of cardboard. The plywood was five feet high and a tree stood behind it. She dropped her cigarette on the dirt, squashed it with her cowboy boot, and banged on the plywood. "Hui," she called.

A hand slid the plywood aside and Johnny stood in the doorway. His face was dark and moles the size of raisins clung to his eyelids. He was my height and his hair was jet black. He wore trunks, a white undershirt, and brown socks. He looked at his wristwatch. "Early," he said.

"Bettah early than late," Gramma replied. She handed him two fives and promised two more when he delivered the manure. She gave him a paper with directions. "No forget," she said, "two hundred pounds."

"How Valdez?" he asked.

"Slow as molasses."

He laughed and gold flashed in his teeth.

"Manuah's already paid fo'," she said and left the shack.

I followed Gramma back to the Scout.

"Watch 'um like a hawk," she said climbing in.

"How long will it take?" I asked.

"Coupla hours."

"That long?"

She shut the door. "Make you guava cake fo' dessert," she said and gunned the Scout through the forest.

Johnny and Valdez had left Manila to work the pineapple fields on the west end. A company rep promised ten dollars a day and free lodging. "Lodging" meant sleeping on a bamboo mat in a room with ten other men. After thirty years of bending their backs, a luna decided they weren't keeping up. Dole Pineapple gave them each a month's pay and evicted them from the plantation barracks in Kualapu'u. Johnny and Valdez had lost touch with their roots and couldn't return to the Philippines. They settled for pick-and-shovel wages on the east end. Gramma gave them my father's hand-me-downs and it was strange seeing them in his old Harvard shirts.

I returned to the shack and stood in the doorway. Johnny was inside eating balut and drinking a bottle of Miller High Life.

"Here's your 'o'io," I said.

He popped the last of the balut in his mouth and washed it down with beer. He took the fish and told me to come inside.

The shack was built beside the trunk of a kiawe tree. The roof was heavy canvas draped over branches. The trunk served as one corner of the shack and the cardboard walls leaned in the direction of the tree. The floor was mismatched carpet and strips of linoleum caked with mud. A Sterno stove was perched on a bald tire. Bottles of hot sauce, ketchup, and salad dressing were on a shelf nailed to the tree. A jar of pickled pigs' feet rested on a folding chair next to the stove. There were no lamps and no faucets.

"Don't you have a refrigerator?" I asked.

"No need."

"How do you keep beer cold?"

"Like 'um warm."

"Where's your phone?"

"Big house," Johnny said pointing toward the place I'd seen in the clearing. He opened a bottle of Vitalis, splashed some on his palm, and massaged his hair. The Vitalis smelled like rubbing alcohol. "Like?" he asked offering me the bottle.

"No."

"Catch planny wahine," he promised.

There was a gold cross on a swimmer's chain around his neck. He put on a shirt with a hula girl print and navy polyester pants. He gazed into an oval mirror taped to the tree and slicked back his hair with a black pocket comb. "Look good fo' wahine," he said.

Magazines were stacked beside the chair. One stack was religious and the other was *Penthouse*. He had removed the covers and was using them to patch holes in his walls. One patch featured a naked woman riding a bicycle. Plastered next to her was the cover of *Awake!* magazine with a story about millionaires destined for hell.

"We go," Johnny said.

I followed him out and he slid the plywood door shut. We headed to the Valiant. I climbed in the passenger seat and springs jabbed my back. Seed pods and leaves had fallen through the holes in the roof—I swept them off the dash. He got in and we drove to the house in the clearing.

"Chy wait," Johnny told me. He got out, tucked the tails of his shirt in his pants, and grabbed the fish. He knocked on the front door while the car puked exhaust. He held the foil-wrapped 'o'io as if it were an aluminum bouquet. The door opened—a Filipina in a red miniskirt and white tube top appeared. She slapped his face. I'd seen her at Our Lady of Sorrows Church with different men. He gave her the 'o'io and returned to the car.

"Is that woman your girlfriend?" I asked.

"We chy make baby."

We took the driveway and the woman dropped the 'o'io. She ran off the porch, pulled limes off her tree, and chased us. The engine rattled.

"Ready or not," I said, "here she comes."

She threw limes as she ran. One of the limes bounced off the hood.

"Aysoos!" Johnny said.

He accelerated but the woman ran faster. A front tire hit a root and the car jerked like a carnival ride. A second lime grazed the roof. She kept chasing and screaming even after she'd run out of limes.

"Humbug," he said.

We turned right onto the highway and headed west for Kaunakakai. The car squealed around turns and the wind whistled through the roof. Johnny squirmed in his seat trying to get comfortable. He said he'd won the Valiant at a cock fight. I asked him about the woman. He told me they'd met when he rented "da big room" in her house. Now a younger man with "planny kala" had that room. The shack was on her property and she let Johnny live there as long as he gave her money. He was three months behind.

"How much a month?" I asked.

"Forty."

"And 'o'io."

He smiled.

The Valiant had an AM radio and Johnny let me spin the dial. A Honolulu station came in strong at Kamalo Ranch but faded. We got past the Seven Sisters Mountains and hit a flat stretch where the highway cut through the marshes. I smelled the brackish water. The signal from Maui was good so we listened to Tom Jones sing "What's New Pussycat."

"Did you know my grandmother when she was married?" I asked.

He told me Gramma and Chipper had thrown "planny pahties." He said Chipper had hired him to dig holes for the pasture's fence posts.

"Was he hard to work for?"

Johnny slowed for a dip. "Chippah stay one good man."

"How was he good?"

"He lemmee borrow kala."

We reached Kaunakakai and cruised the main drag. Smoke spewed from the Valiant. We pulled alongside the pool room. Men crowded a table behind the plate glass storefront. One held a pool cue over his shoulder like a rifle.

Johnny turned off the engine and pointed at the glove box. I pressed a button and the glove box popped open. I saw the Valiant's manual, keys, plastic bags, and a butterfly knife with a mottled handle like the skin of a moray eel. It was beautiful. He took the knife and slid it in his pants' pocket.

"Five minute," he said.

"Can I go?" I asked.

"No can."

"Please?"

He sauntered into the pool room. There were two tables. One table was empty. Four locals shot pool at the other. He approached them and talked to the biggest man. Johnny put his hand in the pocket with the knife. The man laughed and patted him on the shoulder. He returned to the car.

"What was that all about?" I asked.

He started the Valiant. "Cock fight."

We chugged down Main Street and stopped for a Japanese lady crossing at Hop Inn Restaurant.

"Mamma san," Johnny crooned, "I love you so."

The lady reached the curb and gave us the finger.

We kept going. Women were heading in and out of Friendly Market. A hippie with braids chatted with Auntie Esther inside Moloka'i Drugs. A blond boy stood outside Kanemitsu's Bakery eating coconut rolls with Puanani.

"That's Ben!" I said.

"Ai ya," Johnny replied.

Puanani stuffed a coconut roll into Ben's mouth. She giggled and wiped sugar off his cheek.

"He's supposed to be hunting deer," I told Johnny.

"Mo' bettah hunt wahine."

We drove past the courthouse and headed west. Johnny took out the paper with directions and stuck it against the windshield. Two miles beyond The Church of Latter-Day Saints, we turned off the highway onto a gravel road. The tires churned the gravel. We passed a KAPU: PRIVATE PROPERTY sign and followed the road up a hill. Chickens squawked and a pink house appeared. We parked next to the coops. Each coop had two levels enclosed with chicken wire. Hens roosted inside. White garbage bags leaned against the coops.

We got out. The bags were stuffed with manure. Johnny opened the trunk and moved a crab net to one side. A rooster chased a loose hen across the dirt toward the pink house. A girl came out. She was Filipina and about my age. She wore a purple muumuu and her hair was cut short.

"Mrs. Daniels send you?" she asked.

"Yes," I said.

"Twenny bag."

"Wheah Papa?" asked Johnny.

"Town side."

We loaded the bags in. Johnny winced lifting a bag.

"Sore?" I asked.

He stacked his bag on top of mine. "Too much wahine."

The girl crossed her arms and we continued loading. It didn't smell as bad as horse manure. It was almost sweet. I stole glances at the girl.

Johnny took the comb from his back pocket and ran it through his hair. "Alone?" he asked the girl. "Lonely?" She glared at him. He tried Tagalog. He pulled out his wallet and showed her the two fives. "Like haole boy?" She shook her head and returned to the house.

I lifted the last bag in.

"Heartbreaka," Johnny said.

*   *   *

On our ride home, Johnny said the men in the pool room had hired him to tie blades to the roosters. They had to keep changing locations so the police wouldn't catch on. He said Louisiana birds fought to the death and were "numbah one."

"Get girlfriend in Honolulu?" he asked.

I gazed up at the clouds hugging the Seven Sisters Mountains. The faces of girls I'd danced with at Punahou's Canteen drifted by. I settled on Debbie Mills. "Sort of," I said.

"Haole girl?"

"Yeah."

"Soon you marry, make planny babies."

I didn't know how I was going to marry and make babies if I wasn't even going steady. "Were you ever married, Johnny?"

"One time close," he said, "but planny pilikia."

We hit the flat stretch that ran through the marshes. I stuck out my hand. "It's cooling off," I said and we listened to Diana Ross sing "Love Child." He spat out the window. I asked for advice about fishing for papio and mullet. He turned the radio off.

"Bumbye no mo' battah-ree," he said.

The marshes ended and we drove beside the green pastures of Kamalo Ranch. Cows grazed behind the wire. Johnny gripped the wheel with both hands and stared at the road, as if his memories had crept up and overtaken him.

"You all right, Johnny?" I asked.

He looked over. I saw fence posts moving through his eyes.

Big Ruth

I told Ben I saw him with Puanani. He pretended it wasn't him but later admitted he didn't go hunting. He said Kitty's number was scrawled on the Ancient Hawaiian Moon Calendar and he'd phoned Puanani when Gramma was taking her nap. He'd stashed the rifle behind a kiawe tree and hitchhiked west. It had been his third trip. He'd bought Puanani a dress and a necklace at Brucey's Boutique. He'd financed these gifts with booty from pirating wishing wells and admitted he was getting "short on bread."

"Just borrow kala from Gramma," I suggested.

"She's a manju," he replied.

"And okole kala," I added.

"There's a party tomorrow night at the Duvas."

"So?"

"Puanani's going. She's leaving at ten and sneaking over here."

"Gramma's going to catch you."

"Better hope she doesn't," Ben said.

"Why?"

"Puanani's bringing you a date."

"Is she foxy?"

He chuckled. "Beggars can't be choosers."

*　　　*　　　*

Gramma stayed up late the Night of Puanani. It was as if she had ESP. She sat at her table in the big room while we were camped on the pune'e in white T-shirts and Levi's. She wore her red house muumuu and smoked like a chimney watching *KGMB Channel 9 News.* She studied the geckos on her picture window during a commercial for Lex Brodie Tires. Next came a rerun of *Hawaii 5-0.*

"You keeds are damn quiet tonight," Gramma said.

"We are?" I asked.

Ben finger-combed his hair. He yawned a fake yawn, stood up, and stretched. "Time to hit the bunk," he said. "Goodnight, Gramma."

"Aren't you brushin' yo' teeth?"

"Already did."

She flicked ashes in her tin can. "Goodnight, Juicy."

Ben headed down the steps to the lanai and switched on the floodlight.

I looked through the picture window—the moon lit up the front lawn and pasture. I got worried Gramma might see Puanani and mistake her for Billy Duva.

"Going to bed, Gramma?" I asked.

"Aftah 5-0."

"This one's real boring."

"Really?"

"It's about this haole who steals an ulu maika from a kahuna and gets turned into a gecko."

"Ridiculous."

"And the gecko chirps at McGarrett trying to tell him he used to be a human and begs him to find the kahuna to break the spell."

"You shuah? You not foolin' yo' pua Gramma?"

"Oh, no. It's the worst *Hawaii 5-0* ever made. I'm surprised they even show it."

She squashed her cigarette in the tin can and clutched her pack of Chesterfields. "Christ," she said, "I'm gettin' some shut-eye. Goodnight, Peanut."

"Goodnight." I turned off the TV and watched her trail off into her bedroom. I joined Ben on the lanai. All six storm windows were open and, across the channel, the coastline of Maui twinkled with lights.

"Safe and sound?" Ben asked.

"All tucked in," I replied.

He pulled a pack of wintergreen Lifesavers from his pocket and popped one. "Fresh breath," he said extending the pack.

I took one and put it on my tongue. It was so minty that it tasted bitter. "What if the dogs start barking?" I asked.

"They won't."

"How do you know?"

"Puanani's bringing them kalua pig." He snuck into the kitchen and smuggled out three bottles of Miller High Life from the fridge. He figured Gramma wouldn't notice since they were on the bottom shelf. He placed the bottles on the display table between a poi pounder and a conch shell.

"One beer short," I said.

"Only three left, doofus."

"Opening them with your teeth?"

"Shit," Ben said and crept back. He fumbled in the gadget drawer and returned with a can opener. He leaned the can opener up against the poi pounder. "We need tunes," he decided.

I tiptoed into the big room and swiped the transistor radio. I spun the dial to KKUA out on the lanai. The signal was strong and I turned it up for Sly Stone's "Everyday People."

Ben switched off the floodlight and began unscrewing the bulb from its socket. "Hot," he said. He tossed the hot bulb on his bed and stuck in a black light he'd bought at Take's Variety Store. He flipped the switch—the black light turned the walls and rafters violet. The glass balls and the eyes in the deer heads glowed. "Righteous," he said pulling off his tee. His arms were muscular and his chest was filling out. He reached under his bed, pulled out a can of Right Guard, and sprayed his pits. He offered me the can but I shook my head.

I heard giggling and chewed up the rest of my mint. A beam hit Ben's chest—two silhouettes with a flashlight stood at an open window.

"Howzit," Ben said.

"Howzit," a girl answered.

"Back door's open."

"Keep yo' shirt off," the girl said.

The beam hit my face and there was more giggling. The girls scooted around the beach house. The door creaked and

Puanani entered shining her flashlight. She wore a white micromini, a puka shell necklace, and rubber slippers. She had a bracelet made of pikake. The flowers smelled good. A girl loomed behind Puanani—she had her hair in a bun and peered at me as if I were an alien from another planet. Her eyes went past me and fell on Ben.

Puanani turned off the flashlight and hugged Ben. "Dis my friend Ruth," she said.

Ruth was taller than my brother. She wore a muumuu and boots and trudged over to a storm window. She seemed melancholy.

"Howzit, Ruth," Ben said.

"Dey call me 'Big Ruth.' "

"We call my brother 'Peanut.' "

Puanani checked me out, head to toe. "Ho," she said, "Peanut stay cute."

"Who's thirsty?" Ben asked.

"Bof of us," said Big Ruth.

Ben pried off the bottle caps. He handed a beer to Puanani, another to Big Ruth, and took the last for himself. I propped the radio on a sill. The deejay started off the KKUA Top Twenty Countdown with "Wedding Bell Blues." We sat at chairs lined up along the storm windows. Ben sat between the girls and I was on the far end next to Big Ruth. She was tall but she wasn't fat. Her skin was darker than Puanani's and she wore a leather choker. I figured Puanani had been scared to walk through the pasture alone so she talked her into coming.

Puanani sipped her beer and gossiped about the party. It was a birthday celebration for Uncle Billy. She said they'd steamed two pigs in the imu and Billy got a revolver and a shotgun for presents. Puanani tickled Ben's chest.

"Chee," she said, "you get cold nips!"

"Warm 'em up," he replied.

Ben and Puanani kissed hard on the lips. Then came deep kissing. Tommy James & The Shondells sang "Crystal Blue Persuasion." The deep kissing escalated into a grope-a-thon.

Big Ruth fidgeted in her chair and gulped her beer.

"See any good movies lately?" I asked.

"I like *Blue Hawaii*," she said.

"You like Elvis?"

"He some ono."

The Archies harmonized "Sugar, Sugar." Ben and Puanani moved over to the bed. Their lips smacked. He had his hand under her skirt and he said something that made her laugh. She toyed with his zipper.

Big Ruth took my hand and led me out the back door. There was enough light from the moon to see the sand path and the dogs followed us down to the beach. I sat beside her on the stone wall. She swigged her beer and passed it to me. I took a sip and passed it back. I looked over at the lanai—a violet glow came from the storm windows.

"You know Alice da Goon?" Big Ruth asked.

"Doesn't she swim naked in the swamp?"

"Why? You wen see?"

"No."

"She stay my cuz."

"Why do they call her a goon?"

"Gotta be goony fo' swim naked li'dat."

I wasn't sure how talking about Alice the Goon was going to break the ice. Sitting on the stone wall didn't make Big Ruth any closer to my height—she still towered over me. It felt as though we were the most mismatched couple in the world. She polished off the beer and hurled the bottle into the water.

"Puanani stay ono fo' Ben," she said.

"And Ben stay ono for Puanani," I replied.

"Why dey call you Peanut?"

"I'm small for my age."

"You not so small. You get girlfriend?"

"No."

"Fo' real? No mo'?"

"Fo' real," I answered.

"Like smoke?"

"Smoke what?"

"Weed. Ganja. Pakalolo."

"I'd better not," I said, "I've gotta stay alert."

Big Ruth untied her bun and shook her head. Her hair cascaded over her shoulders. She had a delicate nose, pouty lips, and a forehead that reminded me of Princess Kaiulani. There was a look on her face that said this was a night of destiny. "Get chance?" she asked.

"Chance for what?"

"Da kine."

"Oh," I said, "sure. Da kine."

She leaned over and pressed her lips against mine. Her tongue came out and tickled my lower lip. I opened my mouth and her tongue went in. I twirled my tongue around hers. She tasted like haupia. She ran her fingertips along my thigh up to my crotch. I rubbed her breasts through her muumuu as if they were magic lamps.

"Ho, Peanut," she moaned.

A blast of white light came from the beach house. Gramma was on the lanai holding her gas lantern. "God damn keeds!" she said.

Puanani hopped over the sill of a storm window in her panties and raced toward the pasture. Ben darted out in his BVDs and ran after Puanani. The dogs chased Ben.

"Mo' bettah hele," Big Ruth said. "Nice to meet you, Peanut."

"Nice to meet you too, Big Ruth."

She rolled her hair up, tied it in a bun, and gave me a peck on the cheek.

*   *   *

The next morning, Gramma called Ben a devil for sneaking girls over and a thief for stealing beer. She said one thing would lead to another and someday he would land in jail. Ben was hardly apologetic. He told her she was a manju and that he wished she would croak. He said Chipper was smart to leave her and his only mistake was not moving to another island.

"Ben," she said, "promise me you'll nevah see Puanani again."

"Why?"

"Yo' fathah doesn't want you datin' kanakas."

"I'm going to keep on seeing her and that's that."

She cleared her throat. "Puanani's not who you think she is."

"I already know," he said.

"Know wot?"

"She's got Duva blood."

"Theah's somethin' mo'."

"What?"

"Yo' fathah got Kitty hapai, aftah that damn dance."

"He got her pregnant?" I asked.

She crossed her arms. "Lani was their girl. Lani was a wild wahine who had a daughtah and ran off to the mainland. She left Puanani behind fo' Kitty to raise."

"Oh, God," I said. "Is Puanani related to us?"

Ben turned pale. "She's our cousin."

"Worse," Gramma said.

"What could possibly be worse," he groaned.

"Yo' both Puanani's uncles."

"Liar," he said.

"I'm not lyin'."

"I'm her uncle and we're the same age?"

"Ae."

Ben swallowed hard. "Thanks for ruining my whole life."

"You ruined yo' own damn life," she said, "by not listenin' to me from the start."

*   *   *

Ben phoned Puanani the day he found out he was her uncle. There were tears and apologies and promises to stay in touch. He never phoned again.

I didn't discuss Puanani with him. He never brought up her name and, whenever I talked about girls, he either changed the subject or walked away. It was as if he'd given up on the opposite sex after the Puanani fiasco and didn't want to risk losing at love again. Sometimes we'd see her shopping at Misaki's Grocery & Dry Goods with Kitty—Ben would leave the store, walk down Main Street, and sit on the curb. He'd head back only after I loaded in the last of the groceries.

Book Three
The Return of
Wilkins

Norman Wilkins

The postcard from Norman Wilkins arrived the summer
my grandmother said she was through with men. I'd gone up
to the highway to check the mailbox and found a picture of the
ritzy Sausalito waterfront with the message:

> Dearest Julia,
>
> I will be visiting your island next week and plan on
> looking you up. Can you believe how time flies? I do
> understand you have an exquisite ranch on the eastern
> side. Will drive out from the airport so we can catch up
> on old times.
>
> > With Deepest Love and Affection,
> > Norman Wilkins

Gramma pulled out a big magnifying glass she'd bought
at Moloka'i Drugs and examined the words. The wrinkles in
her face seemed to go deeper. "Damn puhi'u," she said and
tucked the postcard between the pages of the *Holy Bible*.

Despite her disgust with the postcard, she hunted

through her garment bag and tried on her Honolulu clothes. I knew she was curious about how Wilkins had held up and I'm sure she wanted him to visit Hale Kia to see how successful she'd become. I don't believe she had any intention of telling him that she'd given the ahupua'a to my father and had little more than a life estate. She swore she'd whack us with her bamboo stick if we mentioned the postcard to anyone. Eighth grade was fast approaching and, although we were too big for spankings, I knew she was serious.

"Keep quiet about Wilkins," Gramma told us.

"I'm telling Daddy," Ben said.

"Pa'a the waha."

"But Wilkins is his father," I argued.

She winced. "Yo' fathah hates 'um fo' leavin'."

"Uncle Chipper should know he's coming," said Ben.

"No."

"Why not?" I asked.

"I don't want Chippah tryin' any funny business."

"What kind of business is that?" I pressed.

"Neva you mind."

Ben laughed. "Chipper might gut the lousy coward."

*   *   *

Wilkins called on a Friday afternoon to say he was heading east from Hoolehua Airport. Gramma seemed stunned after hanging up. She went into a cleaning frenzy that included washing the windows, mopping the tiles on the lanai, and picking ticks off Leo and Spotty.

"You keeds help out," she said.

"What do I get for helping?" Ben asked.

"Anotha summa on Moloka'i," she replied.

Ben vacuumed the Oriental rug while I scrubbed the toilet and polished the chrome fixtures. Our contribution gave her time to decide on an outfit. She settled on a black and white checkered dress, a string of pearls, and black heels. She put on red lipstick, blue eye shadow, and fattened her eyelashes with mascara. She opened her perfume bottle and dabbed Chanel #5 behind her ears and on her wrists. She looked and smelled like she was ready to entertain the Prince of Wales.

"How does Gramma look?" she asked.

"Like a million bucks," I replied.

*   *   *

I watched for Wilkins through the picture window. I wondered if he wanted money. He knew everything about my grandmother because his big brother Fergus had married her sister Sue in Honolulu a month after he'd left for San Francisco. Fergus and Sue had moved to Oregon and he was a frequent guest. Gramma heard about him whenever she phoned her sister. Just what Sue had told her I didn't know but I'd heard her say "Norman Wilkins" and giggle like a schoolgirl.

A green Datsun veered off the dirt road and tooled past the Norfolk.

Ben charged in from the lanai. "The King of England's here!" he called.

Gramma rushed to the big room holding an eyeliner pencil. She peered through the window. "You keeds sit on the pune'e."

"Thought you hated him," he said.

"Kulikuli," she scolded and darted for her bedroom.

The dogs stood in front of the Datsun. Wilkins honked. He drove around them and parked on the slope next to the jeep. His door opened slowly. Spotty circled the Datsun and sniffed its tires. He got out. His hair was silver and slicked back. He wore a white suit with a blue tie and carried a grocery bag. Leo barked as he closed in on the beach house.

When Wilkins was a few feet from the doorstep, Ben flopped on the pune'e and I sat beside him. He punched me in the shoulder and I punched him back.

Gramma returned to the big room and walked awkwardly in her heels. She swung open the screen door. "Aloha, Norman," she said, "long time, no see!"

"Isn't that the gods' truth," Wilkins said with an English accent. He climbed the steps and hugged her. "Oh, Julia," he said, "you're just as beautiful as the day we met at Ala Park."

"I'll bet," Ben whispered.

Wilkins came in. He had blue eyes, a long thin nose, and a narrow jaw. His hair had blond streaks and he was my father's height. He was built like a dancer. "Ah," he said, "these must be your grandsons."

"Come meet Mistah Wilkins," Gramma said.

We popped off the pune'e and introduced ourselves. "You certainly are a pair of fine young lads," he said. We took turns shaking his free hand. His palms and fingers felt soft and his shake was neither strong nor weak. I knew he favored Ben because he shared his refined features. He smelled cool and citrusy, like a basket full of limes and lemons. I asked him if he was from London. He said he was born and raised in Nelson, a town named after a famous English admiral. He reminded me of an aging movie star who still had one foot in the door. Something about him said he'd led a charmed life, a life full of wine, women, and song. He placed his grocery bag on the table. His fingernails were as shiny as cowrie shells. He fished around in the bag and pulled out a green bottle of Tanquerey gin, a carton of orange juice, a pack of Salem menthol cigarettes, and a can of mixed nuts.

"Julia," he said, "fetch us some glasses."

"All right," Gramma said and disappeared into the kitchen.

Wilkins studied Ben and me. "I understand your father is a famous trial attorney in Honolulu."

"He loves suing people," Ben answered.

He pulled off the lid on the mixed nuts and held out the can.

"No, thanks," said Ben.

"Yeah," I said, "we're stuffed from fish and poi."

"Righto," he said. "Is your father a pleasant man?"

"Very pleasant," Ben replied.

"He's the pleasantest father a kid could have," I said, "and he's never run off."

Wilkins smirked. "Clever boy."

Gramma returned with two glasses and he screwed the cap off the gin and filled each glass a quarter of the way. I caught a whiff—it smelled like rubbing alcohol. "I'm concocting your favorite inebriation," he announced.

"Wot's that?"

"Why Julia, don't you remember your drink at the Hale Kuelani? I'm making orange blossoms."

"How nice," she said.

Ben and I returned to the pune'e.

Wilkins pried open the carton of orange juice. He poured until the glasses were full and handed one to Gramma. He raised his glass. "To memories that never fade," he said and clinked his glass against hers.

Gramma sipped her drink and sat at the table with Wilkins. He turned his chair and faced Ben and me. He told us he'd dated a socialite in San Francisco who was a close friend of Giannini, the founder of Bank of America. There were lavish parties on yachts, sipping champagne from the shoes of Hollywood starlets, and run-ins with bootleggers at Half Moon Bay. He claimed he'd put on the gloves against Ernest Hemingway at the Sutro Baths and "thrashed him soundly." His relationship with the socialite fizzled so he bought a winery in Napa Valley and married a Mexican girl. She funneled the winery's profits to her lover and he was forced to declare bankruptcy. The girl ran off. He painted homes in Sausalito to make ends meet and rented a tiny apartment a stone's throw from the Valhalla restaurant. Sally Stanford, a retired madam, owned the Valhalla. They became good friends. He had managed her third run for mayor and, when Sally won, she gave him the deed to a sprawling estate on Sausalito's south shore. The more he talked, the more Gramma got drawn in by his accent and adventurous life. She didn't get in a word edgewise. Her orange blossom was gone in no time and her eyes looked glazed.

Ben nudged me with his elbow. "Drunk as a skunk."

"I know," I replied.

"What should we do?"

"Go get Uncle Chipper."

"You go," Ben said. "I'll keep an eye on things."

I excused myself and walked nonchalantly to the lanai. I slipped through the back door, snuck around the beach house, and jogged through the ironwoods. I wondered how much of Wilkins was in me and whether I'd leave a girl if I got her hapai. I sprinted for the shack. The dogs joined me and racing them made me run even faster. I scooted past the hanging tree and the dump. I rapped my knuckles on the metal frame of the shack's screen door as I caught my breath. The screen was separating from the frame and it billowed like the sail of a ship. "Hui," I called. "Uncle Chipper!"

"Wot the hell?" came his voice.

"Hurry!"

The door to the bathroom opened and he stuck his head out. "Why hurry?"

"Gramma's with Norman Wilkins."

"So the hell wot."

"He's getting her drunk!"

The bathroom door closed. The toilet flushed and Chipper came out wearing an undershirt and BVDs. The gray stubble on his face looked like a mask of splinters and he smelled as though he hadn't showered in weeks. He stood barefoot on his cement floor. "Wot you want me to do?"

"Tell Gramma you love her."

He hobbled to the door and looked over my shoulder toward the beach house. "Brownie don't want me to love her no mo'."

"How do you know?"

"She divorced me, didn't she?"

"She told me part of her still loves you."

"When?"

"In the Scout, on our way to Johnny's."

"Bull crap."

"Please make her stop drinking, Uncle Chipper."

"I'll phone."

"Not the phone! He's got her hypnotized and you've gotta come over."

"Okay. Okay, already."

"Will you shower and shave and put on some nice clothes?"

"That'll take half the god damn day."

"The sooner you come," I said, "the sooner she can get rid of that creep."

He promised to clean up and I jogged home with the dogs. I saw Ben standing by the Norfolk and Leo ran to him.

"Is he coming?" Ben asked as he patted Leo.

"Yeah. How come you split?"

"She wanted to be alone with Wilkins. You won't believe the latest."

"What?"

"Seeing is believing."

I ran to the lanai and eased over the sill of an open window. The radio blared Irving Berlin's "My Sweetie" in the big room. I peered in through the screen door—Gramma was dancing with Wilkins. He held her close and waltzed her over the Oriental rug. She was light on her feet and her face seemed ten years younger. They danced around the Lazy Boy and bumped into the standing lamp. The song ended and they polished off their drinks.

"Remember our first night on Waikiki Beach?" he asked.

She laughed. "Had sand in mah hair fo' weeks."

I opened the screen door and entered the big room.

He poured a generous amount of gin in both glasses and topped them off with orange juice.

"Gramma!" I said.

"Wot, Peanut?"

"You shouldn't be drinking."

She gulped her orange blossom and stared at me as if I were a party pooper.

"Nonsense, young lad," Wilkins said.

"Go to the beach and bring yo' pole," she told me, "catch us a nice big ulua fo' dinnah."

"Brilliant thinking," he said, "and fetch me some coconut milk."

I frowned at Gramma. "You just wanna be alone with El Creepo and his dumb gin."

He lit a cigarette. He puffed and blew a cloud of smoke at me. "A clever boy listens to his elders."

Ben came in and Wilkins told him he should be a fashion model. Ben said he wanted to be an actor like Jack Lord. Wilkins said he had the looks for it. I heard a rumble and looked out the window—it was the Impala. It had eight cylinders but Chipper said only six were firing. He parked behind the jeep and climbed out. He wore a beige cowboy hat with a wrinkled brim and a maroon jacket that hung off him like a tent. Dots of toilet paper covered the spots where he'd cut himself shaving.

"Who's this poor devil?" Wilkins asked.

"Uncle Chipper," I piped up.

He took a long drag on his cigarette. "So this is the famous Chipper Daniels."

Gramma seemed embarrassed watching Chipper hobble up the rise in his Tobbies. She held the door open and he came inside and shook hands with Wilkins. Ben and I returned to the pune'e.

"How'd you know I had a visitor?" Gramma asked.

"A li'l birdie told me," Chipper replied and winked in my direction.

She gave me the stink eye. "Fo' the luva Pete."

"May I fix you an orange blossom?" Wilkins asked Chipper.

"A who?"

"Gin and orange juice," he replied, "one of Julia's favorites."

Chipper reached into his jacket and pulled out a gold flask. "Okolehao's mah tonic of choice," he said and dropped down in a chair.

Gramma and Wilkins sat with Chipper and they talked about the good old days in Waikiki. She brought up the Great War and told Wilkins how Chipper had won the British War Medal for saving the lives of English soldiers. Wilkins swilled his drink. The more Gramma praised Chipper the faster Wilkins drank. He flicked his ashes into the abalone shell and poured a glass of straight gin. He offered Gramma another but she said she'd had enough.

"So, Norman," Chipper said, "why didn't you marry Julia

when you found out she was hapai?"

He ran a hand through his hair. "Well, old chap," he replied, "I was young and wanted to see the world and not be tied down to a family. It was selfish of me, terribly selfish, and heaven only knows how much my son must resent me. I have made many mistakes over the years, things I have come to regret. But life goes on, and god above will not let me live my life over to make things right."

The room fell silent. The speech seemed rehearsed to me, as though he'd used it a few other times. "You could've called or written my father," I said. "You treated him like he wasn't even born."

"You shoulda sent money," Ben said.

Wilkins bowed his head. "You're both right," he admitted. "I should have done those things. But I didn't and for that I am overwhelmed with shame."

"Wheah you plan on spendin' the night?" Chipper asked.

Wilkins looked up. "Why, right here at the ranch, old chap."

Gramma frowned. "Did I say anythin' about bunkin' heah?"

"Well, I thought for old time's sake, after all these years, Julia."

"Camp on mah porch," Chipper offered. "Gotta spare cot."

Wilkins smashed his cigarette in the abalone shell. He finished his drink and snatched the bottle of gin. "Julia," he said, "may I speak to you outside?"

"Shuah," she said.

He led the way and she followed him out the door. The dogs barked and she shooed them away. He put his gin bottle on the hood of the Datsun. He leaned against the door as he talked.

"Whacha think he's saying?" asked Ben.

"Creepy things," I answered.

Chipper sipped from his flask. "That buggah's not givin' up," he said.

A half-hour went by and Wilkins was still talking. I doubted he still owned the estate in Sausalito and figured he'd run out of wealthy women in Northern California. It hurt my feelings he wouldn't recognize me as his grandson. He didn't care about me so he wasn't really my grandfather. If anyone deserved to be called my grandfather it was Chipper.

Wilkins hugged Gramma and she gave him a peck on the cheek. He plucked the bottle off the hood and climbed in the driver's seat. She waved goodbye as the Datsun backed up. He threw a kiss and sped past the Norfolk. She stared at the road like a lovesick girl.

The Spike

Gramma was pleased by Wilkins' visit. She kept trying on outfits and checking herself in the bedroom mirror. I was worried she'd let him back into her life and, a week after his visit, three bottles of wine showed up with the label "Wilkins Private Reserve." The label had a big mansion in the foreground with vine-covered hills behind. She hid the bottles under a quilt in her bedroom closet. Ben examined a bottle on the sly to determine if Wilkins had pasted on a fake label. He lifted the corner of the label with a steak knife but there wasn't anything beneath it but glass.

"The phony peeled off the original," he said, "then slapped on his own."

I figured the bottles were authentic. The stories Wilkins had told us were probably true since his past hadn't been all rosy. He'd admitted to being duped by his young wife and filing for bankruptcy. A phony wouldn't have said those things.

Ben turned the bottle upside down and examined the

glass for markings. Boots clippity-clopped. Ben slipped the bottle under the quilt. Gramma rounded the corner. "Wot you keeds doin' in mah bedroom?"

"Nothing," we answered.

"Nothin', mah foot. Now go wattah the horses."

*   *   *

Ben got so preoccupied with Hale Kia that he started acting like a game warden. He got up when the roosters crowed and scoured the high country with field binoculars issued by the U.S. Army. Gramma thought he was obsessed until he spotted the remains of two does in the foothills. After that, she encouraged him to keep an eye on things.

My brother's concern for the land coincided with Gramma's stories about the Duvas. They were the biggest family on Moloka'i and, because they had a smattering of French blood, they were raised with a sense of superiority. The blood they shared galvanized their souls and inspired a fierce loyalty. If you fought one Duva, you had to fight them all. A Honolulu mobster had beaten up Thomas Duva at the Hele On Bar and twenty Duvas showed up at the bar after midnight. They chained the mobster to a kiawe tree outside the courthouse and scalped him with a machete. The Chief of Police was a Duva so no reports were filed.

Years had gone by since Billy Duva broke into the beach house. Gramma said we'd be her first line of defense against Billy and she gave Ben and me carte blanche authority to kill him if he came within fifty yards of the front door.

*   *   *

I carried buckets of barley to the mares. Ben stood beside

the Norfolk watching the mountain. His camouflage outfit included a shirt, pants, and even a cap. His glasses interfered with the binoculars so he'd taken them off.

"Hui!" he said.

I put down the buckets and jogged over. He pointed at a deer on Kam Highway. A car drove by and the deer jumped our mauka fence. Old Sissy, Sandy, and the other mares neighed and galloped in circles as the deer trotted through the pili grass over to the trough.

He studied the deer through his binoculars.

"Can I look?" I asked.

"Promise not to drop 'em?"

"Promise."

He handed them over. They were our father's binoculars during the war. I stared through the lenses and adjusted the focus. I followed a row of breadfruit trees to the trough—the deer was drinking. Its hide was rust brown and there were white spots on its flanks.

"That spike's growing antlers," he said.

"It's not a doe?"

"You'll never be a hunter, Jeff."

The deer raised its head. The ears twitched. Tiny antlers were on the top of his head. He nibbled the grass growing beside the trough.

A white truck stopped. A man with a buzz cut stood in the truck's bed. He wore an orange muscle shirt and his big arms rested over the cab.

Ben took the binoculars back and readjusted the focus. "They've got guns," he said.

"Who's the bolohead?"

"Billy Duva."

A blue van parked beside the truck. The driver of the van spoke to Billy. The spike kept grazing. A door slammed and a woman from the van joined the men in the truck. The van sped off.

The driver of the truck honked. He continued honking until the spike ran to the middle of the pasture.

"Shut up," Ben said, "shut the hell up!"

"The Duvas won't shut up for you," I said.

"They would if I had a gun."

Billy hurled a bottle into the pasture. The spike made a break for the mountain and the white truck crept along the fence line. A black Fairlane heading the opposite way tooted. The spike froze and Billy shook his fist at the Fairlane. The spike ran past the trough and jumped our makai fence.

"Come on!" Ben said.

We chased the spike into a hala grove. I followed Ben down a narrow path and the spike scampered under a tree. We cornered him against the tree but he dodged my brother, avoided my outstretched hand, and headed for the ocean. We pursued the spike to the beach, where he ran west toward the point of the bay.

A green boat was anchored off the point. The green was so dark it looked black. This was the boat the Duvas used to lay net in the shallow water. Its hull was covered with barnacles. During kai make tides, the boat was marooned on the sand. "That damn boat's watalogged," Gramma had said. Ben had wanted to blast a hole through its hull the day he heard about her history with Billy. She'd talked him out of it by saying the Duvas would retaliate by feeding our mares barley laced with arsenic.

We ran the shoreline to the stone wall in front of the beach house. Three storm windows were open and Gramma sat on the lanai. She wore her lauhala hat and glasses. She'd gotten away with not wearing glasses all of her life but a doctor claimed she needed bifocals for myopia. Each lens had a half-moon floating in it. "Hui," she called, "you keeds get up hea!"

Ben and I left the beach and jogged to the lanai.

Gramma drank coffee from a blue mug. She had on her palaka shirt and denims. "Get inside," she said.

I followed Ben over a sill and banged my knee on the wooden post between windows.

"You keeds got gawky legs," she said.

"Do not," I replied and sat between her and Ben.

A white truck roared through the ironwood forest. It was the same truck from the road. Leo and Spotty leapt up on my sill and jumped down to the lanai. They cowered on the tiles beside Ben's chair. Spotty's head trembled. Moki had told Gramma that Billy kicked our dogs whenever they wandered onto Duva property.

The truck reached the beach and its tires sank in the sand. The rear tires began to spin. The men got out with their guns.

Ben held up his binoculars. "Carbines," he said.

The passenger door opened and three pit bulls went for the spike. The spike bolted into the water. Billy whistled and the pit bulls stopped. I heard a crack from a rifle. The spike bounded through the shallows like a rabbit through a meadow.

Gramma stuck her bifocals in her shirt pocket. "Lemmee

see those glasses," she said. Ben gave me the binoculars and I handed them to her. She propped her elbows on her sill and looked through the lenses. "Damn that Billy Duva," she said.

I heard more cracks. Two men had rifles and they kept firing. Billy pulled a cane knife from the truck. He walked with a swagger and swung at a kiawe tree. A branch sheered off.

The spike kept going. He was a hundred yards offshore when the shooting stopped.

"Headin' fo' Pailolo Channel," Gramma said. She passed the binoculars and I gave them back to Ben.

"He'll never make it," he responded.

"How do deer know how to swim?" I asked.

Gramma slipped on her bifocals. "They just do."

The spike made the blue water before the reef. It was too deep for him to spring off the bottom so he paddled like a dog. Surf crashed over the reef, sending waves against him.

One man waded to the boat and heaved up the anchor. Billy and the others took turns lifting themselves over the sides. Billy jerked the starter cord. The outboard sputtered and died. He jerked a second time and it died again. On the fifth try, the engine caught and they headed out. Billy turned the engine over to another man when the boat was halfway to the reef.

"They'll eat anythin' with hair on it," Gramma said.

The boat churned through the shallows. The men had guns and Billy stood up to check their progress. I felt helpless as the boat closed in.

"Gramma," Ben said, "get your rifle."

"Wot fo'?" she asked.

"Shoot over Billy's head."

"And have that puhi'u fiah back?"

Ben put his binoculars down. "We can't just sit here."

"Not a damn thing we can do."

Hale Kia began and ended at the shore. The Duvas made the rules in the ocean. They could drop nets in the shallows in front of the beach house whenever they wanted.

"Does the spike have a chance?" I asked.

"If he can just make the reef," she said. "Billy can't follow 'um ovah the reef."

The water was too shallow for a boat to pass safely over the coral ledge. The propeller would tear into the ledge and the hull would scrape. They'd be forced to go east and use the harbor. By that time, the spike would be in the open ocean and he'd be hard to spot. I knew the spike had the stamina to swim the seven miles to Maui. Gramma had seen herds of deer make the crossing.

"Go, li'l fulla," she said, "go."

"Go!" I pleaded.

The man at the outboard wedged the boat between the spike and the reef. The spike lost momentum and his head went underwater. The boat pulled alongside. Hooves kicked the boat and it seemed as though the Duvas were making a rescue. Waves broke over the bow, showering the men. Billy aimed his rifle down and I heard a crack. A second crack followed.

Gramma shook her head. "Disgustin'."

"Can't believe it," Ben said watching through the binoculars.

"Believe what?" I asked.

"Billy missed," he answered, "at point blank!"

The spike swam frantically for shore. The pit bulls ran up and down the beach barking. Billy put the gun down and said something to the driver. The boat turned. This time, they went straight for the spike and the bow slammed into him. The spike's front legs came high out of the water and kicked as if he were trying to run through the sky.

"Why don't they just end it," Gramma said.

"He's still gotta chance," I said.

Ben smirked. "You're a fool, Jeff."

Billy got on his knees. He held the cane knife. He kept the blade low and dragged it across the spike's neck. The deer's cry sounded like a baby's. He kicked his hooves against the boat and pushed away. The driver floated the boat closer. Billy leaned over again with the cane knife and the spike reared up off the bottom and struck him in the head with his hoof.

"Yes!" Ben said.

Billy put a hand to his forehead to check for blood. He reached down and grabbed the spike by an antler. He lifted the spike's head and used the cane knife with the other. The spike kicked but Billy wouldn't let go.

"Don't know about you keeds," Gramma said, "but I've seen enough." She got up with her mug and retreated to the big room. The theme song for *All My Children* played.

"That spike's pau," Ben said.

One man held the spike by the legs and a second helped drag the body into the boat. Billy dipped his cane knife in the water and ran his hand over the blade. The boat headed back.

Laughter and shouting came from the point. Children were playing on the beach. A boy sat in the truck with his hands on the wheel. A woman in a muumuu waved at the boat. Billy waved from the bow. His orange shirt flapped in the breeze like a flag.

Ben stood and offered me the binoculars.

"No," I said.

He placed them on the sill and joined Gramma in the big room.

I watched the ocean. The trades howled and whitecaps danced the surface. There was so much water out there that it made me feel empty and lost, as if part of me was sinking beneath the waves.

The Poachers

Turning fourteen was a milestone for Ben. Besides getting his braces off and convincing our father to buy him contacts, he received a .22 rifle for Christmas. He shot a coconut in the backyard and, after digging out the slug, knew he had the power to kill. His .22 could rain fifteen shots as fast as he could pull the trigger. He bought a telescope with a tripod and brought that with the rifle to Moloka'i.

Gramma wasn't crazy about Ben having his own gun. She thought he'd let his emotions get the better of him and suggested he stow it in the garage. Ben refused. He kept the .22 in a black case beside his bed. He found a beach chair that had washed up on shore and hunkered down on the front lawn with his telescope. He watched everything from the foothills to the high country.

"Wanna go fishing?" I asked Ben.

"I'm busy."

"Doing what?"

"Protecting our land."

I thought he was wasting his time on Moloka'i. But then he spotted the poachers. This was the second time he'd seen trespassers on our mountain.

"One's a popolo," he said, "take a look."

I squinted through the lens—there were two men. One was haole and the other black. They wore camouflage jackets. Rifles hung from their shoulders and they hiked like they owned Hale Kia.

"I'm going up," he said.

"Want company?"

"Willing to fight?"

I took my eye off the lens. "Sure."

"You'll chicken out."

"Will not."

Ben had spotted a gang of poachers earlier that summer. "Only good poacher is a dead poacher," he said loading his gun. Gramma appeared at the doorway holding her .219 rifle. "Shoot ovah their heads," she said. They started blasting and I slid open the ammo box and counted out Ben's next fifteen rounds. They kept firing until the poachers disappeared. It had been great fun. You could get away with crazy things like that with Gramma. Ben said he'd intended to kill the poachers all along and that he shot higher only to make up for the distance.

*   *   *

We climbed the first hill in our jeans, T-shirts, and sneakers. Gramma had given us her blessing. Ben carried his rifle and a hunting knife with a deer bone handle. The knife was in a leather sheath attached to his belt.

"Too bad you don't have a gun," he said.

"So?"

"What if they start shooting?"

"I'll run."

"Chicken."

I'd wanted to bring the BB gun but I knew that would do little against the poachers. I didn't ask my brother if he had a plan. I just hiked. The dogs were back at the beach house— Gramma didn't want the poachers mistaking them for deer. I tried matching his pace but he walked so fast that I had to jog to keep up. I huffed and puffed after the first hill.

"Bet Daddy never scouted like me," he said.

"He used to run up this mountain," I replied.

"According to who?"

"Gramma."

"She's full of kukae," he said.

I knew Ben had been waiting for this day, the day he could match deadly force with deadly force. He'd just seen William Holden in *The Wild Bunch* and loved how Holden's character was willing to fight to the death for a noble cause. His noble cause was protecting Hale Kia. He said the thing that separated a hero from a coward was knowing when to pull the trigger. The idea that our enemies were men made him more determined to defeat them—that way he'd surpass what our father had done as a boy. Our father had never gone up after anyone and he didn't mind me tagging along since I'd be a witness to his exploits.

We snuck through two fence lines that kept cows from reaching the highway. Narrow trails in the scrub brush were loaded with goat droppings. Gramma had told us the land between fences was inhabited by the 'uhane, ghosts that killed hunters.

We reached a third fence line. I looked south and saw the blues and greens of Pailolo Channel and coral reefs fingering toward Maui. Turquoise pools in the reef marked where fresh water bubbled up through the ocean floor. A marlin boat cruised the water between islands. A breeze blew off the channel and there was the wild scent of blooming lantana.

Ben pointed to a KAPU NO TRESPASSING sign nailed to the gate. "Punks can't read," he said.

I ran my hand over the sign—white paint flaked off and snowed on the red dirt. The fence line ran east and west. The wire was smooth and the posts were ironwood that Chipper had cut in the flatlands. Mounds of cow manure baked on the dirt flats to the north.

We ducked between strands of wire.

He pulled the lever of his rifle and loaded the chamber. He handed me his knife. "Kill him if he shoots me," he said.

"Who?"

"The popolo."

I waited while Ben snuck through the plum trees. I brandished the knife and climbed to a dirt flat. To the east, an outcropping overlooked a gulch. The black poacher was perched on a boulder watching the eastern ridge through his rifle's scope. He had a moustache and his jacket sleeves were rolled up past his elbows.

Ben crawled to a plum tree next to the boulder, popped up, and jammed his barrel against the poacher's neck. "Drop it!" he said.

The poacher stood up and raised his hands.

I ran through the brush gripping the deer bone handle. I reached them and the poacher had his hands behind his head.

Where's your haole friend?" Ben asked.

"Came alone."

"Liar. Get his rifle, Jeff."

I picked up the rifle by its strap and slung it over my shoulder.

"Who are you boys?" the poacher asked.

"The owners," I said.

"The owners of what?"

Ben tapped the .22's trigger. "Move."

"I go nowhere with you two."

"You're going to jail for trespassing," Ben replied.

The poacher kept his hands behind his head and led the way to the road. A pheasant scurried through the ferns. A strange feeling took hold, something that made my chest burn and my legs tingle. I caught up to the poacher and slashed the air with the blade of the knife. "Where's your friend?" I demanded. The rifle fell off my shoulder and the poacher shoved me aside. His hands were on the rifle's stock when Ben fired. Blood sprayed the ferns.

"Fuck!" the poacher said holding his ear. Blood spurted out from between his fingers and spattered his camouflage jacket. "You shot my fucking ear!"

"I ventilated it," Ben said.

"You fucking little bastard!" The poacher took out a handkerchief and held it against his ear. The handkerchief turned bright red in seconds.

Ben kept his .22 on him.

"Won't stop bleeding," the poacher moaned.

"Get his gun," Ben told me.

I held the knife in my left hand and picked up the rifle with my right. I heard an engine—the Scout was charging up the mountain with Gramma at the wheel. The tires churned over rocks and ruts in the road and the cab jounced violently. Chipper rode shotgun and our dogs raced through the trees.

She pulled alongside. Her .219 was resting on her lap. "Fo' the luva Pete," she said, "why'd you shoot 'um?"

"Went for his rifle," Ben answered.

"This mountain's kapu," she told the poacher.

"Thought it was state land."

"You thought wrong," Chipper said.

Gramma looked past Ben and me. "Now who's this fulla?"

The haole poacher was hiking down. He was muscular with brown hair and his arms were tattooed. He held his rifle in one hand and kicked up dust as he walked. His jacket was knotted at his waist. There was something cocky about the way he carried himself. The dogs charged up after him and sniffed his pants and boots.

"He might shoot," I said.

"He won't shoot," the black poacher said.

Ben glared. "Thought you said you came alone?"

The black poacher said nothing.

The haole poacher squinted when he saw the bloody handkerchief. His pace quickened and he put both hands on his rifle. "Roy," he said," What the hell happened?"

"Boy shot me."

"I'm calling the cops," said the poacher.

"Call, nothin'," Gramma said. She told him he was trespassing and "damn lucky" she hadn't notified the game warden. Chipper asked for his rifle but the poacher refused. Gramma slid her bolt action. Ben jammed his barrel against Roy's neck.

"Cades," Roy said, "do what they say."

Cades lowered his rifle and passed it to Chipper. I gave Chipper the second rifle and Ben dropped the tailgate for Leo and Spotty. Ben and I stood in the bed and Gramma made the men march down in front of us. They seemed tiny as we leaned over the cab's roof. The dogs whined for attention but Ben kept his rifle trained on them while I brandished the knife. Roy held the bloody handkerchief against his ear.

We made it to Kam Highway and Chipper unloaded the rifles. He threw the bullets in the brush and gave the men their guns.

"Don't evah lemmee catch you again," Gramma warned.

"Next time," Cades said, "we'll ask permission."

"Won't be a next time," Ben said.

The men walked east toward the bridge at Kainalu Stream with their guns slung over their shoulders. They didn't speak to each other and they didn't look back.

Ben lowered his rifle and patted Leo.

"Proud of you boys," Gramma said.

We headed to the flatlands. I held the knife up and the blade glinted in the sunlight. I felt like a soldier who'd marched off to war and returned victorious. Drops of blood had dried on my shirt. I begged Ben to let me borrow his knife.

"No," he said.

"Just one day."

"All right. But no throwing it against trees. I don't want it busted."

I held the deer bone handle tight. "I won't bust it."

The Scout turned off Kam Highway and we took the long driveway to the ocean. White blossoms from the oleanders were scattered over the stones and gravel. It was great having Uncle Chipper with us. I gazed over the flatlands. The mares were safe in their pasture and the ironwood forest was protecting our coast. For the first time I felt connected to Hale Kia. Ben and I had proved we loved the land enough to risk our lives.

Uncle Bobby

Wilkins called on the Fourth of July and gabbed for an hour. Subsequent calls escalated into talking marathons that drove Ben and me pupule. Whenever the phone rang, Gramma scrambled to it like a teenager. If she had on her bifocals she removed them for her conversations—it was as if she thought he could see her through the phone and might find her less attractive. He was oblivious of the time difference between California and Hawaii and called at strange hours of the day and night. Once he called at four o'clock in the morning and Gramma nearly busted a hip when she tripped over Spotty.

The phone rang during *The Lawrence Welk Show* and Gramma rushed to the kitchen. "Oh, Norman," she said. Ben turned off the TV. The conversation was one-sided, with Wilkins doing most of the talking and Gramma listening like a girl with a crush. He must have asked about the land because she said Hale Kia was over three hundred acres and that it was free and clear except for Chipper's life estate.

"Think she loves El Creepo?" I asked Ben.

"Sure," he replied. "Bet you ten bucks they shack up."

"You're on," I said and we shook on it.

She hung up an hour later. She appeared in the doorway holding her bifocals. Her face was flushed with excitement.

"Wha'd Wilkins want?" I asked.

"Nothin'," she answered.

Ben winced. "Did he ask for money?"

" 'Course not. And don't tell yo' fathah he phoned."

"What do I get if I don't?" he asked.

"I'll bake you a bloody cake," she replied.

*   *   *

John Danford was Gramma's second lover and the father of my Uncle Bobby. Danford had competed with Duke Kahanamoku in surfing, outrigger canoeing, and rough water swimming. He'd beaten Kahanamoku only once, in an unofficial swim sprint at Alakea Slip, but that victory was enough to make him a legend on Oahu.

"What was Danford like?" I asked my father.

"He was a big rugged Portagee."

"Do you have any pictures?"

"No."

"So how do you know he was big and rugged?"

"Just look at Bobby," my father replied.

I compared Wilkins to Danford. Wilkins was English and Danford was Portuguese. Wilkins was blond and Danford was dark. Wilkins was a pretty boy from England and Danford was a tough guy from the islands. Wilkins spoke with an English accent and Danford spoke pidgin English. Despite their differences, the two men had something in common—they'd both deserted Gramma before their sons were born.

*   *   *

Uncle Bobby loved crouching and showing me his fighting pose. "One punch," he said throwing an uppercut. He was more a brawler than a boxer. He'd beaten up a Duva one summer and Gramma sent him home to Honolulu to avoid a blood feud.

"Did you ever beef in the ring, Uncle Bobby?" I asked.

"Heavyweight Champ of da Seabees."

"Did you ever fight my father?"

He threw a second uppercut. "Knock out."

Bobby and my father spoke pidgin English, but my father only used it to get better deals from local merchants and mechanics. In pictures of Bobby as a boy, he holds up his fists to the camera. If my father is in the same picture, he stands apart from his younger brother with his arms crossed. Gramma said Bobby had been in Bobo Olson's corner the night Olson fought Sugar Ray Robinson for the middleweight championship of the world. Now Bobby managed the best restaurants and bars in Honolulu, including Queen's Surf and Prince Kuhio's. His affair with Miss Hawaii had caused him to lose Dolores, his wife of thirty years. He proposed to Dolores again a year after they'd divorced.

"Can't live without you, babe," he told Dolores, "let's go anotha t'irty."

"No cheatin'?" she asked him.

"No cheatin'."

A year after his second marriage to Dolores, he met Donna

Fushima at Prince Kuhio's. Donna was a cocktail waitress with shiny black hair cascading down to her eighteen-inch waist. They drank mai tais after work and he gave Donna an emerald bracelet. Dolores showed up the next day and invited Donna into the restroom. Donna followed her in.

Dolores yanked Donna's hair. "You slant-eyed bimbo!"
Donna threw a hook. "Portagee bitch!"

Bobby sipped cognac at the bar while screams echoed through the restaurant. The walls shook. A painting of Queen Lili'uokalani fell and patrons thought it was an earthquake. Dolores left Prince Kuhio's with two black eyes and a squashed bouffant. Bobby married Donna Fushima at the Kahala Hilton's porpoise lagoon the week after he divorced Dolores for the second time.

*   *   *

Bobby knew my father didn't like him so he rarely visited Moloka'i in the summer. There'd been bad blood between them ever since they lived in Kaimuki with Granny, their grandmother. Dad Hinkle, the star boarder, was jealous of my father's close relationship with Granny. Hinkle treated Bobby like a son and beat my father every chance he got.

*   *   *

My father built an A-frame cottage east of the beach house after Gramma gave him Hale Kia. He wanted to keep the cottage a rental and he told her it was off limits to Bobby. Bobby flew over with Donna when the cottage was unoccupied and my father was in Honolulu. They stayed in Gramma's bedroom and kept to themselves. The morning after their arrival, Bobby and Donna ate papaya halves in the big room.

I joined Ben on the lanai, where he was cleaning his .22. He had on his camouflage outfit and matching cap. The storm windows were open and there was a sweeping view of the coast and the sea. The islands of Maui, Kahoolawe, and Lanai were beyond the deep blue of the channel.

"Hey, Juicy," I said, "Daddy should let the newlyweds stay in the cottage."

He squirted cleaning fluid on a cloth swab. "The General hates Bobby." He'd started calling our father "the General" because he loved giving orders.

"How come he hates him?" I asked.

"He thinks Bobby wasted his life getting drunk and poking squid."

"Sounds like fun."

Ben looked up from his work. "The General's secretly jealous."

"Why?"

"He'd like to poke Donna himself."

"The General digs Asian chicks?"

"I've seen him looking."

"Think we'll be friends later in life?"

He ran the swab through his barrel with a metal rod. "I'm no psychic," he said inspecting the dirty swab.

I was worried what my relationship with Ben might become. Back in Honolulu, we were hardly the picture of brotherly love. We were in the same grade at Punahou and I was a constant reminder he'd failed to match up with kids his own age. He ignored me whenever we crossed paths on campus and encouraged the school bully to throw me in the lily pond.

He treated me better on Moloka'i because I was his only friend at Hale Kia. Our father had wanted to mold him in his image and likeness but his attempt at playing god produced a sad boy. Ben had attempted to shore up his sense of self-worth by establishing himself as our father's equal in Gramma's eyes. Competing with her myths was a losing proposition.

I understood my brother but didn't trust him. Ben could be your best friend one minute and your mortal enemy the next. At times I felt he was on a quest to find new reasons to hate me. We co-existed on a superficial plane, a place of feigned friendship and temporary alliances. We'd had only one fight on Moloka'i but that fight was a doozy. I'd lost his silver lure and he got me in a headlock and rubbed my face against the screen door. The screen cut like sandpaper. I got away and grabbed a spear gun. I pulled the sling, locked it on the spear's shaft, and fired. The spear narrowly missed his head and I bolted across the lawn to retrieve it for a second try. He ran behind the beach house, where our grandmother was hanging out the wash.

"Gramma," he said, "Jeff's trying to kill me!"

"That's wot you get fo' fightin'," she replied.

He saw me coming—he sprinted down the beach and ran around the point.

*   *   *

Ben put the .22 down on his bed and picked up his old BB rifle. He sat at an open window and rested an elbow on the sill. He sighted down the barrel and fired at a can on the sea wall.

The dogs were resting on the sand path to the beach. They saw the gun and scampered under the beach house.

"Someday," he said, "the General's going to get his."

"Think he sends Puanani any money?" I asked.

"That manju? If Gramma didn't have dentures he'd yank the gold outta her teeth."

"Let's ask him about Lani."

"What for? He'll just deny she's his daughter."

I leaned against the sill. "I'd like to ask Kitty about him."

"Fat chance she'd squawk," he replied and took aim again. "You know," he said, "you look just like the General."

"Do not."

"Have you seen Gramma's old pictures?"

"I don't have thin lips."

"You've got momona ones from gobblin' donuts."

"Do I look like Wilkins?"

"No," he said, "and be glad you don't."

"How come?"

He fired. "That guy's a royal pussy."

Gramma came out with her transistor radio and a mug. She had on her ranch clothes. She placed the radio on the sill next to Ben and sat down. Her gray hair was wavy because a transsexual named Kimmi had given her a perm. She slipped on her bifocals and sipped coffee. She hadn't said anything bad about Donna yet so I knew she wasn't comfortable with her. She turned on the radio and "Someone To Watch Over Me" played.

The screen door creaked and Donna walked down the steps. She wore yellow capri pants and a white tee with the slogan GEEV 'UM! Her hair was up and held in place by a pair of red lacquered chopsticks. Bobby followed her out in his tank top and denims. He was a bald man who reminded me of Telly

Savalas. He slid two chairs in front of an open window and
Donna sat next to me.

Bobby stood beside Ben's chair. "Lemmee see dat gun."

He handed Bobby the rifle.

"C'mon, Bobby," Gramma said switching off the radio,
"show these keeds how to shoot."

He braced the gun against the post between windows.
His opu hung over his belt. "Could outshoot yo' old man any
day of da week," he said and shot standing up.

"Miss," Ben said.

Bobby gave the rifle to Ben and sat on the other side of
Donna. His chest was a forest of gray hair and he smelled like
English Leather. "Forgot about da wind," he told Donna.

"Did you play football with my father?" I asked Bobby.

"He tell you dat?"

"No."

"Yo' faddah was a bookworm."

"We call him 'the General,' " Ben said.

Bobby smiled. "I called 'um 'Captain Norm.' "

"He's moved up in rank," I said.

"Pass that rifle," Gramma told Ben.

He gave her the gun.

She cradled it in her arms, sighted down the barrel, and
fired. "Theah," she said, "that's how to shoot."

"You missed," Ben told her.

"Bobby," she said, "didn't I hit that can?"

"Sounded like it to me, moddah."

"I'll go check," Ben said.

"Peanut," she said, "go down with yo' bruthah."

I hated being called "Peanut" in front of guests. I was a teenager now and that nickname made me feel like a first grader. I'd told her to quit it but she couldn't get "Peanut" out of her head.

Ben and I hustled down to the beach. He picked up the can and turned it over. "What a dud," he said handing me the can. There were no marks.

"Can I take a shot?" I asked.

"Sure. Bet you're better than Bobby."

I put the can on the wall and we walked the grassy incline up to the beach house. Hawaiian music played on the radio and Bobby was doing the hula. Donna giggled as he gyrated his hips to the slack key sounds of Gabby Pahinui. My grandmother had on her polite face with the half-smile, the one she used for strangers. This was the first time she'd met Donna and she didn't know how to act. The song ended and Bobby took a bow.

Donna clapped. "No ka oi!"

"My Bobby can dance," Gramma said.

Bobby sat and Donna gave him a peck on the cheek. Another song played but Gramma turned the radio off.

I followed Ben over a sill.

"Did I hit that can?" Gramma asked Ben.

"You missed."

"You shuah?"

"I'm sure I'm sure," Ben replied.

Ben loaded the rifle with BBs and gave it to Donna. Bobby showed her how to steady the gun by pressing it against her shoulder. The emeralds in her bracelet glistened as the muscles in her forearm flexed to steady the gun. A gold band glowed on her finger.

"Good girl," Bobby said. "Now squeeze da triggah."

"Will it kick, Honey?"

He laughed. "Like a mule."

The barrel jiggled when she squeezed.

"Miss," Ben said.

She passed the gun to Bobby and he missed again. Ben was next and he held the rifle confidently and fired. There was an unmistakable plink of a BB striking.

"Hit!" I said.

"Good shot," said Bobby.

Ben and I went down to check. The BB wasn't strong enough to penetrate tin but there was a dent in the middle.

I ran my finger over the dent. "Aim right for it?"

"Yeah. Why shouldn't I?"

"Uncle Bobby said to watch the wind."

"Wind blowing outta his okole," he said.

The morning became a contest of teenagers against adults. Ben gave me the rifle and I felt the pressure. I sighted down the barrel, touched the trigger, and pulled. There was no plink.

"Eh, Jeff," Bobby said, "scoop me a beah."

"So early, Honey?" Donna asked.

"Puts hair on mah chest," he claimed.

I went to the kitchen and returned with a cold bottle of Primo. I was glad my uncle hadn't called me "Peanut." I handed him the beer and he took down half in his first gulp. Sweat beaded up on his head.

"Ah," he said, "dat's da kine."

I sat down and it was my turn. My heart beat fast. I

raised the barrel, lined up the sights, and fired. I heard a plink.

"Yowza!" Ben cheered.

We went down to inspect the damage. Now there were two dents. Mine was a little higher up than Ben's. We were winning by two.

The next round, Gramma turned the radio back on. The news played. It seemed like five minutes before she pulled the trigger.

"Miss," Ben said.

"I hit that can," she insisted. "Wot you lyin' fo'?"

We returned to the beach but this time Bobby tagged along. "Gramma was a crackah-jack shot in her day," he told us. He said she hiked the mountain at sunset to hunt dove. He picked up the can and burped. There were two dents. Leo and Spotty joined us and Bobby patted them. He told us he owned three golden retrievers and that they slept in bed with him and Donna. We returned to the lanai.

"Well?" Gramma asked.

"No, moddah," Bobby said.

"You shuah, Bobby?"

"Musta grazed it."

We started in again. Ben hit the can and we were winning by three. That's when Bobby decided to go for a swim.

"Donna loves da waddah," he said.

Donna smiled. "So clean on da east end, Auntie Brownie."

The newlyweds returned to the bedroom.

"Grad-oo-lations," Ben told me. We did our tiny handshake where we shook with thumbs and index fingers.

Gramma fidgeted in her chair while drinking coffee. She scowled at the channel. She listened to a report about trouble with the pineapple industry. The song "Zippity Doo Dah" came on and she switched off the radio. She threw the last of her coffee through the open window. She picked up her radio, walked into the kitchen, and tossed silverware and dishes into the sink. The freezer door opened and slammed.

"What a grouch," I told Ben.

"Poor sport," he said.

Bobby and Donna came out and walked toward the point. He had a towel from the Outrigger Canoe Club draped over one shoulder. Donna wore a black bikini and had a silver chain around her belly. She seemed to glide while he waddled. He wrapped his arm around her waist and pulled her close.

"Donna's a fox," Ben said on the lanai.

"A Twentieth Century Fox," I added.

"You keeds go catch some fish fo' dinnah," Gramma called from the kitchen.

"Let's make tracks," he said.

We went spin-casting near the point while the dogs chased crabs. Donna swam with her head out and Bobby sat on the beach. She waved for him. He waded until the water reached his knees. She splashed him and he caught her and they laughed. He held her in the shallows.

Ben reeled in his line. "Uncle Bobby did all right for himself," he said, "the bald skebbe."

"Why'd she marry him?" I asked.

"Not for his kala."

"He's broke?"

"Bobby doesn't have a pot to pee in."

"How'd he lose all his money?"

"On alimony," he said, "and emerald bracelets."

"So why's she with him?"

He cast his lure and it sparkled when it hit the water. "Gramma says love's a funny thing," Ben said, "and I believe her."

Arlene

Arlene was married to Rocky Robello, a dock worker who beat her whenever he drank. Rocky lost his job at Kaunakakai Wharf for siphoning gas and stealing bags of Moloka'i onions. I'd see Arlene at Our Lady of Sorrows Church sitting in the back row wearing sunglasses. She never went up for Communion. She was a brunette with a pageboy haircut and she had the high cheekbones of a model.

"That girl's got Indian blood," Gramma said.

Arlene seemed out of place on Moloka'i. She never spoke pidgin English and she never swore. She was from San Francisco and had met Rocky at the Monterey Jazz Festival, where he played lead guitar in an acid rock band. She'd married him when the band broke up and they moved to his family home on Moloka'i. He went on drinking binges, partied with local girls, and accused Arlene of cheating. Arlene was hired as a reservation agent by Aloha Airlines. Someone poured sugar in her gas tank and Rocky blamed her when the engine seized.

Arlene was thumbing a ride so Gramma stopped and drove her to Kaunakakai. Arlene said she wanted to divorce Rocky and start a new life. Gramma offered her the saddle room until the divorce was finalized. Arlene accepted. She arrived at Hale Kia wearing a peasant dress, sunglasses, and clogs. Her luggage was a sleeping bag and a pink suitcase with flower power stickers. Ben and I piled saddles in one corner while Gramma pulled bridles and lassos off the walls. Ben broomed webs out of the bathroom and I polished the fixtures in the sink and shower.

"Get some air in hea," Gramma said cranking open the louvered windows.

Arlene took off her sunglasses—her eyes were black and blue. She was so happy that she started to cry.

Gramma hugged her. "Yo' safe with us, Arlene."

*   *   *

Gramma civilized the saddle room by putting in a refrigerator, an oven, and a twin bed. She gave Arlene fabric for curtains and Arlene earned money cleaning the beach house, washing clothes, and mending. Her eyes healed and she quit wearing sunglasses. I would see her at the end of a long day picking lemons in her green bikini. She'd sit on the top step of her stairway, sip lemonade, and watch the sun drop below the ironwood forest.

*   *   *

Arlene asked Gramma about the man wearing BVDs on his front lawn.

"Thin as a bean pole?" Gramma asked.

"Skin and bones."

"Slow as a turtle?"

Arlene nodded.

"That's Chippah."

Arlene made extra money doing Chipper's laundry and sewing. She had coffee with him on his porch. She worked at Chipper's first since the saddle room was close to the shack. Gramma quizzed Arlene when she got to the beach house.

"Wot's in Chippah's ice box?" she asked.

"TV dinners."

"Any greens?"

"Frozen peas."

"Fruit?"

"Two papayas hanging off a rope."

"I'll bring 'um a li'l somethin'," Gramma said.

Arlene made Chipper a pill calendar that told him the day and hour he was supposed to take his medication for a laundry list of ailments, from migraines to ulcers. He was good about taking his pills except that he washed them down with shots of okolehao. Once he'd spent all night in bed with a centipede. Booze and pills had deadened his senses and he didn't feel the bites until morning. Arlene cleaned and bandaged his wounds.

"His whole body's swollen," Arlene said.

"That's wot the damn fool gets," Gramma answered.

*   *   *

Arlene worked for my grandmother weekdays from ten to two. Gramma prepared lunch and they watched *All My Children* at noon. They went on and on about men when the soap broke for commercials. Gramma said men were overgrown boys and that women had to learn how to mother them to make things work. Arlene asked her about Chipper and she said being married to him was paradise in the beginning but "a livin' hell" at the end. Arlene said her first boyfriend became a priest and the second sold drugs. Gramma mentioned Wilkins. She claimed he was the love of her life and that she still had feelings for him. Arlene said it sounded "so romantic" and that she should give him a second chance. I couldn't believe Arlene. The soap ended and Arlene swept the lanai. I snuck into the big room and reminded Gramma that Wilkins had ignored her for over five decades and that if anyone deserved a second chance it was Chipper.

"That ol' fool's half-dead," she replied.

*   *   *

Ben and I were watching Honolulu All-Star Wrestling when a white Falcon with gray primer rumbled past the Norfolk. The Falcon stopped next to the saddle room and a husky man with long, dirty blond hair got out and banged on Arlene's door. She answered in her bikini. She let the man in and the door closed.

"Gramma," Ben said, "some hippie's over at Arlene's."

She looked through her picture window. "That's that damn Rocky's cah."

"What's Rocky doing here?" he asked.

"He brought Arlene the divorce papahs to sign."

"Want us to spy?" I asked.

"Shuah," she said. "And lemmee know if that puhi'u tries any monkey business."

We ran outside and snuck up to the saddle room. Ben

climbed a hala tree and stood on a branch. The wind rustled through the lauhala.

"What's Rocky doing?" I asked.

"Bangin' Arlene."

"No!"

"Sucker," he said.

I peeked through the branches and saw the yellow curtains on the window and the steps leading to the front door. A myna pecked at a mango next to the garbage can.

"All quiet on the western front," Ben said.

Arlene screamed. She screamed again and was out the door running down the steps with Rocky behind her. She knocked over the garbage can and the bird flew off. He caught her and slammed her down on the hood his car. He pulled her pageboy hair and she clawed his face. "Bitch!" he said. She got away. He caught her again and dragged her up the stairs into the saddle room. The door slammed.

"Let's go!" Ben said sliding down the trunk.

We ran home and he whipped open the door. Gramma was sitting at the table smoking a Chesterfield.

"Rocky's beating Arlene!" he said.

She crushed her cigarette in her tin can. "Crumb bum," she said and walked to her bedroom. She returned with her rifle.

"I'll get my .22," Ben said.

She slid two bullets into her magazine. "A big buck needs a big gun."

We followed her out. The dogs saw the rifle and crawled under the beach house.

We climbed in the jeep. The canvas top had rotted off and I sat on the rusted metal floor in back. Gramma sped to the saddle room and pulled alongside the lemon tree.

"Hui," she called. "Oh, Arlene!"

There was no answer so we got out of the jeep.

"Arlene's dead," Ben said.

"Dead, nothin'," Gramma said grabbing her rifle. "Rocky's hushin' her up. You keeds got lungs, use 'um."

"Arlene!" we called.

The door opened. Arlene stood in the doorway holding one hand over her eye. "Everything's fine, Brownie."

"Tell Rocky get out hea now."

She ducked inside, said something to Rocky, and returned. "Rocky says, 'Go jump in the swamp.' "

Gramma cranked the lever on her rifle and aimed at the Falcon. She pulled the trigger and the bullet pierced the front and rear windshields. The shot echoed through the gulch. Dogs barked and our mares ran to the mauka side of the pasture.

Rocky pushed Arlene aside and ran bare chested down the steps. His long hair swung over his shoulders and his face was scratched. "Fockin' bitch!" he said.

She cranked the lever and aimed. She held the butt of the rifle against her shoulder and sighted down the barrel. "This one's got yo' name on it, Mistah Rocky."

Rocky quit running. "You won't shoot."

"Shoot 'im, Gramma!" Ben pleaded.

She kept her rifle on him. "Yo' trespassin' and hurtin' Arlene."

"You go prison, Brownie."

"I had a good long life," she replied, "but Rocky, yo' young."

Rocky brushed the hair out of his eyes. He made his way to the Falcon and opened the door. He got in slowly. She kept her gun trained on him as he drove off the ranch.

"If you keeds evah see Rocky again," she said, "come get Gramma."

*   *   *

Rocky never returned. It was a good thing because Ben kept a bullet in the chamber of his .22 and vowed to shoot Rocky before Gramma had a chance to load her rifle. The divorce went through and my father told Gramma it was all right for Arlene to continue living at Hale Kia as long as she didn't invite men over. I guess he figured she was good for his mother.

*   *   *

I was filling up the horse trough when my father crossed paths with Arlene for the first time. My mother was visiting her relatives on the east coast and he'd flown over from Honolulu for the weekend. Arlene walked down the saddle room steps and I jogged over and introduced them next to the lemon tree. I noticed a space between her two front teeth like the model Lauren Hutton. Arlene was twenty years younger than my father. She wore a white blouse and jeans cut mid thigh. I knew she was attracted to him by the way she smiled. She reached up and picked a lemon.

"Thanks for helping with my mother, Arlene," my father said.

"Oh," she replied, "Brownie's a sweetheart."

"Are you enjoying Hale Kia?"

"It's paradise."

"That's right," my father replied, "it's paradise found."

They just stood there smiling not knowing what to say. He gazed up at the sky. She raised the lemon and smelled it. A sparrow sang in the lemon tree.

"I've got to catch up on my sewing," she said. "So nice to finally meet you, Mr. Gill."

"Please, Arlene, call me 'Norm.' "

"I will," she said and walked through the high grass in the pasture. She reached the stairs and stared at my father before disappearing into the saddle room.

"Daddy," I said.

"Huh?"

"You should see her in a bikini."

He laughed. "I think you've gotta crush, Jeff."

We walked through the pasture to check for mangoes. My father glanced at the saddle room as he reached to pick a ripe one.

                    *   *   *

The saddle room was built beside the mangrove on the edge of the pasture. Arlene brought life to those dreary acres. I smelled her bacon frying when I fed the mares their morning barley. Her porch light came on at dusk. One evening I walked to the Norfolk. The wind whipped the branches and pushed the clouds over the stars. I checked out the saddle room. TV light flickered through the curtains. Arlene had a black and white set with bent rabbit ears and a screen that snowed. I wondered how it felt to divorce someone you once loved. I heard footsteps.

Ben came out of the dark. "What's going on, Peanut?"

"Nothing."

"You're spying on Arlene, trying to catch her naked."

"I'm looking for Venus."

"You can't see Venus through all these clouds."

"It'll clear."

"Pre-vert," he said before vanishing into the darkness.

*   *   *

I teased my father about Arlene whenever he visited. He was a seasonal bachelor—my mother left him every summer for Boston as a reward for being a housewife the rest of the year. I told my father about Arlene when we were alone because Gramma and Ben would say I was lying. "Arlene lives in her bikini," I'd say and "Arlene wants you to go swimming with her past the point." My father knew I was a kidder, but he probably wondered if there might be a kernel of truth in what I said.

"Arlene said something very interesting today," I told him while we watched *Mission Impossible*.

"Oh?" he replied. "And what was that?"

" 'Norman Gill is a handsome man.' "

He crossed his legs on the Lazy Boy. "She didn't say that."

"Oh, yes, she did."

"Arlene knows I'm married."

"Haven't you heard of free love? It's the latest craze."

He blushed. He gulped his martini during a Polydent commercial. "Arlene really said that?"

I made the peace sign. "Scout's honor."

He pulled a lever and his footrest popped up.

"She really digs you."

"Jeff," he said, "you're full of bullshit."

But when my father called my mother in Boston the next day, he made a point of mentioning the young woman in the saddle room.

"Arlene's been through a messy divorce," he told my mother.

My father handed me the phone and I went on and on about Arlene. "She wears bikinis," I said.

"Isn't that nice," she replied.

"She said Daddy's a dead ringer for Tom Jones."

There was silence on my mother's end. "Isn't that something," she finally said.

"She hopes to remarry soon."

"Let me speak to your father."

My father enjoyed the intrigue of having Arlene stay at Hale Kia and never contradicted anything I told my mother about her. Maybe he thought the idea of a cute divorcee living at the ranch would make her think twice about leaving him every June.

Joe

Gramma had run out of supplies so she said we were driving to town in the Scout. Arlene needed a few things too so she put on her peasant dress and hopped in the passenger seat. Ben and I climbed in the Scout's bed. Gramma drove to Kaunakakai and bought poi, potatoes, oatmeal, and rice. Then she headed west into the foothills. We sped past the Phallic Rock, a five-ton upright boulder. The Phallic Rock was supposed to make women fertile. *The Moloka'i Action News* reported that a grandmother from Minnesota had given birth to twins after camping beside it. We veered off the asphalt and took a red dirt road through the pineapple fields. We reached a plantation town with rows of green bungalows.

We parked in front of Kualapu'u Suprette, a general store that had once served as a mess hall for the first wave of pineapple workers from China and the Philippines. It stocked everything from meat to wigs. Aisle signs hung from the ceiling on lines of catgut. Fluorescent lights tinted the cans and bottles blue. A

buck's head was mounted on the far wall. The buck wore a
wreath around his neck and white lights on his antlers during
the winter. Now that it was summer, the buck had on sunglasses,
a visor, and a plastic lei. Beside the register was a glass case
filled with donuts. Flies were trapped in the case.

Joe Leong owned Kualapu'u Suprette. He was seven
years younger than my father and had a baby face. Joe's father
had sent him to Saint Louis High in Honolulu and then on to the
University of Hawaii, where he majored in business. Joe had a
spring to his walk and that made him appear even younger. He
was in great shape from hiking all over Moloka'i hunting the
elusive white buck. Locals claimed the buck was the
reincarnation of Lanikaula, a kahuna who'd empowered
Kamehameha's warriors with superhuman strength. Sarah had
warned that stepping in the footprint of the white buck would
bring a decade of suffering.

Joe loved spying for shoplifters from his second floor
office. He never called the cops if he caught you stealing. Instead,
he gave you the choice of either having a finger broken with a
small mallet or getting your mouth washed with Lava soap. Ben
had tried slipping packs of Violets candy and pieces of Bazooka
bubble gum into my pockets in the hopes I'd get nabbed. Pastor,
a Filipino boy, had gotten five fingers busted in two months. I'd
seen him in Kualapu'u with finger splints on both hands.

"Next time you get caught," I'd told him, "just get your
mouth washed."

"No can," Pastor had answered, "stay allergic to Lava."

Gramma and Arlene started in Canned Goods. There
was a sale on tomato paste and Arlene got excited.

I walked the length of the meat counter and examined the mullet and papio stacked on crushed ice. Their eyes were clear—that meant they were fresh. Pig, cow, and deer carcasses hung off giant hooks behind the counter. The smell of raw meat mixed with the aroma of donuts.

I continued down the aisle and saw Joe staring at me in the round mirror hanging above Sporting Goods. I waved at the mirror. He waved back and walked down the creaky wooden steps from his office to a cement floor painted sky blue. Ben had opened a box of .22s and was examining a hollow point.

Joe wore a button-down shirt and khaki slacks. He put his hand on my brother's shoulder. "Ben," he said, "who's this wahine with your grandmother?"

"Arlene," he answered, "Gramma's helper."

"Local wahine?"

"She's from Frisco," I said.

"I'll be damned," said Joe.

Gramma introduced Arlene to Joe in the Wigs aisle. Arlene examined the wigs while he rambled on about the toilet paper shortage.

"Use lauhala," Gramma recommended, "but watch fo' thorns."

Joe laughed. "Arlene," he said, "you can have anything in my store for free."

"Are you sure?" she asked.

"My treat."

This sudden burst of generosity was out of character for Joe. He'd slip fat in our meat orders and always overcharged for donuts. "That Joe's a sneak," Gramma'd said. Yet here he was, giving things away.

Arlene tried on a blonde wig.

"You look just like Marilyn Monroe," Joe said.

"I do?"

"Marilyn's dead," I blurted.

"Dead as a doornail," Gramma said.

He scowled at me.

Arlene put the wig back on its Styrofoam head and darted to Personal Care. She fingered everything from mouthwash to hair spray.

Gramma charged our groceries and paid cash for a half-dozen Long John donuts. The Long Johns were a foot-long and they had twists in them. Gramma pushed a cart full of boxed goods through an open door out to the sidewalk. She held open the bag of Long Johns. "Take two," she told Ben and me.

"Two each?" Ben asked.

"That's right."

Ben reached in and grabbed two. I pulled mine out of the bag and Gramma took one. We ate on the sidewalk in front of the Scout and watched Arlene run up and down the aisles. The Long Johns were coated with sugar and the dough was light and buttery.

"Can I have the last Long John?" Ben asked through a mouthful of dough.

"Don't be a damn hog," she said, "that's fo' Arlene."

I finished my second Long John and opened the tailgate. Ben rolled the grocery cart over and slid the boxes across the Scout's bed.

"Christ, Arlene," Gramma called, "make it snappy."

Arlene snatched something in Personal Care. Joe escorted her to the Scout and opened the passenger door. She slid in and thanked him again. She was holding a jar of Dippity Doo.

He shut the door. "Hope to see you soon, Arlene."

"That would be nice, Joe."

Ben and I climbed into the bed and sprawled on the bench seats. The pineapple fields behind Joe were fallow with the ashes from a recent burn. A harvesting machine squatted on the western horizon. The pickers seemed like ants as they worked the rows of pineapples. Joe stood on the curb with a big toothy smile. He stuffed his hands in his pockets and rocked on the balls of his feet.

"Arlene took such a dumb thing," I told Ben.

"What would you take?" he asked.

"Long Johns. How about you?"

"Bullets."

Gramma fired up the Scout and Joe waved goodbye. We left Kualapu'u and I watched Arlene through the Scout's rear window. She examined the Dippity Doo label. I put my ear to the glass and heard her recite a litany of ingredients. Gramma handed her a bag and I watched Arlene eat the last Long John.

*   *   *

Joe Leong was a big shot on Moloka'i. But the truth made him ordinary. He'd inherited the store from a miserly father who'd cashed in on the pineapple workers during the boom years. Joe's father had the market cornered. Now that pineapple was being phased out and everyone had cars, the monopoly had ended. His prices were rock bottom but the pineapple workers

from the old days had passed on their dislike for Old Man Leong
to their children. That meant avoiding Kualapu'u Suprette. Then
Joe's Chinese wife caught him with a Filipina at Maximo's Movie
House and filed for divorce. After that, most of the Chinese
community drove to Kaunakakai to do their shopping.

*   *   *

Joe called Gramma and said Arlene should have a phone
in the saddle room. "We live in the Twentieth Century," he
declared. Gramma thought that was extravagant. She offered
to relay messages but Joe insisted on paying for installation.
"That's big money," she said when the Hawaiian Bell truck
arrived.

*   *   *

Joe's first date with Arlene was on a Saturday. He'd made
dinner reservations at Pau Hana Inn, a restaurant with a view of
the wharf. A silver Firebird pulled up to the beach house and
Joe dropped off a package before heading down to Arlene's.

"That Joe's a perfect gentleman," Gramma said carrying
the package to the kitchen. She slipped off the string, opened
the paper, and blood spilled over the counter.

"Righteous," Ben said, "T-bones!"

"Gross," I said.

Gramma frowned. "Wot's bettah than steaks, Peanut?"

"Custard pie."

"Momona," Ben teased.

"I'm not momona."

He poked my opu. "Will be if you keep gobblin'."

The Firebird roared up the dirt road and cruised past the
Norfolk. I thought it was going to be a long night but Joe had

Arlene home before *Mannix* was over. "Arlene could do a lot worse than Joe," Gramma said watching the Firebird rumble back to the highway. The Saturday night dates continued until one night Joe and Arlene didn't go to dinner and the Firebird was still there Sunday morning.

My father was up for the weekend. He sat in his Lazy Boy carving out the flesh of a mango with a spoon. "Mother," he said, "how long has Arlene been living here?"

"Since last summa," she answered.

"It's time we started charging rent."

"Joe's bangin' her in the saddle room," Ben said.

"Kulikuli," she scolded.

My father finished the mango and put the rind down on the end table. "Know what your problem is, Mother?"

"No, Normy. Wot?"

"You let people take advantage."

*   *   *

Before the summer ended, Arlene took the pressure off Gramma by moving to Kualapu'u. Joe sent his meat truck to get her things. They lived in a cottage behind Kualapu'u Suprette. I remembered Joe hosing down the sidewalk and blood from the butchered meat running under the cottage.

"Why would Arlene live there?" I asked Gramma.

"She loves Joe."

"But why Joe?"

"Love is aiwaiwa."

"What's that?"

"Mysterious," she said, "damn mysterious."

Gramma received a call from Arlene saying she was very

happy and not to worry. Joe was planning a big wedding on Chinese New Year and we were all invited. Then Arlene got hapai and the wedding was off. Joe paid for her to fly to Honolulu to have an abortion. She never returned. There was a rumor she spent her nights walking Hotel Street but Gramma dismissed that as idle gossip. "Puhi'us up hea got nothin' bettah to do," she said. She was quick to defend Arlene whenever someone insulted her. I think Gramma considered her the daughter she'd never had.

*   *   *

Gramma received a letter from Arlene saying she'd met a wonderful man from the state of Washington and that they'd gotten married on the mainland. The city on the return address was Tacoma. There was a stamp with a salmon jumping out of water and it made me think their house was on a river and that they ate lots of fish. A wedding picture was enclosed. Arlene wore a blonde wig and a red dress with a plunging neckline. Her face was heavy with make-up. Her smile looked forced. The man had gray hair and wore a blue tux.

"I'm happy fo' Arlene," Gramma said.

"Her husband's as old as Moses," I replied.

"Maybe, but he's got kala."

"That's a wedding dress?" I asked.

She tucked the picture in its envelope and hid it in her bedroom. She never showed it to anyone, not even to my father.

*   *   *

Gramma's relationship with Joe didn't change much. She still drove up to Kualapu'u for meats. He still slipped fat in her orders and overcharged for donuts. Sometimes he asked if she'd heard from Arlene. Gramma always said Arlene was busy tending to her apple orchards in Washington. He gave us his predictions on shortages and advised stocking up on things like white sugar and toothpaste. Joe's face lost its youthful glow. He put on weight and moved slowly behind the counter, as though being the owner of Kualapu'u Suprette was his cross to bear. He no longer had a spring to his step and he frowned at simple chores like sweeping the steps and tearing off sheets of butcher paper. He stopped decorating the deer's head and quit tracking the elusive white buck. I knew he cared for Arlene not by what he said but the way he said it. His voice quivered whenever he said her name. He was a man being torn apart by guilt and loss.

Joe was dying inside, a little at a time.

Luau at the Moloka'i Shores

Merv Machado was a local boy with a good tan who liked flashing his capped teeth. He flirted shamelessly with women and girls and rarely appeared in public with his Hawaiian wife. Gramma smiled coyly whenever she ran into Merv. She told him he should be on *Hawaii 5-0*. I knew she had a crush when she said he was "the spittin' image of Engelbert." She loved the *Engelbert Humperdinck Show* and had told me Engelbert was sexier than Tom Jones. Merv bought twenty of her fan palms and she liked him even more.

Merv was the GM of the Moloka'i Shores. A year had passed since the official opening and the word was out the resort was a bust. He was having trouble selling the condos so he advertised the vacant ones as "Luxury Vacation Rentals." He sent postcards inviting everyone on the island to a Grand Opening Luau.

"I'm ono fo' kalua pig," Gramma said studying her postcard.

Moloka'i Shores was ten miles west of Hale Kia, across the street from an abandoned Union 76 station. The resort was built after two years of backbreaking ground work. The developers had chainsawed a ten-acre kiawe forest, burned the stumps, and flattened the earth with bulldozers. There were rumors the 'O'io Marchers walked the land on their way down to Ali'i Fishpond. Sarah told Gramma she wasn't going to the luau. She said sacred aina had been desecrated and that eating Merv's kaukau would bring bad luck.

*   *   *

On the day of the luau, Ben and I slicked down our hair with Brylcreem and put on Aloha shirts, slacks, and loafers. Gramma wore a purple dress with a slit skirt, heels, and a new bouffant wig. Kimmi had stopped by that morning to style the wig and the smell of hair spray permeated the beach house. Gramma applied rouge, mascara, and red lipstick. She asked Ben if she should get contacts and he said glasses made her look more sophisticated.

We rode in the cab with Gramma. She sang "She'll Be Coming 'Round the Mountain" and "Oh My Darlin' Clementine." Her voice cracked when she reached for the high notes. We saw Moki at Honomuni—he was picking limu out of a fishnet hanging off his clothesline. We waved at Johnny as he bicycled east balancing a fishing pole across the handle bars. Gramma got tired of singing after the Puko'o Fishpond so I belted out "The Marine's Hymn" and followed that up with "Caissons Go Rolling Along."

"Good boy," she said when I finished. She asked Ben to sing but he said singing was stupid. He told her she'd put on her wig backwards.

"You don't wanna look like a kua'aina," he told her.

She stopped beside Ah Pong's and spun the wig around. "How's Gramma look now?"

"Like a movie star," I said.

She raced through Kamalo. It was three when we reached the Union 76. The station's plastic sign had been shattered and it looked as though a big rock had hit it judging by the size of the splinters lying on the dirt. We pulled off the road and followed a caravan of cars and trucks into the resort. A wisp of white smoke from the imu curled into the sky.

"What if we see Billy Duva?" Ben asked.

"Wot if, wot if," Gramma said, "wot if the rabbit hadn't stopped?"

We parked in a red cinder lot next to Auntie Esther's Buick. Keikis with rubber slippers ran ahead of parents. Kupunas used canes. An old Hawaiian couple wore matching lauhala hats with akulikuli leis around their brims. A young mother rocked her crying baby. The only time I'd seen as many locals was when Lord "Tally Ho" Blears brought Honolulu All-Star Wrestling to Kaunakakai.

"Hot as blazes," Gramma said rolling up her window.

I got out after Ben and shut the door. The heels of my loafers crunched the cinders. The trades carried the aroma of kalua meat. The lot was full and drivers parked along Kam Highway. Ben and I walked on either side of Gramma. She had trouble negotiating the cinders in her heels but got used to them after holding my arm and taking a few baby steps.

A Portuguese woman wearing a black silk holoku and a

feather lei shuffled over the cinders. Her bowler hat sported a boar's tusk pin. "Oh, Auntie Brownie," she said, "you look so no ka oi!"

"Hello, Sophie," Gramma said. She introduced us as "Norman's boys." She'd told us that Sophie was a wealthy cattle rancher who'd married a school teacher half her age. Sophie said her husband was attending a seminar on Maui. She talked about taxes, the price of beef, and hoof-and-mouth disease. She spotted Joe and charged across the cinders to gab with him.

"What a blabber mouth," I said as we followed the crowd.

"Yo' fathah liked Sophie," Gramma said, "in the ol' days."

"Was there any girl he didn't like?" Ben asked.

"Kulikuli," she told him.

We made our way through the lot. I saw Chipper's Impala. Dr. Lucky's truck was there and so was Rocky's Falcon. The windshields had been repaired and the paint was new. I thought about Arlene and wondered if she was happy in Washington. The cinders ended and the centipede grass began. Fan palms were spaced ten feet apart along a cement path. We followed the path to a three-story building with a sloping plantation roof. The northern wall was made of stone and a white seahorse logo was attached to the stonework above the resort's name. Pink antheriums, gardenias, and yellow heliconia bloomed in a garden outside the lobby.

Everyone headed to a stage built fifty feet from the imu. Kaui, Sarah's grandson, hugged Gramma and dropped a white ginger lei around her neck. He wore a niho palaoa, an ivory hook suspended from a necklace of human hair. The niho palaoa warded off evil spirits. He thanked her for the Easter ham and said he had to go check on the imu.

"Let's find Chippah," Gramma told Ben and me.

A giant lauhala mat was spread out in front of the stage. Picnic tables were set up on either side of the mat and most were already taken. Three Hawaiian men onstage tuned their slack key guitars and ukuleles. They wore white shirts and pants with red sashes around their waists. The men joked with family and friends in the crowd. A "Halawa Valley Boyz" banner billowed above the stage.

Auntie Esther and two Asian transsexuals huddled beside a tiki torch. Esther wore red hot pants, a halter top, and red stilettos. She'd broken up with the Chief of Police after catching him with a woman. She tried seducing Dr. Lucky when he checked up on her cat, but he'd already proposed to Keiko, the Japanese girl who baked coconut rolls at Kanemitsu's Bakery.

"Theah's Chip," Gramma said pointing to the mauka side of the stage.

Chipper was smoking at a table beside a coconut sapling. He wore sunglasses and a tan leisure suit. The crown of his head gleamed in the sunlight. He spotted us and waved us over. I pulled out a chair and Gramma sat beside him. She took off her glasses, tucked them in their case, and slipped the case in her purse. He told us he was the first to arrive and that he took a tour of the condos with some investors from Honolulu. Gramma said she couldn't understand how people could live "packed togethah like rats."

Ben nudged me with his elbow. "Let's ditch these fuddy duddys," he whispered.

"We're going cruising," I told Gramma.

"Cruisin'?" she asked. "Wot the hell's that?"

"Nothing," I answered.

Gramma squinted at us. "No mischief."

Ben and I hustled to a shore lined with tiki torches. Benches perched on the grass overlooked the channel. We reached a mud beach loaded with green limu and clumps of pickleweed. Tiny waves rolled in. The muddy water extended to the reef and the long gradual slope of Lanai was on the southern horizon. Ali'i Fishpond was to the east. A man threw net next to the fishpond wall. The water was to his knees.

"Shallow," I said.

"Yeah," said Ben, "and mud instead of sand."

I knew he was thinking we were lucky to have Hale Kia. Our beach wasn't wide but the sand was golden and we had it to ourselves. Gramma had told us one day the ranch would belong to us.

"Guess who's here," he said.

"Who?"

"Ruth."

"Big Ruth?"

"She's not really big," he said, "she's just tall."

The stench of rotting limu drifted in with the trades.

"Pee-U," I said.

He wrinkled his nose. "We'd better get back."

We returned to the table just as Merv Machado took the stage wearing a gold Members Only jacket, white pants, and black Beatle boots. A girl kissed him on the cheek and draped an orchid lei around his neck. She did the same for the musicians. Merv snagged the microphone. "A-lo-ha!" he said and congratulated Dr. Lucky and Keiko on their engagement. He introduced the band members: Ford, Alvin, Kalena, and a boy named Israel who played soprano ukulele. He told us dinner would be served in an hour and said, "Let's pahty!" Everyone cheered. He pulled a small flute from his jacket pocket, put the flute to his nose, and played "Pearly Shells" through his left nostril.

"Wot next," Gramma said.

Merv finished and everyone clapped. He turned the stage over to the Halawa Valley Boyz and they played the lively "Ka'a Ahi Kahului." Dr. Lucky and Keiko did a rumba on the lauhala mat. Mr. Mendoza escorted his wife up and Jesse Duva two-stepped with Becky Lima. Esther asked a blond man to dance. Big Ruth was alone at a table on the makai side of the stage. She wore a muumuu of gold satin and had a yellow hibiscus behind her ear. She still wore her choker. The song ended and Alvin said they were going to sing a medley starting with "I Kona." Ben stared at Big Ruth.

"No sked 'um," I said.

He got up, crossed to the other side, and talked to Big Ruth just as a slack key guitar played the first notes. She smiled and got up. They danced the Hitchhike beside our table.

Gramma chuckled watching them dance.

"Ben's good," I told her, "don't you think?"

She nodded. "Just goin' it."

Chipper pulled a hip flask from his jacket pocket and took a swig.

"May I have this dance, Gramma?" I asked.

"I'm too ol' to be dancin'," she replied.

A brunette wearing a tie-dye blouse, white shorts, and pink sandals danced with her back to me. Her okole moved in sensual circles and a plumeria lei bounced off her shoulders. She did a spin—it was Lucy Seville from Punahou. Her partner was the older Ciacci boy. Lucy had wanted to go steady with me in seventh grade but I turned her down. I spotted Dr. Seville dancing with a blonde lady I knew was Lucy's mom. Dr. Seville had been my principal in junior high—he reminded me of LBJ. The song ended and the Ciacci boy escorted Lucy to the beverage table.

I hustled over and dipped a paper cup into a bowl of red punch. "Hi, Lucy," I said holding out the cup.

She took the cup and said, "Sir Jeff!" She had piercing blue eyes and her hair was full of chunky blonde streaks from the sun. "Whacha doing here?"

"I spend summers with my grandmother."

She sipped the punch. "West end?"

"East."

"I saw Ben dancing," she said flipping her hair over her shoulder. "Do you know Albert?"

"Sure," I replied, "we chased the same pig."

"I nevah wen catch," Albert said. His breath smelled like opihi.

"I didn't catch the pig either," I admitted.

"Anyway," Lucy said, "My Dad's thinking of buying a condo."

"He should," I replied.

"How come?"

"You could visit me on Moloka'i."

"He wants to rent it out."

"Laydahs, Lucy," said Albert.

"Can we dance again?" she asked.

"Shoots," he answered and took off.

"Albert's in charge of the imu," Lucy said. She wore frosted pink lipstick, eyeliner, and turquoise eye shadow. Her breasts pushed out her blouse and her tan legs were long and muscular. She'd filled out since junior high. She finished her punch. "Is your grandmother here?" she asked me.

"She's at that table by the coconut tree."

Lucy glanced over. "Wow, she's mod!"

"Can you do me a big favor?"

"What favor have you ever done for me, Jeffrey Gill?"

"I won you that bunny at the carnival."

"That was light years ago," she said fingering her lei. "What's this big favor?"

"Ask that man with Gramma to dance."

"Is he your grandpa?"

"He's her ex. We call him 'Uncle Chipper.' "

"Uncle Chipster's too busy smoking to dance."

"You ask him and I'll ask her. I'll cut in on you and he'll be with Gramma."

She crushed her cup and shot it like a basketball at a garbage can—it bounced off the rim and dropped in. "He can ask her himself."

"He's too shy," I replied.

"He doesn't look shy."

The Halawa Valley Boyz finished singing "Hi'ilawe." Alvin asked for requests.

"Moloka'i Nui Ahina!" Mendoza called.

"Chee," said Alvin, "dat's da kine." He strummed his ukulele and sang the opening lines. Marv, Kalena, and Israel joined in. Their voices formed a lively harmony and couples crowded the mat. Lucy approached Chipper and whispered in his ear. He shook his head and puffed his cigarette. She snatched the cigarette, threw it on the ground, and stomped it out. She grabbed his hand and pulled him out of his chair. He put his hand on her shoulder and started an awkward fox trot. I extended my hand to Gramma and this time she took it. I danced her over to Chipper. Lucy got tired of the fox trot and showed Chipper how to do the Watusi. I danced closer to Lucy and winked at her. She winked back. I left Gramma, put my hands on Lucy's waist, and we did the cha'-cha'-cha'. Chipper and Gramma just stood there. Finally he wrapped an arm around her and they started to waltz. I saw Ben rocking out with Big Ruth, Esther doing the Frug with Kaui, and Jesse spinning Becky. Lucy held my hands tight and whipped her hair up and down. The song ended and the Halawa Valley Boyz put down their ukes and guitars.

"Hana hou!" Kaui said.

"Auwe," said Gramma, "good fun."

I introduced Gramma to Lucy. She said Lucy reminded her of a girl on *One Life to Live*. Dr. Seville moseyed over with his wife. Seville talked to Chipper about investments while Mrs. Seville chatted with Gramma.

Alvin took the mike. "We go eat!" he said.

"Peanut," Gramma said, "bring me and Chip plates heavy on kalua pig."

"Any lomilomi salmon or squid luau?" I asked.

"And laulaus?" Lucy suggested.

"That'd be nice."

Lucy and I headed for the imu. Albert and his younger brother shoveled away the dirt mounded on top. Steam rose up through a blanket of burlap bags. Kaui and Joe removed the bags and beneath that were layers of taro and banana leaves. Merv pulled the leaves off to reveal ten golden turkeys surrounded by sweet potatoes, yams, and breadfruit.

"No mo' oink, oink?" Mendoza joked.

"Gobble, gobble mo' bettah," said Becky.

Everyone laughed. Merv and Kaui carved the turkeys on a koa cutting boards. Women arranged foil pans on picnic tables covered with ti leaves and pala'a ferns. I saw laulaus, poi, weke, ahi, chicken long rice, steamed crabs, inamona, limu, and squid luau. Becky chopped a raw salmon filet and mixed it with rock salt, diced onions, and tomatoes.

"Hungry?" I asked Lucy.

"Famished," she replied.

"Gramma and Chipper first," I said.

We found paper plates and plastic forks and got in line. Ben was talking to Big Ruth beside a pair of unlit torches. Lucy and I piled the plates high and I snatched two 7-Ups. We delivered everything to Gramma and Chipper. Gramma didn't mind it was turkey instead of pig.

We returned to get our dinners. The turkey was shredded and I piled it on the main course section of my plate. I filled up the other sections with chicken long rice, opihi, and squid luau. The poi was fresh so I scooped some on my plate. I picked up a shred of turkey and put it in my mouth—it was moist and tasted smoky. Lucy selected a laulau, lomilomi salmon, and poke. We sat beside a bougainvillea trellis and ate. Families hunkered down on quilts and blankets. Keikis played tag around a tree fern. "Hele mai 'ai!" a mother called.

I speared an opihi and studied it on the end of my plastic fork—it had a black rubbery body and a yellow sucker that it used to hold on to stones along the shore. I put it in my mouth and it tasted like a clam. "How's the poke?" I asked Lucy.

"Good. Wanna try some?"

"Sure."

"Open wide," she said and put a piece in my mouth.

It was salty and tender. "Ono," I said.

"How'd you get the nickname 'Peanut?' "

"It's a long story."

We finished and it was time for sweets. We found the dessert table and gorged ourselves on guava cake, kulolo, caramelized pineapple-on-a-stick, and slabs of haupia. We headed to the stage just as Merv ignited the tiki torches. The Halawa Valley Boyz played an instrumental called "Ku'u Ipo Onaona." Dr. Lucky slow danced with Keiko. Albert went up with Big Ruth—he put his hands on her waist and she rested her chin on his shoulder.

"Let's go for a walk," Lucy suggested.

We strolled to the beach. It wasn't dark but the tiki torches were lit. A fishing boat moved through the channel with its cabin light on. Lights flickered on the coast of Lanai. There was supposed to be a moon but it hadn't risen. We sat on a bench overlooking the water.

"We'll be graduating before we know it," Lucy told me.

"We're only sophomores," I said.

"I know. But Dad says growing up means saying goodbye to all your high school friends."

"Why would you wanna say goodbye to people you're close to?"

"Are we close, Jeff?"

"I always thought we were."

She crossed her legs. "Ever wonder where you'll be after Punahou?"

"College."

"Think we'll stay in touch?"

I scooched beside her. "Sure."

She stared straight ahead at the channel.

"Something wrong?" I asked.

She turned to me. "What could possibly be wrong, Jeff?"

I tried kissing her but she turned away and my lips grazed her cheek.

"Don't," she said.

"Why not?"

"Remember the carnival?"

"That was light years ago. You said so yourself."

Lucy looked me straight in the eyes. "It's not the same anymore," she said, "at least not for me."

"Let's pretend we've just met."

She got up and wandered to the edge of the grass. I joined her and we watched the waves lap at the shoreline. I draped an arm over her shoulder but she just stood there as if I were a ghost. She seemed as far away as Lanai.

"I'm going steady," she said.

I took my arm off her shoulder. "With who?"

"Arnold Lepine. He's a senior this year."

"He's too old for you."

Lucy sighed. She picked up a strand of pickleweed and examined it.

I heard footsteps. I turned and saw Ben standing beside a tiki torch.

"Time to hele, Peanut," he said.

"Gramma wants to go?"

"She's waiting in the Scout."

*   *   *

The moon balanced on the rim of Haleakala on our drive home. Yellow clouds hovered over the kiawe trees to the south. I thought about the old days on Moloka'i when the road was dirt and my grandmother and Chipper used to ride it on horseback. Sometimes they had only the stars and the moon to guide them. We turned north toward the Seven Sisters Mountains. The mountains were blue with black gulches. We made a sharp right and our headlights lit up the white walls of Saint Joseph's Church. I felt cramped in the cab because I had to spread my legs around the transmission box to fit in.

"How come we had to leave so early?" I groused.

"It was past Peanut's bedtime," Ben said.

"I got sick of Chip," Gramma admitted. She said he polished off his hip flask of okolehao and started in on lilikoi punch laced with vodka. He went down Memory Lane and some of the memories weren't too pleasant.

I thought about Lucy. We'd hugged goodbye and I held

her and there was a moment where anything was possible. But the moment passed. I trudged past the stage on the way to the parking lot as Alvin crooned "I'll Remember You." Hearing that song made me feel like the only boy in the world without a girl. Lucy felt right on Moloka'i but I'd hurt her at Punahou and she'd moved on.

We braked for a long slow curve through the papaya plantation at Mapulehu. Halfway through the curve, our headlights died. "Fo' chrissakes," Gramma said easing to the side of the road. She popped open the glove box, snatched a flashlight, and shined the light in our faces. "You keeds sneak any kaukau from the luau?"

I shielded my eyes. "No."

"Turkey," Ben said.

"Give it hea."

"What for?"

"Akua want it."

"I thought ghosts only ate pork?"

"If it was cooked in the imu," she said, "they want it."

He reached under the seat, pulled out a paper plate, and handed it to Gramma. She yanked off the plastic wrap and grabbed the hunk of turkey. She headed to the mauka side of the road and disappeared behind a kamani tree. The aroma of papaya blossoms drifted up from the plantation.

Ben yawned and stretched. "Guess where she's going."

"To the heiau," I said, "to put turkey on the sacred stone."

"This ghost stuff is royal bullshit."

"You're not supposed to steal from a luau."

"Big deal."

"It is a big deal if a ghost stops us."

"You're pupule if you believe that."

"Guess I'm pupule."

He shifted in his seat. "By the way," he said, "what happened with Lucy?"

"She's going steady with Arnold Lepine."

"That punk's a mahu."

"You get to first base with Big Ruth?"

Ben swung open the passenger door. He climbed out, unzipped his fly, and peed in the roadside brush. "Ruth's got the hots for Albert."

"Dat buggah get hauna breath," I said.

"Yeah, and Lane, his kid brother, beat him to the pig."

"Lane's such a lame name."

He zipped up. "Too bad you didn't score Lucy," he said. "Lucy the Narc."

"Lucy's no narc."

"She's the principal's daughter, isn't she?"

"That was junior high."

He sat in the cab and kept the door open. "It's in that girl's blood. She would have squealed if Tenant hadn't ratted us out first."

"Lucy's not like that."

"Sure she is."

"You're just peeved Big Ruth dumped you for Hauna Breath."

"I'll bet Lane's making out with Lucy this very second."

"Not in a jillion years."

"Funny, she was kissing him at the luau."

"Liar."

"Let me get my crystal ball," Ben said plucking an imaginary one from thin air and waving his hands over it. "Why, will you look at that," he said, "Lane an' Lucy go make poke squid on da beach."

"Jerk," I said.

He laughed. "No wahine in her right mind would want you."

"Look who's talking, Romeo."

He shoved his middle finger in my face. "Put dees wheah da sun no shine."

I made a fist with my left hand and hit him in the cheek. He punched me in the eye and I threw another left that struck his forehead. He shoved me into the corner of the cab and put all his weight on me. I couldn't move. I squirmed and pulled the lever on the driver's door—we tumbled out and my head hit asphalt. He stayed on top of me and pinned my shoulders and arms against the road with his knees. I jerked my hips trying to buck him off.

"Quit fighting," he said, "you sonuvabitch!"

"Fuck you!"

He squeezed my throat with both hands. I freed my left hand and hooked him hard to the belly. He gasped and rolled off just as lights cut through the papaya plantation. A car was coming. Heels clicked over the road and Gramma blinded me with her flashlight.

"Wot you damn keeds doin'?" she asked.

Ben popped up. "Nothing."

"Nothin', mah foot. Now flag this drivah down."

I got to my knees and stood. Something barreled around the curve and lit up the road. The lights were low on its frame and spaced far apart. Its paint shimmered in the moonlight and a chill went through my body thinking it was Rocky's Falcon. I heard a familiar rumble. "Chipper," I waved, "it's Uncle Chipper!"

"I'll be a monkey's uncle," Gramma said.

The Impala pulled over and idled. Chipper rolled down the driver's side window. "Miss me?" he asked.

"Like the bloody plague," she answered.

"Wot's the pilikia?"

"Blew mah fuse."

Chipper smelled like booze. "Ride mah tail home, Brownie," he said, "follow me close."

"You okay, Uncle Chipper?" I asked.

"No ka oi."

We got in the Scout and Gramma fired it up. She hugged the Impala's bumper and kept her emergency lights flashing. She followed him on straightaways, around curves, and through dips. She banged my knee shifting from second to third.

I didn't say a word on the ride. Neither did Ben. I was sure Gramma knew something was wrong but she was concentrating on getting us home. My eye was swelling and I had trouble swallowing. I hated my brother. His desperation to find someone to love had turned him mean.

I wished he'd never been born.

The Mountain House

A month after her divorce, my grandmother had a dream she owned a house in the clouds. She liked the idea and had Thomas Duva bulldoze a two-mile trail up her mountain. Then she hired Moon Matayoshi to build her a home. Chipper told her she was a fool. She chained together redwood beams and tied the chains to her jeep's rear bumper. Chipper and Moki drank okolehao and watched the jeep drag its tail of lumber up the first hill.

The mountain house began as a cabin with a tiny kitchen, a shelter for hunters to escape the rain and brew a cup of coffee. But strange things started happening. Hunters said cups swung on their hanging nails and chairs were found turned upside down. Chipper drove up and saw burners on the stove flare to life by themselves and a pair of antlers fly across the room. Gramma disregarded his story since he spiked his coffee with Wild Turkey. She called in Sarah after dreaming she stood in the path of the Night Marchers. Sarah drove up with her and they walked the cabin's perimeter.

Sarah sniffed a gardenia blossom and frowned. " 'Oi'o ovah hea," she said. "Sacred trail."

Gramma lit a cigarette. "Wot you want me to do?"

"Lawe aku, da soona da bettah."

Moon dismantled the cabin. Sarah found a safe spot nearby and Moon started in on a second cabin. Gramma surrounded it with red ti plants because Sarah said ghosts would not cross the sacred boundary of the ti. Moon built an outhouse on the old site. I always heard voices in the darkness below the toilet seat and the toilet paper spun off the roll by itself.

"Gramma," I said, "your outhouse is haunted!"

"Good haunted," she replied, "make you dump fasta."

*   *   *

We visited the mountain house every summer. Ben was sixteen the first time he took along his rifle. On the drive up, Ben rode in the cab with Gramma and I rode in back. My job was to prevent our supply boxes and water jug from sliding over the bed and slamming into the tailgate. I gazed down at the shrinking flatlands and saw our mares in the pasture and the Norfolk. I watched for the 'uhane, spirits who took either human or animal form by day. They lost the power to shapeshift when the sun went down. The 'uhane were trapped between past and present and had committed grievous crimes in the world of the living. They'd kill if you surprised them. Gramma said the best thing to do if you saw one was to pretend you didn't and go about your business. She said the 'uhane lived in the lantana below the second gate and sucked sap from the kiawe trees. Ben and I had once explored the land between gates. I discovered bite marks on a branch but he said the marks were probably from goats. Locals swore by the 'uhane after three hunters were found gut-shot on a ridge in Puko'o. I thought that if Wilkins returned, we should send him on a hunting expedition. He was still calling and wanted to visit again. Gramma said she was thinking of taking "a li'l trip to Sausalito." I knew she'd be vulnerable if she went alone so I told her I'd carry her bags and tip cab drivers and porters if she ever wanted to go to California. She said that would be nice and promised to pay my passage.

We reached the beginning of the rain forest and the mountain house loomed before us. It seemed like a fort with its steel roof, boxy design, and lack of glass windows. Its exterior walls were covered with green shingles. It was built on stilts like the beach house. Wooden storm windows protected its face and a stairway led to the main floor. The grass had been cut and shaped into a ragged lawn and a circle of stones enclosed a garden of orchids, hibiscus, and red ti. It smelled like it had rained but the sky was clear. Gardenias bloomed in a grove fifty feet makai of the house. This was the grove where Gramma had killed Charlie—she aimed for his shoulder and shot him through the neck.

We parked beside a kauri pine. My grandmother shifted the wide brim of her lauhala hat, pushed her bifocals over the bridge of her nose, and gazed up at the mountain house as if reuniting with an old friend. Towering Cook pines rose up behind the house and Norfolks flanked either side. Mist drifted through the hills to the north.

Gramma reached behind the bench seat. She pulled out a rifle wrapped in a pair of denims and secured with laundry cord. The munitions companies had stopped making the .219 caliber she needed so she only had a handful of bullets left.

Ben got out of the cab and stretched. He wore jeans and a camouflage shirt.

"Befoa you keeds go runnin' off," Gramma said, "pack everythin' up."

She carried her rifle up the stairs. A wooden water tank was perched on its own set of stilts beside the house. A hole in the tank dripped water to a garden of red torch ginger, wild orchids, and ferns. Aluminum gutters were positioned to funnel rain from the roof into the tank. The tank water was a breeding ground for mosquitoes but the filter kept the larvae from reaching the spigot. I'd told Gramma I was worried about drinking mosquito eggs and she filled a glass with water and held it up to the window. "Christ," she'd said, "you can hardly see 'um."

She jammed her shoulder against the front door and it sprung open. She picked up her rifle and disappeared inside.

Ben opened the tailgate. "Slide those boxes over," he told me.

"Aye, aye, Captain Ben." I slid two boxes over the metal bed. They contained a loaf of Holsum bread, cans of tomato soup, powdered cocoa, pilot crackers, rice, butter, eggs, a duck wrapped in pink butcher paper, and a carton of Chesterfields. He took the heavy box and I took the light one. We walked up the steps into the kitchen and placed the boxes on the counter top. The only light came from a tiny window above the sink.

Ben opened the kerosene fridge and touched the top rack. "Not cold yet," he said.

"Give it time," Gramma replied. She turned on the water

valve in the sink and a brown stream shot from the spigot.

"Mosquito water," he said.

"Wheah's mah wattah jug?" she asked.

"In the Scout," I answered.

"Go get it."

I returned for the jug. A pool of water was in the bed and I knew we'd lost some drinking water. Gramma had misaligned the metal cap with the grooves on the jug. Her hands were weak but she insisted on doing all the packing. The mountain house had been her sanctuary—preparing for a stay was a ritual. It was here she'd mixed her oils in glass jars, prepared her brushes, and completed her first paintings. Ben and I had crawled under the house the previous summer and found redwood planks, a brass spittoon, and dusty magazines. There'd been the smell of dead air and things decaying. He rooted through the magazines until he found Brigitte Bardot on the cover of *Life*. "Watch out for centipedes," he'd warned as he brushed a web off Bardot's face and crawled into the sun. Canvases had been stacked next to the lawn mower and I shuffled through paintings of trees with gnarled trunks, a house with walls that seemed to undulate, and a white horse standing in a pasture with high fences.

I grabbed the jug by its handle and swung it out of the Scout. The dogs scampered through the high grass and ferns.

Ben climbed up on a stilt and looked in the water tank. "Gross," he said and jumped off. He tried sliding down the handrail at the top of the stairs but it wasn't slippery enough. He inched his way down by pushing his combat boots against the stairs.

"Watch it, Juicy," I called, "you'll catch a splinter!"

He reached bottom and ran to the Scout. He slid the bench seat forward, grabbed his black gun case, and pulled out his rifle. The gun had a white star on its chestnut stock. He checked the chamber for a bullet and walked to the kauri pine. He turned a branch toward me—it was rubbed raw. "A buck was here this morning," he said. He walked behind the water tank and headed for the outhouse. Its tiny steel roof glinted in a nest of ferns.

I carried the jug up the steps into the kitchen. Gramma was kneeling on the linoleum pouring kerosene from a can into an aluminum funnel. The funnel was sticking in a tank at the bottom of her stove. The smell of kerosene made me hungry. Orange cast-iron pots and skillets hung off hooks attached to a beam. A shelf under the counter was crammed with supplies from previous visits: Worcestershire sauce, a bottle of sliced pickles, a pack of Mandarin orange peel, cooking sherry, curry powder, and cans of tuna and water chestnuts.

"Ready to light the pilot," she said.

I walked into the back room. Lauhala mats covered the floor and deer hides were nailed to the walls. Balls of steel wool had been stuffed into the channels between the corrugated roof and the end beams to discourage rats but rat droppings had fallen on the chairs, the mats, and the canvas cots. A gecko ran the length of the wall. The green coils of mosquito punks were perched on fruit plates in the corners.

When I was five, Chipper had gone with us to the mountain house. He'd finished a quart of okolehao by dusk and, after dinner, started in on the cooking sherry. I was sleeping on a canvas cot with Gramma when he stumbled over holding a kerosene lantern. His face was a mask of orange light and shadow. "Brownie," he said, "get in mah cot."

She held me close. "Go away, Chip," she said.

He yanked her arm.

"Stop, Uncle Chipper!" I cried.

He left and rummaged through the bottles in the kitchen. She got off the cot, took his hands off the bottles, and put them on her shoulders. She hugged him and rocked him back and forth saying, "Chip, oh, Chip," in the kerosene light.

A window in the back room had a view of the opposite ridge and a meadow. A white ribbon of water fell from the edge of the meadow to the gulch below. I remembered Chipper sitting here with my brother on his lap talking story about hunting grizzlies in Alaska.

Ben hustled in with his gun case and I followed him to the front room. Termite sand peppered the varnished floorboards. He checked out the heads mounted on the wall. There were three bucks and a goat. The eyes were amber-colored marbles that Narakiro had glued in after dipping the heads in embalming fluid. The biggest buck had been shot by Beebe, my father's partner at the firm. Gramma said the goat looked Chinese so she called it her "Pake Goat."

I noticed all the noses had holes. "Do rats eat the noses?" I asked.

"Rats eat everything except rubber," Ben replied. "When I shoot my buck, I'll have 'em put on a rubber nose. The best taxidermist lives on Maui."

"What about Narakiro?"

"He's a puhi'u."

Gramma swept droppings off the lauhala mat in the back room. "You keeds open two windows," she called, "get some light in hea."

Ben shook his head. "I'm opening them all."

"Fo' wot?"

"So I can take a panoramic shot."

She stopped sweeping and frowned. "When I say 'two,' I mean 'two.' "

"Bitch," he muttered.

Ben swung open a storm window and I opened a second. Below us, the dogs charged through the garden. We suspended the windows on hooks attached to the beams. He opened a third window. The light made the amber eyes in the heads glow.

I looked down the mountain and over the channel—a tug towed three barges west. The barges were spread out and it appeared they were powering themselves. But I knew chains and heavy rope connected the barges to one another and to the tug. Maui's Nakalele Point jutted out into the indigo water. The Maui coast was brown but that gave way to green hills of sugar and pine. The peak of Haleakala was hidden by clouds. Sometimes clouds drifted in through the open windows and, when we were little, we'd pretend to be angels and run the length of the room flapping our wings.

Ben flipped open his gun case and pulled out his rifle. He aimed it at the biggest buck head. "I'm shooting one bigger than Charlie."

"A .22 can't kill a buck," I said.

He lowered his gun. "Gramma has a .219 and look what

she did."

"Her bullets have more powder."

He pulled a cane chair to the middle window and sat. "I'll hit one in the eye."

"That's a tough shot."

"Whose side are you on anyway?"

"Yours."

"You'd better be." He rested the rifle on the sill of the middle window, held the butt of the gun against his shoulder, and sighted down the barrel. He put his combat boots on the wall to steady himself. "Won't be long now," he said.

Gramma entered the room. "Long fo' wot?"

"My first trophy."

"You couldn't hit a hapai horse's okole."

Ben whistled as he held his rifle.

"Cut that whistlin'," she said.

"What's wrong with whistling?" I asked.

"He's callin' the devil."

"I am the devil," he said.

She sat on a pune'e wedged against the wall and lit a Chesterfield. "Holdin' that gun like a li'l girl."

"Nice," Ben said.

"Buy you a pink dress fo' Christmas."

"Don't forget a pink bow for my hair."

She blew a puff of smoke. "Wot in hell you aimin' at?"

"Trees."

"Ridiculous. Yo' fathah thinks yo' a damn sissy."

"Why would you suddenly care what he thinks?"

"Why wouldn't I care?"

"You didn't care enough to raise him. Didn't your mother raise all your bastards?"

Gramma glared at Ben.

"Maybe it's time for a snack," I suggested.

"I'm callin' yo' fathah the second we get down," she said.

"Good," he shot back. "I'll tell him how you got drunk with Wilkins."

"Take yo' filthy boots off mah wall."

He took his boots off. "Like it or not," he said, "I'm going to shoot a buck."

"You couldn't hit a damn thing, not on yo' life."

"I shot that poacher."

"You scratched his ear."

"I shoulda killed him."

"You'll be in jail soon enough," she said and flicked her ashes into an abalone shell on the night stand.

"Ben's a good shot," I told Gramma.

"Christ," she said, "yo' bruthah couldn't even hit that can on the beach."

He took his gun off the sill, spun it around, and aimed it at her. "I could hit you," he said, "then I could mount your head."

"Cool it," I told him.

"Take a hike, Jeff. This is between me and her."

She balanced her cigarette on the lip of the shell. A line of smoke stretched from the pune'e to the corrugated roof. "Go ahead," she said, "pull the triggah."

He worked the bolt action.

"Miles from a docta," she said, "you can bleed to death up hea."

He stared down the length of the barrel. "Don't worry,"
he replied, "I'll make it quick."

Gramma picked up a stiff pair of denims tied with
laundry cord.

"Drop it!" he said.

She untied the cord, pulled off the pants, and brought
up her rifle. She cranked the bolt action and aimed at Ben. Her
gun had a light brown stock and a long black barrel shiny from
oilings. "Don't miss yo' first," she told Ben. Her aiming eye
looked huge through the lens of her bifocal.

"Put it down, Ben," I said.

"No way."

I walked to the pune'e. "Gramma, please?"

"This bullet's got Mistah Ben's name on it," she said,
"unless he drops his gun first."

"You'll shoot me," he said, "and then Jeff."

"Why would she kill me?" I asked.

"No witnesses. She'll say we shot each other."

"Silly business," she said.

That's how it went in the mountain house, a Mexican
standoff between my grandmother and brother. Ben had me
convinced Gramma would shoot me after she shot him. I was
prepared to run out the door and down the mountain. I imagined
running across the ragged lawn and zigzagging through the
gardenias so she couldn't shoot me through the neck the way
she'd shot Charlie. I saw my blood spatter the white blossoms
and the dogs standing over my body. Fifteen minutes went by
and the standoff continued. An hour passed and they were in
the same position. I squatted below the Pake Goat. A cricket

chirped in the back room.

Gramma lowered her rifle and rested it on her lap. "Peanut," she said, "light the punks."

"This early?" I asked.

"Damn mosquito's flyin' around."

Ben steadied his gun. "What a dumb thing to worry about," he said.

She put her gun on the pune'e. "Shoot if you want," she said, "but I'm makin' tomato soup."

He lowered his rifle. "With pilot crackers?"

She nodded and slapped at a mosquito. "And I'll light the pilot and cook that duck. Duck's ono way up hea." She got up and left.

He looked up at the heads on the wall.

I walked over. "You weren't really going to shoot, were you?"

He brought up his barrel and aimed it out the window. He pressed the butt against his shoulder. There was something sad in his face.

"Were you, Ben?"

"I don't know," he said. "I really don't know."

Three Bottles of Wine

Ben rode in the bed of the Scout on our way home. It was late morning and I kept Gramma company in the cab. She'd picked a bouquet of gardenias before we left and wrapped them in a red cowboy handkerchief. The bouquet rested between us and the aroma of fresh gardenias flooded the cab. The Scout jerked over the ruts in the road. We'd gotten a late start. The dogs had chased after a doe and it took Ben and me an hour of searching before we found them panting beside a stream. Now the dogs trotted alongside the Scout as we entered a grove of mountain apple trees.

Ben had avoided talking about the Mexican standoff. So did Gramma. I was sure she wouldn't tell my father because Ben would blab about Wilkins. I knew they both wished the standoff had never happened. They'd been cordial during scrambled eggs and cocoa but I was sure their relationship was damaged.

"Can you see our Norfolk?" Gramma asked as she drove.

I looked down the mountain. "Not yet."

"Yo' bruthah's gotta hot head," she muttered and said she'd never trust him again. She told me I reminded her of my father and that I was capable of great things if I learned to buckle down. I told her Ben was capable of great things too. She said he had too much of his mother in him to go very far in life. I could feel the judge and jury in my grandmother and I resented her for exiling Ben from her heart.

We stopped at the third gate. I pulled the wire loop of keys off the shifter and climbed out. I opened the lock, dropped the chain, and swung the gate open.

"Peanut's the gate keeper," Ben teased from the bed as the Scout passed.

I closed the gate, locked it, and climbed up on a boulder. A cold wind blew off the channel. I looked south—the land opened up and I spotted the Norfolk. It seemed as if a black tarp had been draped over the land. "Ben," I called, "the pasture looks funny."

He studied the flatlands. He leaned over and stuck his head in the cab. "There's been a fire!"

Gramma let the Scout idle. "You keeds go on ahead."

I handed her the loop of keys. "Don't you need me to open the gates?"

"I'll open mah own damn gates. Now get goin'."

Ben led the way in his combat boots and we raced down the mountain with the dogs. My Keds were easy to run in and I built up so much momentum that it felt like I was flying. I caught my brother and we were neck and neck. I knew if I tripped on a rock or a root I'd get hurt so I ran in the tracks the Scout had made on the way up. We reached the second gate and I slowed down enough to spot the mares on the green side of the pasture.

"Hurry!" he said.

We reached the first gate and Kam Highway. The dogs beat us to the pasture. We crossed the highway, slipped through the fence, and trudged over ashes and clumps of burnt grass. I shielded my eyes from a swirl of soot. The fire had died twenty feet from the mango tree and the mares were safe on the west side of the pasture.

"Let's go see Chipper," Ben said.

"Think he started it?" I asked.

"Either him or the Duvas."

The lemon and papaya trees were stumps and one still smoldered. We reached the dirt road and jogged toward the shack. The burn extended from the pasture to the dump. We arrived at Chipper's porch—his Tobbies were outside the door. A black swamp crab scuttled across the cement.

Ben banged on the door frame. "Hui," he called, "Uncle Chipper!"

"Comin'," Chipper said.

Through the screen I saw the rope hanging down from the ceiling. Sheets and a plastic pad were balled up on the mattress. The nightstand was crammed with pill bottles, cough syrups, Bandaid boxes, a pair of binoculars, and cans of insecticide. The air smelled bad. Newspapers and magazines were scattered everywhere. A trail of red ants from the dump had found safe passage under the door. Chipper hobbled out to the porch wearing an undershirt, gray shorts, and navy socks. His arms and legs were bandaged.

"You all right, Uncle Chipper?" I asked.

He plucked his binoculars off the nightstand. "Gotta few burns."

Ben frowned. "How'd the fire start?"

"Tell you when Brownie gets hea." He walked to the lawn and raised his binoculars. "Gonna catch hell," he mumbled.

I saw the Scout easing down the final hill. We talked about hunting and fishing until Gramma reached the road to the shack.

The Scout pulled up and she climbed out. "Chip," she said, "who started it?"

He said the fire sparked the day we'd left for the mountain house. Moki had dropped a cigarette near the dump and, in ten minutes, the flames spread west to the pasture and north to the saddle room. Lemons and papayas sizzled on the trees. The mares galloped in circles looking for a way out. Sandy tried jumping the fence line so Moki roped her and tied her to the mango tree. He put the rest of the horses in the corral. Chipper called the fire department while Moki soaked horse blankets and thumped the flames. Chipper turned on the faucet for the trough and flooded the western side of the pasture. The firetruck arrived and Chief Lima discovered there were no hydrants and that he'd forgotten to fill the firetruck tank. Chipper told him to fill it with swamp water but Lima said brackish water would destroy the tank. The fire was within twenty yards of the saddle room so Chipper and Moki used the horse blankets. The firemen broke branches off the ironwoods and beat at the fire. Even the Duva boys helped. When it was over, five acres of pastureland were torched. Chipper had third degree burns on his arms and legs. Chief Lima drove him to Moloka'i Hospital in the firetruck. I thought it was heroic for an old man to sacrifice his body to save the horses and the saddle room. Gramma just stood there after his story but I knew she recognized the qualities in Chipper that first drew her to him.

"Christ, Chip," Gramma said, "what in blazes were you wearin' fightin' that fiah?"

"An ol' swim suit," he confessed, "and Tobbies."

"Fo' the luva Pete."

I thought about the loss Chipper must have felt when his first house burned. This fire made me feel as though I'd lost something too. The ranch felt different, this landscape of ashes, stumps, and charred fence posts. It wasn't just the burning of the trees and the grass and the posts that bothered me. It was the way I perceived things to be at Hale Kia—green and ordered and impervious to destruction. But here was proof things could be destroyed in my grandmother's world. Some day, like the trees and grasslands that had perished, she would be gone too.

*   *   *

The next morning, Gramma had us hack down the stumps with machetes while she changed Chipper's bandages. Later, she drove to Moloka'i Drugs to buy an antibiotic ointment. She told Valdez to replace the damaged fence posts with steel ones and she bought a feeding trough and twenty bags of oats to see the mares through until the winter rains. The fire hadn't touched Fizz's lot but she had me bring Fizz oats so she wouldn't feel excluded.

I watched Ben spill two buckets of oats into the feeding trough. Sandy, Cody, Jetty, and Sparkling Eyes heard the oats fall and trotted toward us. "These mares are spoiled to the max," he said.

"Without oats they could starve," I argued.

"The fire only got a third of our grasslands."

I spilled in a bucket of oats. The mares fought for positions along the trough. They stuck their mouths in and started grinding the oats. My spare bucket was for Old Sissy because the younger mares never made room for her.

* * *

Ben and I were watching hunters shoot ducks on *American Sportsman* when the phone rang. Gramma hustled to the kitchen. Ben turned the TV off and we listened to her gossip about Wilkins.

"Chewing the fat with Sue," Ben said.

She mentioned the bottles of wine and her promise to visit him in Sausalito. She quit talking and all I heard were a few mumbles before she dropped the receiver in its cradle. "No fool like an ol' fool," she said.

Ben turned the TV back on.

Gramma walked in. She plucked matches and a pack of Chesterfields off the table and lit a cigarette.

"What's wrong?" I asked her.

"Nothin'."

"Is it Wilkins?" Ben asked.

She puffed her cigarette and blew smoke. "Ae."

"Wha'd he do now?"

"He found out yo' fathah owns Hale Kia. Last week he married a widow from Saint Helena and now he's managin' her winery."

"El Creepo," I said.

"I know what to do," Ben said.

"Wot?"

"Blow his wine to smithereens."

"Go ahead," she said, "I don't want his damn bottles in mah house."

Ben rushed into the bedroom and lifted the quilt. I snatched one bottle. He took two. We carried them to the stone wall on the beach. We spaced the bottles a foot apart and ran to the lanai. We pulled three chairs up to the storm windows and Gramma huddled down in her favorite chair at the window farthest east. I sat between her and Ben. He pulled the .22 from his case.

"Oldest first," he said.

Gramma slipped on her bifocals and he handed her his rifle. She placed an elbow on the sill and nestled the butt against her shoulder. The brown stock was made of plastic and the .22 seemed like a toy in her hands. She aimed, re-aimed, and finally fired. There was no crack and the bottles were intact on the wall.

"Somethin' wrong," she said.

"Jeff's turn," he told her.

She gave me the gun. I pulled up the barrel and aimed for the middle bottle. I got the rear and front sites lined up and pulled—my bullet ripped through the neck of the bottle and wine dribbled over the wall. The bottle was there but the cork and neck were gone.

"Nice shot," Ben said.

I passed him the rifle, he fired, and a bottle splintered. Wine spurted over the wall and spilled on the sand.

"Good one!" I cheered.

"Gramma's turn," he said.

She left. I heard her rooting around in her bedroom. A bureau drawer opened and slammed.

"What's she doing?" I asked.

"Don't know," he replied, "but she's still a dud."

"You owe me ten bucks."

"For what?"

"Remember our bet about Wilkins?"

"I'll put it in my will," he said.

Gramma appeared at the screen holding her rifle. She swung open the door and walked down the steps. She made her way to her chair but didn't sit.

"How many bullets you got left?" Ben asked her.

"Foah."

"That's it?"

She cranked the lever. The light reflecting off the water made the wooden stock on the .219 glow. She aimed and fired— the bullet blew the third bottle off the wall.

I clapped. "Bull's-eye!"

"That'll fix 'um," she said.

Book Four
Капи

The Hanging Tree

My father arrived at Hale Kia the first day of August. He planned on spending the rest of the summer at the beach house so Gramma put sheets on the pune'e. He hunkered down in the big room and buried himself in work—he edited contracts for clients, scrawled daily chores for Valdez on yellow legal pads, and examined Gramma's charge accounts at stores in Kaunakakai. If he considered a charge extravagant, he'd give her a tongue lashing. She told me arguing was a no-win situation. "He just needs to blow off steam," she said.

*   *   *

I headed for the pasture to check on the horses. The grass had returned to the eastern side and the mares stood under the mango tree. The level in their trough was low so I spun open the valve and stuck my hand under the nozzle. The water was cool. I let it run and walked to the fence. I leaned over the top strand—the steel flexed down and tightened to accept me. It felt good hanging there, with just my toes touching the ground.

The wire felt warm against my bare chest and I followed the red scar of road cutting along the ridge. An orange truck crawled through the pines like a ladybug through pili grass. The hunters had come early for the keys. One was Moki. Gramma was worried her deer were dying off so she'd made him promise never to shoot a doe. Beebe, now senior partner at the firm, had gone up and slaughtered six does during Easter vacation.

Water spilled off the lip of the trough so I ran over and shut the valve. I headed back to the beach house. My father was waiting for the hunters. Hale Kia belonged to him but he wanted locals to think his mother still owned it because they respected her. He equated that respect to fear since they knew she had an itchy trigger finger. He also realized Bobby had friends and, if they found out about the change in ownership, they'd tell him.

Ben was on the front lawn wrestling Leo and Spotty. The dogs took turns charging him and he gripped their snouts and flipped them over on their backs. His blond hair went past his ears and he'd bulked up from lifting weights. We were going to be juniors at Punahou and were both in the bottom half of our class. Neither of us ran with the popular crowd. He stood up and hunched his back like our father. "Now, Jeffrey," he said, "did you water those horses like I told you?"

I saluted. "Mission accomplished, General Gill."

Leo pawed his trunks. He flipped him over and drummed on his opu. "This honay's a momona," he said using his baby voice.

"Moki's coming down," I said.

He rubbed Leo's ears. "Sounded like a war up there."

"Think they got anything?"

"Hope not," he said. "Let's go report to the General."

We walked past the jeep and stood beside the garden. My father was behind the screen door looking through his binoculars. He wore a V-neck with holes and wrinkled khaki shorts. He'd developed poor posture from hunching over his desk at the firm. His habitual slouch made me think of his back as a shell and his hands as claws.

"Second gate?" Ben asked him.

He didn't answer. His hair was greased back with Yardley's Brilliantine and his face sprouted black and white stubble. He didn't own a rifle and never went hiking. He said he'd given up on hunting since he never had any luck tracking deer. My brother considered him a tenderfoot.

"Daddy?" Ben asked.

"What."

"Are they near the second gate?"

He lowered the binoculars. "Get inside."

I followed Ben in and the door closed.

A football game was playing on TV. My father plopped down in his Lazy Boy, put on his glasses, and swung his feet up on the footrest. He drank Miller High Life from a bottle. "God damn 49ers," he said.

Gramma sat at the head of the table wearing her ranch clothes and bifocals. She flicked ashes from a Chesterfield into her tin can. A copy of TV Guide was open with shows circled in pencil. She no longer rolled bales of lauhala. She got a monthly fee from a Hawaiian woman who came with her family to harvest leaves. She had escaped more and more into television, as if the world portrayed on that tiny screen were more important than the real world. Her imagination kept humming right along—she kept seeing Ben in commercials despite my pleadings to the contrary.

"He would tell you if he was on TV," I'd told her.

"Oh, no, he wouldn't."

"Why not?"

" 'Cause he's a sneak."

The only time I was able to distract her from television was when I talked about Chipper. He still had a claim on Hale Kia and, although his acre was hardly desirable, he was connected to the land. I believed this connection kept him going. I knew he liked her—he'd bring her loaves of Portuguese sweet bread and custard pies from Kaunakakai. They were the only two people living year round at Hale Kia and I imagined they took turns visiting one another. I wasn't sure if he was still an alcoholic, but she said he'd cut way back.

A Dallas Cowboy intercepted a San Francisco pass and ran for a touchdown.

"Cowboys all the way!" Ben cheered.

"That Brodie's the bunk," Gramma said.

"It's only preseason," my father replied, "these games don't count."

I sat at the table and searched for the orange truck through the picture window. Moki had once returned with a headless, gutted deer he swore was a spike. Gramma had asked him why he beheaded the spike and he said that made it easier to pack down. "That's no spike," she'd said when he returned to his truck. She was caught between a rock and a hard place—he would just end up poaching if she didn't let him hunt. An angry Moki might burn down the mountain house or poison the mares. He'd married a Duva and she didn't want anyone with ties to that family getting upset.

"Jeff," my father said, "how many shots did you hear?"

"Six or seven."

He finished his beer and belched. "Gramma says twenty."

"Don't worry," Ben said, "they didn't get anything."

"Yeah," I said. "Buncha duds."

"Why duds?" he asked.

"Why would they take all those shots?"

Gramma chuckled. "Keed's gotta point, Normy."

"Time will tell," he said. He peeled the label off his empty bottle and rolled it up into a ball. He dropped the balled up label into the bottle and jammed the cap over the bottle's mouth. "Why the hell didn't they punt?" he asked.

*   *   *

The truck pulled up. Ben and I followed our father out. The dogs lifted their legs over the tires and sniffed the tailgate. A tarp was pulled over the bed. Two men got out of the truck and stretched. They smelled like a day's work.

"Hello, Moki," my father said.

"Long time no see, Mistah Gill," Moki answered. He wore blue overalls and a puka shell necklace. His hair was gray and coarse. He placed a boot on the front bumper and tied the lace.

The driver wore a black tank top. His arms were red and stained with tattoos. He pulled a rifle from behind the seat and slid the bolt action. He had on camouflage pants and a black cap with "Hanoi Hilton" embroidered in gold. An unlit cigarette hung from his lips like a fuse.

Gramma came outside. "Any luck, Moki?"

"A'ole, Brownie," he said handing her the wire loop strung with keys. "Cades hea get all da luck."

Cades put his rifle in the truck. He scratched a wooden match over the truck's roof and carried the flame to his mouth. He took a hit and blew smoke through his nose. I recognized him as the poacher we'd caught all those summers ago. He pretended not to know us.

My father looked at the men as if watching them from a distance, as though he still held up the binoculars.

Cades walked to the tailgate and signaled Moki with his eyes. They rolled back the tarp.

Ben stood on the bumper and I joined him. A buck was lying on its side in the bed. The hide was rust-colored with white spots. The antlers seemed to be made of velvet—I touched one and it felt spongy.

Ben brushed his fingers over the hide. "Where'd you shoot 'im?" he asked Cades.

"In the heart."

"Skin 'um hea, Brownie?" Moki asked.

Cades took off his cap and put it on backwards. "You folks take the hind quarter," he offered.

She put her hands on her hips. She looked at the mountain and back at the men.

"Use that big ironwood near the dump," my father said. "You know the one, Moki."

"Short on rope," said Cades.

"My mo'opuna'll run some ovah," Gramma said. "Come on, Ben."

"Jeff can do it," he said.

My father glared. "You heard your grandmother."

Ben followed her inside.

The men climbed in the truck. Cades fired it up and drove down to the dirt road.

My father muttered something to himself. He walked to the hala tree next to the beach house and peed on its trunk.

*   *   *

The hanging tree marked the western edge of Chipper's property. I'd swung from its branches and felt the scars from the ropes. Now I stood under it watching the truck back up over the ironwood needles. The ground was a shifting puzzle of light and shadow. I heard the ocean but I couldn't see it.

Ben jogged barefoot across the lawn. He held three coils of rope in one hand and a Buck knife in the other. The dogs trotted beside him and he joined me.

"Ever see that guy Cades before?" I asked.

"Yeah," he said. "The poacher."

The men got out and the dogs crowded the tailgate. Ben handed Moki the rope and he tied slipknots at the hooves. Cades tossed the ends over a branch.

My father stood on the grass in the light. "Need any help?" he asked.

"No need," said Moki.

Cades nodded. "Dirty work."

Moki and Cades pulled on the ropes and hoisted the buck out of the truck's bed. There was a snapping sound as the head twisted down and the body swayed. The tips of the antlers made patterns in the needles. The men pulled their skinning knives and the dogs panted. Moki cut the hide at the hooves. Cades did the same. They'd gutted the buck in the mountains but blood still fell. A fly buzzed the carcass. The dogs licked the blood off the needles. Ben ran the blade of the Buck knife over the blond hairs on his forearm.

"Going to mount that head?" my father asked.

"No can, Mistah Gill," said Moki. "Stay one velvet horn."

"He's a beaut," my father said.

Cades held his cigarette in the corner of his mouth and stared at my father. He pulled the hide down over the meat.

"Can I help?" Ben asked.

"Cut da hind quarta," Moki said.

He raised the Buck knife and sawed at the meat. Blood trickled down the blade and fell on him. Leo licked the blood off his feet. The smell of raw meat and blood made me nauseous. More flies came.

My father crossed his arms. He shifted his weight from one foot to the other as they butchered the animal.

"Like hunt?" Moki asked Ben.

"Sure."

"My son's a good shot," said my father.

"Next time," Cades said, "we'll take the boy."

"Would you like that, Ben?" my father asked.

"Yeah."

Cades slipped his knife into the chest cavity and carved through the cartilage. "What kinda gun you got?" he asked Ben.

"A .270."

"That's a good gun," said Cades.

Ben had killed his first buck earlier that summer. But the buck only had one antler and the antler was small. He'd fired from the mountain house to the opposite ridge and I helped him pack it down through the gulch. Gramma called it "Ben's one-horn trophy."

Ben hacked through the hind quarter. Meat fell and Leo gobbled it up. "My blade couldn't cut butter," he said.

"Mine's like a razor," Cades said and handed him his knife.

Ben jammed the blade of the Buck knife into the trunk. He resumed cutting with Cades' knife. "Now this is more like it," he said.

Flies came in swarms. Cades twirled the end of a rope but they kept coming. The flies were blue and it became a frenzy of wings.

"Cheesus," my father said.

"No worry, Mistah Gill," Moki said. "We wash da meat."

"I'll get a hose," my father volunteered. He walked to the water pipe next to the shack, picked up the end of the hose, and slung it over his shoulder.

A door squeaked and Chipper appeared. He wore an undershirt and pajama bottoms. "Wot's this monkey business?" he asked from the porch.

"Oh, hello, Chip," my father said, "just borrowing your hose."

Chipper rubbed his eyes and watched the men.

"Give you some meat?" my father asked.

"I'm sick of venison," he answered. He flung his screen

door open and let it slam behind him.

I was mad at my father for not getting permission. He didn't own all the land yet and he acted as though he did. I left the hanging tree and headed for the swamp.

"Jeffrey," my father called, "help Daddy wash the meat!"

I jogged through the sour grass along the bank. The grass stung my legs. I followed a narrow path through the naupaka until I reached the ocean. I put my hands where the water was clear and washed my face. I put my feet in and felt clean.

I wondered what the men were talking about. My father was probably running me down. "That kid's a damn sissy," I imagined him saying. It would get back to Gramma. Even my mother would know when she returned from Boston.

"Hey, Peanut!" Ben said. He ran along the path holding the Buck knife and he jumped on the sand. Blood had spattered his arms, chest, and shoulders. "How 'bout that Cades?" he asked.

"Pretended not to know us," I said.

"I'd like to gut 'im."

"Did you see the General dragging that hose?"

He washed the knife in the ocean. "Notice he didn't help with the buck?"

"Yeah," I said. "How come?"

Ben snickered. "He didn't wanna get his li'l hands dirty."

Telling Futures

My father received a phone call at the beach house saying there was big trouble at the firm. "Another god damn emergency," he said. Seniority had dictated his rise to partner and that meant more responsibility. He considered the associates too stupid to handle serious situations so he had us take him to Hoolehua Airport with two weeks left in August. On the drive west, my father talked about how Uncle Chipper had refused his offer of venison.

"That guy's damn peculiar," he said.

"Maybe he's turned vegetarian," I suggested.

"That'd be the day," my father replied.

*   *   *

I'd been guilty of sophomore slump at Punahou and was eager to change things my junior year. I was also curious about Mindy Birch. Gramma was chopping water cress when I asked her to read my cards.

"Can't read no mo'," she claimed.

"How come?" I asked.

"God took mah powah."

"True power never leaves."

"Who says?"

"A psychic on *Merv Griffin*."

The blade nicked her finger. "Gunfunnit," she said.

I followed her to the bathroom. She held her finger over the pedestal sink and blood fell in the basin. I found a Bandaid in the medicine cabinet and wrapped it around her cut.

"Wot you wanna know?" she asked.

"Does Mindy Birch like me?"

"Silly business," she said.

*   *   *

I kept bugging Gramma to read my cards. I bugged her morning, noon, and night. I bugged her from the J. Akuhead Pupule morning radio show to *All My Children* at noon to *Channel 2 Eyewitness News* at night. One morning she carried a knotted yellow scarf into the big room. She sat at the table, untied the knot, and pulled out a deck of playing cards. The edges of the cards were worn and some were so wrinkled that they'd started to crack. I told Ben to come inside and we flopped on the pune'e.

"Who's first?" she asked.

"Ben," I said.

"You're just chicken," he told me.

"Am not."

"Chicken of the Sea."

She frowned. "You keeds wanna readin' or not?"

He got up and sat beside her.

Gramma shuffled the cards and he cut twice. She made

three piles. She placed the pile that came from the bottom on top and gathered up the other two. She smacked down a pair of queens and surrounded those with eight more cards. She lit a Chesterfield and blew a puff of smoke that rolled over the table. "Queen of Spades and Queen of Clubs," she said.

"So?" he asked.

"You like two dahk wahines."

"Is that true, Juicy?" I asked.

"Maybe."

"Will Ben go steady?" I asked.

"No."

He frowned. "Why not?"

"Spades surround the queens. Spades spell trouble."

"Two girls in the bush," I said, "none in the hand."

"Shutup, Peanut. What else does it say?"

She contemplated the cards. "Wish doesn't come true."

"Will I shoot another buck this summer?"

"No."

He stood up. "These cards are bogus."

"Men traveled miles for mah readings."

"Big deal."

Gramma puffed her cigarette. "Was a big deal back then."

"They liked listening to your drunken lies."

"Wot you mean, 'drunken?' "

"Weren't you and Chipper big alchies?"

"Who told you that?"

He plucked the binoculars off the table. "Everyone."

"Who's everyone?"

"Joe Leong and Ah Pong for starters," he said looking

up at the mountain through the binoculars. "A Hawaiian lady at the luau said you drank like an ugly old mullet dying of thirst."

"I'll have you know I was once the most beautiful woman on Moloka'i."

"You were the only woman on Moloka'i."

She tapped her finger on the table. "At least I wasn't a li'l sissy like you."

"You were too busy being a drunk."

"C'mon, Ben," I said, "cool head."

He put the binoculars back.

She raked up his cards, put them in a pile, and placed the pile on the bottom of the deck. She shuffled and took another drag off her Chesterfield. "You'll never shoot a buck big as Charlie," she said.

"You were in the right place at the right time," he replied. "Even my mother coulda shot him."

"Yo' muthah neva pulled a triggah in her god damn life."

He chewed his lower lip. "You're right," he said, "but she was never a slut like you."

She puffed her Chesterfield and flicked the ashes into her tin can. "How's yo' one-horn trophy?" she asked. She winked at me and chuckled. She kept chuckling and went into a coughing fit.

He walked across the Oriental rug. He opened the screen door to the lanai and headed down the steps.

"Look up on that wall," she called after him, "then you'll know what a real buck looks like." She smashed the tip of her Chesterfield against the bottom of the can. "Come sit by Gramma," she told me.

"Quit egging him on," I replied.

"Yo' bruthah can take it."

"Remember last summer in the mountain house?"

"Ben was bluffin'," she replied. "Do you wanna readin' or not?"

"No."

"Then go turn on Gramma's set."

I got off the pune'e, turned on the TV, and walked out to the lanai. Ben was leaning against a window sill.

"Ignore her," I said.

"I know something she didn't predict," he replied.

"What's that?"

He dragged a chair over the tiles. He stood on the chair, reached up, and grabbed Charlie's massive antlers. He pulled but Charlie didn't budge.

"Are you nuts?" I whispered.

He pulled a second time and Charlie didn't move. On his third try, the head tilted and the tip of an antler banged the frame of a seascape. I hopped on his bed and righted the painting.

"Wot's that noise?" Gramma called from the big room.

"Nothing," I answered.

"Don't sound like nothin'."

He put all his weight into a fourth pull—nails hit the floor and the trophy fell in his arms. Charlie's nose was against his chest as he climbed off the chair. He slung the antlers over one shoulder and lugged Charlie out the back door.

Gramma stood at the screen. "I heard somethin'," she said.

"Juicy's taking Charlie to the beach," I told her.

She rushed out to the lanai. "Ben," she said. "Ben!"

He reached the shore and kept going. He powered through the shallows in his T-shirt and trunks and churned past an anchor pipe one hundred yards out. The dogs ran to the water's edge and barked.

"That god damn devil," she muttered.

I plucked Ben's telescope off the ledge behind his bed, propped its tripod stand on a sill, and adjusted the focus—my brother was chest deep in water. Charlie's chin rested on his shoulder and it seemed as if he were taking a pet deer for a swim.

"He's gettin' it this time," she said.

"It's only a dumb deer head," I replied.

She went inside and returned with her .219 and three bullets. She loaded the bullets into the magazine and cranked one in the chamber. "He's plumb run outta luck," she said.

"You've flipped your wig, Gramma."

"Yo' no hunta," she snarled, "you don't undastand." She brought the barrel up and fired a warning shot.

"Jesus!" I said.

Leo and Spotty scrambled under the beach house.

I used the telescope—Ben was closing in on the deep end of the harbor. He carried Charlie to the edge of the reef, raised him over his head, and tossed him in. Charlie bobbed on his plaque and his antlers dug into the water. He seemed anchored in place, his marble eyes gazing back at Hale Kia. The current skirting the reef caught him and he floated west through the deep water.

"Peanut," Gramma said, "go save my Charlie."

I quit looking through the telescope. "I could get caught

in that current and drown," I told her.

"Yo' fathah would."

"What about sharks?"

"Yo' nothin' like yo' fathah."

Ben followed the reef in along the edge of the harbor. He stumbled over a coral head, dove in the water, and swam for shore.

She brought up her rifle. I made a grab for the barrel and she shoved the tip into my chest. "Stay cleah," she warned, "this is between me and Mistah Ben."

"You wanna shoot your own grandson?"

"This all started a long time ago," she replied, "and today I'm ending it."

"Ending it? Ending it how?"

"You'll see."

Ben reached shore down from Chipper's shack, pulled off his wet shirt, and ran into the forest.

Gramma returned to the big room. She plopped on her lauhala hat and headed out with her rifle. I went after her. She hustled over the lawn between the beach house and the cottage. She checked the dirt road, scanned the pasture, and took a sand path cutting through the ironwoods. The forest smelled like pine and doves cooed in their nests.

"You're just going to scare him," I said, "right?"

She eased over a fallen tree and studied a footprint in the sand. "Damn keed's got luau feet," she muttered.

We were near the graves of Abigail and Skippy when she spotted Ben. He was talking to Uncle Chipper. Chipper had on his green cap and jeans. Gramma raised her rifle. Ben saw her and ducked behind Chipper.

Chipper turned. He held a bouquet of gardenias. "No, Brownie!"

"Step aside, Chip."

Chipper pleaded with her to put down the rifle and she told him to move. He continued pleading and she finally lowered the gun.

"Yo' safe," Chipper told Ben.

He stepped out into the open. "Knew the bitch wouldn't shoot," he muttered.

Gramma raised her rifle and fired. Doves flew from their nests. Ben sprinted past the hanging tree and ran for the dump.

Chipper just stood there looking at us. The gardenias fell and his knees buckled. He dropped beside Abigail's grave.

*   *   *

It's strange how you can wound someone you love without meaning to. It's stranger how the wounded can forgive. Maybe true love can never be extinguished in the soul of a man living off memories. Chipper was face down beside the cross I'd made for Abigail. We rushed over and turned him on his back. His cap rolled off. He had a chain around his neck with a gold band attached to it. "Flesh wound," he mumbled spitting ironwood needles. The bullet had entered his forearm, missed the bone, and passed clean through. Gramma pulled the bandanna off her lauhala hat and pressed it against the wound. Blood soaked through the bandanna so I ran to the beach house to get a roll of duct tape. She pulled off the bandanna and wrapped duct tape around his forearm. We rushed him to Moloka'i Hospital. A doctor sutured his forearm and gave him a transfusion. He told Officer Duva he'd shot himself cleaning his rifle. Officer Duva looked at Gramma suspiciously. Chipper was home in his bed the next morning with my grandmother hovering over him like Florence Nightingale.

*   *   *

Ben broke into the saddle room and lived there the final week of August. He kept his rifle loaded. Gramma left meals on the saddle room's doorstep on her way to see Uncle Chipper. His final meal was shrimp curry with mango chutney and she'd wedged an apology note between a slab of coconut cake and a bottle of Coca-Cola. He told me she wasn't sorry and that he was mad at himself for wasting so much time over the years trying to please her. He said she was wrong about his future and that he was going to get his driver's license and ask Monica Apianni to go steady. We joked about Charlie. I told him that surfers had probably seen Charlie bobbing in the waves and thought they'd gotten some bad pakalolo. Despite our kidding around, I sensed his fear and knew he would never spend another summer with the woman who tried to kill him.

*   *   *

My grandmother's accidental shooting of Chipper had an unexpected consequence—instead of creating a permanent rift, it brought them together. She did all of his shopping in Kaunakakai, including picking up his prescriptions at Moloka'i Drugs. She visited him three times a day. She changed his bandages, brought him meals, and gave him a daily sponge bath. They watched *Hollywood Palace*, *Mannix*, and *The Lawrence Welk Show* on his new Trinatron. She hid his okolehao and only let him drink a glass of wine with dinner. He suggested hiring a girl. She told him he was her responsibility.

I left Moloka'i that summer feeling bad about what had happened between Gramma and Ben. But I was glad she was devoted to Chipper. Sometimes good things are born from tragic situations. I knew now they'd be more like a couple and I said a prayer for them as our plane flew over the ranch and away from Moloka'i.

Puko'o Fishpond

Ben took a job in Honolulu with Mahuka Roofing the summer before senior year. Gramma seemed relieved he hadn't come to Moloka'i but I knew she missed him too. She said it felt funny not having him with us. She framed a picture of Ben posing with his rifle and imagined him in more and more commercials. "Isn't that Mistah Ben?" she asked squinting at the tube. One night she convinced herself he had a guest role on *Mannix*.

Gramma had placed an ad in the *Moloka'i Action News* offering fifty dollars and a half-dozen spiny lobsters for the return of Charlie. Nobody responded so she purchased a buck's head from Narakiro to replace him. The new buck had smaller antlers and a bigger nose but nobody noticed.

I spent June and July helping around the ranch. The machete became my best friend as I cut off dead fronds and branches on trees around the beach house. I took long swims in the deep water past the point and speared manini in the coral near the harbor. Gramma wanted me to learn how to drive so she gave me lessons in the jeep. It was strange having her sit in the passenger seat while my hands were on the wheel. I wanted to impress her with my driving skills but I had a bad habit of popping the clutch. We drove Kam Highway and, when I turned into Hale Kia, I forgot to apply the brakes coming down the incline and tore through a fence.

*   *   *

My father owned the Puko'o Fishpond, an oceanfront site he'd purchased for five thousand dollars at an auction on foreclosed properties. He wanted to turn the fishpond into a resort. He became partners with a Canadian investment group and they hired Sam Fong Construction to knock down the stone walls and fill in everything with sand and coral dredged from the ocean. He'd convinced the Canadians that tourists would flock to Moloka'i to escape the madness of Waikiki.

I accompanied my father to Puko'o the first Sunday in August. I sat in the suicide seat of Gramma's jeep while he sped west. Rust had eaten holes the size of quarters in the hood and fenders. The muffler delivered a sporadic ratta-tat-tat. My father wore leather sandals, khaki shorts, a striped shirt, and a lauhala cowboy hat. A knotted shoelace secured the hat to his chin. He drove in the middle of the road, cut turns sharp, and grazed the roadside brush. There was no pause in him, just push-push-push. He zipped by a station wagon with its headlights on. "Fool doesn't know day from night," he said. He believed most people were "just plain stupid." Surviving battles in the South Pacific and making it through Harvard had swelled his brain to godlike proportions. He believed he knew everything about every subject. He knew more about psychology than psychiatrists, more about medicine than doctors, more about stocks than brokers, and more about running the country than Presidents. I asked him if he believed in God and he said no, but that religion was beneficial since it saved husbands the cost of sending their wives to shrinks.

"What's the most important thing in life?" I asked as we drove west.

"Security," he replied.

At first I thought that was a pretty good answer. Then I realized he hadn't said "love." I wondered if my mother abandoning him every summer for Boston had something to do with him not valuing caring and affection. Maybe he figured if he were broke she would never return.

"Now, Jeff," my father said, "I want you to take more of an interest in Puko'o."

"I'm interested," I said.

"Not like your brother."

We swerved right to avoid a rock in the road. Ilima branches swept across the paint and whipped my jeans.

"Ben really cares," he continued.

"Ben hates Puko'o."

"Then why does he ask me so many questions?"

"To kiss your okole."

"It shows he's concerned. It's like pulling teeth getting you to come along."

"I'm here, aren't I?"

"I can tell you don't wanna be." He braked for the curve at Buchanan Fishpond and the jeep squealed like a pig. Ducks

waddled the pond's mud banks. It was here Gramma had seen
the Squid Lady, a blonde woman with the body of a squid,
running across the road. She had a dream she was riding a
swimming horse when the Squid Lady surfaced and tried pulling
her off. She grabbed a machete and lopped off her head.

My father stared at the pond and we drifted across the
yellow line. A truck barreled straight at us.

"Cheesus!" he said cranking the wheel.

The truck swerved and there were shouts but he kept
going. "This road's too narrow for these damn trucks," he said
and pushed his glasses back with his thumb.

We entered a dark stretch through a kiawe forest. This
was where the kahuna Lanikaula had been buried. A branch
dragged along the jeep and a thorn stabbed my thigh. Blood
soaked up through the denim.

"You and Ben," my father said, "both have your mother's
brains."

"She's smarter than you think."

"Punahou sent me your IQ scores. You're both way below
average."

"Dean McQueen said we couldn't study for it."

"Neither of you has the smarts for law school."

"Who says we wanna go?"

"Go ahead, be a ditch digger."

"Digging ditches isn't all there is."

"That's right," he said, "you'd make a great clerk."

"What's your IQ?"

He adjusted his side view mirror. "In the one-fifties."

"Is that genius?"

"Practically."

He said my low IQ, combined with my lazy streak, was a sure fire formula for disaster. The future seemed bleak by the time we reached the outskirts of Puko'o. It was routine for him to search for weaknesses in Ben and me and make us aware of our shortcomings. He said giving us everything had destroyed our drive and ambition.

We swerved off Kam Highway and, after a dip, the tires grumbled over a coral road. He braked hard in front of a gate, plucked a wire loop of keys off the shifter, and handed me the loop. "Open it," he said, "the big brass key."

I got out and unlocked the aluminum gate. The chain fell in the coral. Bulldozers, end loaders, and dump trucks surrounded a Quonset hut behind the gate. The construction boss used the hut but nobody worked on Sundays. It was a ghost camp. Barrels of oil were stacked beside the hut. A barrel with its top cut off was stuffed with bottles and cans. I swung the gate open.

"Lock it behind you," he said driving through. The tires kicked up coral dust that stung my eyes.

I retrieved the chain and fumbled with the padlock. The gate felt flimsy compared to the mountain gates. My father watched me in the side view mirror. I finished and strolled to the jeep. The heat made me angry. I knew I could hurt him by bringing up Lani. I slid into the jeep and dropped the loop over the shifter.

"Something wrong?" he asked.

"No," I answered.

"You move like a slow motion person."

"So how come I keep beating you at swimming?"

"Next time we're racing," he said, "lemmee in on it."

He floored it through the mounds of coral and sand dredged from the ocean. The mounds would be used for landfill. Weeds and lantana flourished in the mounds. The mounds gave way to a coral desert. The coral was bleached bone-white from the sun. Nothing lived in the desert, not even weeds.

We drove beside a canal used for runoff. My father didn't want water spilling over the banks and flooding Kam Highway because he might get sued if there was an accident. The canal was low and choked with algae. A bald tire was stuck in the mud and polliwogs swam in schools around a dead hau tree. Dragonflies skimmed the canal's surface. As boys, my father and Bobby had helped Gramma and her friends drag a hukilau net from one end of the pond to the other. They'd caught hundreds of mullet and weke and she threw a luau on the beach at Puko'o. Everyone on the east end had been invited, including the Duvas.

"This canal stinks," I told my father.

"It'll be buried," he replied.

We turned south and headed for the ocean. Blue lagoons glowed beyond the coral. A wall flanked the middle lagoon. My father had used stones from the fishpond to build the wall. He planned on pumping in sea water and spilling it down the wall to flush the lagoons. "It'll work like a toilet," he'd said, "keep things fresh."

We parked beside the wall and climbed out. He pointed to an oblong boulder propped on top. "That big boulder," he said, "know what it is?"

"The Naha Stone."

"Don't be a wise guy," he said. "It's a you-know-what."

"What's that?"

"A penis," he laughed, "a giant penis."

"It's your Phallic Rock."

"That's right." He stacked loose stones at the base of the wall.

The boulder that was supposed to be a penis stood guard over three lagoons. The lagoons formed a cloverleaf marina. It had taken three sets of steel teeth from a dredge to carve them out of the reef because the teeth kept breaking. Sarah had told Gramma the project was cursed.

The shores of the lagoons were powdered with golden sand. I walked the manmade beach while my father worked. You couldn't please him if you tried to help so it was best to leave him alone. I dug my heel in the sand. I remembered Silva, the Portuguese trucker with the bum leg who'd hauled sand from the west end. Ben and I had helped Silva by climbing his rig and rolling back the tarp. Silva had rewarded us with "hamburgah sandwiches" he bought at Dairy Queen. When my father had found out the sand was stolen, he washed his hands of the matter. "None of my business," he'd said, "I'm the innocent buyer." The stealing of sand had occurred the previous summer, when my father paid Ben and me minimum wage to build ripraps for the lagoons. The stones for the ripraps had come from the fishpond walls.

I looked toward Maui and saw a boat gliding for the lagoons. It floated low in the water. "Daddy!" I called.

He continued placing stones. "What?"

"Someone's coming."

Two men were in a fiberglass boat with poles mounted on either side. The man up front looked Hawaiian and the driver was Japanese. They drank Olympia beer in cans and both had long hair. Their poles flexed as they trolled the banks of the lagoon.

"Who in hell," my father said. He waded until the water reached the bottom of his khaki shorts. The brim of his hat bent back in the breeze. "Kapu," he said as his shadow spilled on the beach, "private property!"

The man up front held a hand to his ear.

"Can't hear you," I told my father.

He took off his hat and waved it as if shooing away flies. "No trespassing!"

The man turned and said something to the driver. The driver shifted gears on the outboard and the boat idled. They reeled in their lines and the engine belched exhaust.

He put his hat back on. "Kapu," he continued, "get the hell out!"

The driver said something to the man up front. The waves edged the boat closer. I saw their red fuel tank and the black line feeding the outboard. They were twenty feet offshore.

"Wot?" the man asked from the bow.

"You're trespassing!"

The man stood. He wore a Ski Hawaii shirt and his trunks went below his knees. I guessed he had some haole blood. He finished off his beer. "Like one good whippin'?" he asked.

"This is private property."

"No ack."

"I'm warning you."

The man crushed his can and threw it in the lagoon. It bobbed like a float. The tide worked the hull against the coral and there was a scraping sound. The impact caused the man to lose his balance and he sat back down.

"I'm calling the police," my father threatened.

The man swung one leg over—he was in the water wading for shore.

My father retreated to the stone wall as he approached. "Look here," he said, "I don't want any trouble."

"You get one big mout'," the man said.

"And you're breaking the law."

"Billy," the driver called.

He looked back. "Wot?"

"Leave 'um alone."

"Why?"

"Dat punk's one lawyah. He make sue job."

The man stopped a few feet away from my father. He was Billy Duva. Years had gone by since he'd slaughtered the spike in the ocean and, besides growing his hair long, he'd gained some weight. His hand came up and struck my father's face. The cowboy hat came off and his glasses went flying.

"Fockin' lawyah," Billy said, "dis Hawaiian land."

My father held one hand over his cheek. He dropped to his knees and picked up his hat. He put the hat on his head and dug through the sand searching for his glasses.

I approached Billy from behind.

The driver whistled.

Billy turned. "Wot," he told me, "you like beef?"

I wanted to run. But I couldn't stand seeing what he'd done. "Right now," I said holding up my fists.

Billy kept his hands low. He was only a little taller than me but was heavy with muscle and fat. I knew he was waiting for me to lead so he could counterpunch. I threw a right at his jaw that he dodged. I came in closer and threw a combination— my right missed again but the left struck him just below the throat. Billy rushed me. He rammed me like a linebacker and I fell to the sand. He lifted me up and tossed me in the water. He stood on the beach with his hands clenched.

"Next time," Billy told me, "you go hospital." He waded to the boat, placed both hands on the hull, and pushed it free. He lifted himself over the side and the boat returned to the harbor.

"Jeff," my father called, "help Daddy find his glasses."

I got out of the water and helped him search the sand. My jeans were soaked. I kept an eye on the lagoon but the boat was gone. I found the glasses between two stones in the wall. A lens had cracked. I handed them to my father.

"Christ," he said. He put on the cracked glasses and walked to the jeep.

"I'm sorry," I told him.

He slid into the driver's seat. "Let's get the hell outta here," he said and adjusted the rearview mirror.

We followed the tire tracks through the coral desert. Heat waves shimmered over the landfill. I opened the gate and we headed home. Everything felt wrong about the day and there was no going back to make it right. It made me feel funny my father had killed the soldier who stabbed him but couldn't defend himself. He's older now, I thought. Older and weaker. And I wasn't strong enough to fight off his enemies.

"Wish I had Ben's rifle," I told my father.

"What for?"

"To shoot that bastard."

"They coulda had a gun on that boat."

I cursed myself for not standing by my father's side when Billy came on shore. But it had all happened too fast. We reached the curve at Buchanan Fishpond and my father took the turn slow.

"Did Gramma ever tell you about Billy Duva?" I asked.

"What about him?"

"He was in her bedroom."

"I know."

"I wanna kill him."

"Now, Jeff," he said, "you don't wanna ruin your life killing a bum like that."

"It'd be worth it."

"Going to jail is never worth it," he said.

I gazed across the channel at Maui—a black plume was rising from the fields. They were burning the cane. My father shifted gears and I felt close to him. I wasn't sure how much of the Billy story he knew but I suspected he felt powerless like me. There were so many things in my grandmother's life that I wanted to fix. My father sped up and drove in the middle of the road. The jeep rumbled over the wooden slats of a bridge and two boys leaned against the railing. One hitchhiked and the other peeled a mango.

"Hui!" the hitchhiker said.

My father waved.

"Wot?" the boy with the mango said. He gave us the finger and the other boy laughed.

I wanted to stop and push them off the bridge. I was bigger than them but Billy was bigger than me.

Being fair was the last thing on my mind.

Book Five
Under the Kamani Tree

Wailau Valley

My father talked Gramma out of attending our graduation from Punahou. He thought her presence might trigger an avalanche of well-wishers with family ties, such as Bobby and Donna. He'd worked hard to keep his half-brother and a trio of uncles at arm's length and didn't want a happy occasion wrecking his estrangement.

Ben was relieved Gramma didn't show, but I felt bad not having her in the audience at the Honolulu International Center when I went up for my diploma. It was as if I didn't have a grandmother at all and all the summers we'd shared on Moloka'i were nothing more than meaningless vacations.

*   *   *

I flew to Moloka'i after graduation while Ben worked for Mahuka Roofing. I spent my time trimming trees and taking care of the dogs and horses. Valdez was still working but his days of heavy labor were over. He was content raking, weeding, and mowing the lawn. Sometimes Gramma made us tuna sandwiches and I'd have lunch with Valdez under the Norfolk.

Gramma liked snacking on green mangoes dipped in soy sauce, red chili peppers, sweet onions, and rock salt. She'd get ono for barbecued fat. I'd toss steak fat on the hibachi, cook it crispy, and serve it over rice. I told my father over the phone that barbecued fat was bad for her health. He said to let her eat as much as she wanted. He suggested I grill some for Chipper too.

Gramma wanted to paint again so we scoured the beach house for her supplies. We found stiff brushes and old tubes of paint stashed in a rusty Folgers Coffee can in the wash room. I spotted an easel and a blank canvas wedged in the wash room's rafters. She mixed colors in pickle jars and set up her easel. She sketched a meadow with fences and I helped her outline mares and stallions.

I drove her down to Chipper's every morning after the J. Akuhead Pupule radio show. She always brought him leftovers. We'd sit on his porch and they'd talk story about all their wild times on Moloka'i. I think the stories they shared made them feel young again.

*   *   *

I was two weeks away from leaving for the University of Colorado when Ben called asking if I'd explore Wailau Valley with him on the north coast of Moloka'i. I made arrangements for our trip knowing this would be our last chance to bond before our paths diverged. I felt bad for Ben. My father had told him he "wouldn't amount to a hill of beans" without a college degree. But any empathy I had for my older brother was tempered knowing he hated me for doing exactly what our father wanted.

*   *   *

The highest sea cliffs in the world were on the north coast. Wailau was only accessible by boat and only in the summer. The swells were too dangerous the rest of the year. The cliffs were sheer rock with blue swells slamming against them. Instead of beaches, there were narrow walkways of shattered lava. Getting stranded there during the winter months would be deadly. If you tried making your way along a walkway, you'd get knocked off by swells pounding the cliffs. If you tried going straight up, you had to scale one thousand feet of jagged lava. Gramma said a shark trail ran from Makanalua Peninsula to Wailau and that tiger sharks cruised the edges searching for goats that had fallen. I imagined climbing a cliff—I'd place a bloody hand over the top and, not having the strength to pull myself over, fall a thousand feet into the blue abyss.

*   *   *

Ben told me he'd pitch a pup tent in the ravine on the mauka side of Hale Kia. I warned him about the 'uhane. He laughed and said he'd suck all the sap from the kiawe trees to starve them out. His encampment wasn't visible from the flatlands. I hiked up with leftovers and found him in his tent wearing fatigues and combat boots.

"Howzit, Juicy," I said.

He climbed out holding his .270 rifle. He saw my paper plate covered with foil. "Wha'd you bring me, Peanut?"

"Chop suey over rice."

He rested his rifle on a boulder. "Bitchin."

I handed him the plate and fished out a plastic spoon from my pocket. He peeled off the foil, sat beside the tent, and wolfed down the chop suey. His dirty blond hair fell past his shoulders. Fellow roofers called him "Jesus." He spat out a water chestnut and it rolled down the hill.

"Ono?" I asked.

"Onolicious."

"Gramma has your picture framed."

He scooped up meat, bean sprouts, and rice with the spoon. "Don't tell that bitch I'm here."

"She misses you."

"I don't miss her. How's Chipper?"

"Pretty good," I said. "He's gotta garden and grows corn."

"Bet he's raising pakalolo."

"Gramma thinks you're in the new Zippy's commercial."

"Oh, yeah?"

"You're a blond surfer who orders shrimp tempura."

He finished the chop suey and licked his fingers. "Where does she think you are now?"

"Fishing past the point."

"Good."

"Leo and Spotty miss you."

Ben folded the paper plate in half and then in quarters. His fingers were yellow with calluses. "I love those dogs," he said.

*   *   *

Spida Kaimikaua picked me up at Hale Kia in a red Ford truck with a missing front bumper and a cracked windshield. He was a wiry man with glasses and deep lines in his face. Silver sparkled in his black hair. He wore a long sleeve Ocean Pacific shirt and denim shorts. A pink scar ran the length of his right leg from a hunting accident he wouldn't discuss. He tooted when we reached the public road.

Ben walked out to Kam Highway in his fatigues. "Howzit, Spida," he said.

"Eh, Big Boy!" he replied. "Get planny room in back."

Ben climbed into the bed and we drove east through the high meadows of Pu'u O Hoku Ranch down to Halawa Valley. We passed a green church with white trim and abandoned cars ensnared in vines. The road ended and he parked on a hill above a black sand beach.

"You haoles get baggies?" Spida asked.

"Under my fatigues," Ben said.

"Hemo da clothes."

We stripped down to our trunks and waded to a cream-colored boat anchored offshore. *Betsy* was painted in magenta on the boat's side. We had packs with sleeping bags slung over our shoulders. The barrel of a rifle poked out of the top of Ben's pack and he carried a fiberglass pole. I'd left my pole at the beach house. I didn't want to challenge him in any way, especially knowing how bad he felt for not getting into UH. He lifted himself over the boat's side and I followed. A green sea turtle surfaced and gasped for air.

"Why'd you name your boat *Betsy*?" Ben asked Spida.

"Dat's mah uncle's sistah's niece," he said climbing in, "on mah faddah's side."

"You must really like her," I said.

"Nah. I like da name."

The outboard had a faded green bonnet. A mottled black

hose connected the outboard to a blue tank. One of the propeller blades had a chunk missing. "Think we can make it?" I asked.

Spida lifted the tank. "Planny gas."

"What about the engine?"

"Dis one Evinrude, brah," he said patting the bonnet. "Sixty horse stay inside."

Ben ran his hand over the gunwale. A section had been repaired with duct tape. "This is had-it," he said.

"Get too close to da cliffs," Spida said, "pay da pipah."

A tennis ball was crammed in the drain at the bottom of the boat. "Where's the regular plug?" I asked.

"Wot, boddah you?"

"No."

"You haoles no miss one trick, eh?" Spida cranked the starter cord and the engine purred. "Garans ballbarans we make 'um," he said and took the seat next to the outboard. "Pull da ancha, Big Boy!"

Ben pulled up a chain rope and placed a triangular anchor on the bow. Spida powered us into the open ocean. Limu boiled up behind *Betsy*. The water changed from green to blue and we headed toward the leper colony at Kalaupapa. Cape Halawa blocked our view of Maui. Moloka'i's Makanalua Peninsula looked like the shore of another island. We rode through swells that buffeted the lava cliffs. Waves pounded us and water splashed into the boat.

"You guys like haole chicks?" Spida asked.

"Sure," I said.

"I get one t'ing fo' Filipinas. No can help."

"They're juicy," Ben said.

"Get da bess okoles." Spida cranked the wheel and we curved away from the cliffs.

I saw lava just below the surface—a cliff had fallen into the ocean.

"Unreal," Ben said. "There's a mountain down there."

"Planny boat smash up ovah hea," Spida said, "den come da shahk."

Swells crisscrossed in front of us and *Betsy* lifted up and slammed down. The water was up to my ankles. We continued along the cliffs, where storm birds roosted in the lava crevices.

"Let's troll," Ben said.

Spida slid open a panel. "Get feaddahs," he said and showed us an assortment of feathered lures. The steel leaders were tangled and he handed them to Ben. Spida dug for lines in a compartment near the engine. The swells rebounded off the cliffs and came at us as waves. *Betsy* rocked violently. We hit a valley and the propeller whined.

Ben gripped the side of the boat. "Whoa!"

"*Betsy* doin' one hula!" Spida joked.

"Forget about trolling," I said. "Let's just get to Wailau."

*   *   *

The sea cliffs folded in and gave way to a bay. Hala, wiliwili, and loulu palms dotted the hills. Three thousand Hawaiians had lived in Wailau before Captain Cook. "Leprosy came," Gramma'd said, "and every otha damn disease." The few surviving Hawaiians lost their taro when the tsunami swept through the valley in 1946. Wailau was deserted. Spida said only twenty tourists had visited that summer. He told us how he'd laid net one night the width of the bay and, when he woke the next morning, the floats were all bunched.

"Tigah shahk stay inside," he said.

"How big?" Ben asked.

"Mo' longa dan *Betsy*."

"How'd you get the net back?" I asked.

"No can," he said. "I let 'um drif'."

We motored past a tiny atoll and headed for a stone beach.

"Da end of da line," Spida said shifting to neutral. "You haoles gotta wade in."

I looked down and saw stones blanketed in green limu. Convict fish skittered by.

Ben put one leg over the side. "Any sharks?"

"See da fin firs', Big Boy."

Ben slid in and the water reached his chest.

I handed him his pack and pole. I went feet first and the water was up to my neck. I stood on a stone, Spida passed me my pack, and I swung the strap over my shoulder. I waded in behind Ben.

"See you haoles foah days time," Spida called. He shifted gears and *Betsy* puttered along the shore before heading into the deep blue.

The bay was calm and the water turquoise. Purple parrot fish swam near my feet. On shore, waves splashed the stone beach. Two canvas tents ringed by a low stone wall had been set up in a clearing.

"Somebody beat us over," I said.

"Tourists," Ben replied.

A woman walked out of a tent. Her hair was reddish-brown and down to her waist. She wore a pink bikini top and a

white sarong. She saw us and put her hands on her hips. I
wondered where her man was and figured he was hunting in
the valley or catching prawns upstream. The wind came up and
blew her sarong open. Ben stumbled on a stone and fell in the
water. He got up wincing.

I helped him steady his pack. "You okay?"

"Yeah," he said.

"Eh, brah," I said, "you wen spahk dat wahine?"

He squinted. "What wahine?"

"Da one stay on da beach with ehu hair. Cute, no?"

"What's she doing here?"

"Waitin' fo' you, brah."

The woman retreated to her tent and knelt at the entrance.
We closed in on the beach and she stood up. "Howzit!" she
waved. " 'Membah me?"

"Uh, oh," Ben said.

The woman's lilting voice sounded familiar and I realized
she was Kimmi, a transsexual who'd worked for Gramma. She
was different now because, back then, her hair was bobbed.
Kimmi was really an Asian man but she did everything possible
to disguise it. Her features were delicate so the illusion was not
difficult. She'd developed breasts from daily shots of estrogen
and was planning a trip to Sweden for a sex change.

Once, after she had finished styling Gramma's new
bouffant wig, she approached Ben. "Get sweet toot'?" she'd
asked.

"I'd rather eat sweets than meat," he'd said, "and I love
meat."

"Bake you one pie," she'd promised.

298

KIRBY WRIGHT

Kimmi had baked him custard pies and lilikoi cakes and even mango petit fours. Ben had plumped up that summer and Gramma gave her a selection of old bras, panties, and even her salt-and-pepper wig.

"Can dye da wig?" she'd asked.

"Shoot yo' pickle," Gramma'd said.

Kimmi dyed the wig platinum. She looked like a blond Beatle at the Fourth of July Parade in Kaunakakai. Ben and I sported fern-and-berry wreaths around the crowns of our cowboy hats and, as we escorted Gramma, we crossed paths with her. Besides the wig, Kimmi wore a sleeveless white top, gold lamé shorts, and platform zoris with cork heels. She had to rush to the Pie Eating Contest to put out pies.

"Cute li'l breasts," Gramma'd commented as she bounced away.

I'd nudged my brother in the ribs. "Someone should enter her contest."

"I'm not hungry," he'd said.

Now, after years of estrogen, Kimmi had the hourglass shape of a woman. Any man would think she was a model. She waded out and lifted up her sarong. Her legs were long and tan. "Ben an' Jeff," she called. "How Auntie Brownie?"

"No ka oi," I said.

We reached shore and Kimmi hugged us. She invited us over to a tent carpeted with a quilt of orange ginger lilies intertwined with pink hibiscus. The tents belonged to her and, since she was alone, she said we could have the one without the quilt. She'd cleared stones and stacked them to form a barrier three feet high that encircled the tents.

"Protec' from wild boah," she explained stroking her hair. A diamond sparkled on the ring finger of her right hand.

"There's boar here?" Ben asked.

"Big kine tusk."

We thanked Kimmi and I followed Ben over to the second tent. He lifted the flap—the ground was hard and filled with small pebbles. We placed our packs against a canvas wall and unfurled our sleeping bags.

Ben pulled jeans from his pack and put them on over his trunks. "Wanna go exploring?" he whispered to me.

"Sure," I said. "Shouldn't we invite Kimmi?"

"No."

*   *   *

We hiked up to the falls through the emerald leaves of wild taro. The taro claimed the valley floor. We followed a path covered with Surinam cherries and Chinese plums. The cherries and plums were fermenting and they gave off a pungent odor. Ben spotted two goats grazing on a ridge.

"Tomorrow," he said, "I'll bring my rifle."

"We don't eat goat."

"I need the practice."

"Shoot coconuts."

"Coconuts don't bleed," he said.

We hiked along the edge of the river. The entire basin was stone. We reached the eight-foot walls the Hawaiians had built to designate districts. The walls ran parallel to the river and stretched north to Olokui, the mountain looming ahead. We continued and the valley closed in on us. We entered a kukui nut grove and a brown nene goose ran for cover. We made our way through a forest of tree ferns and monkey pod trees. Orange fungi shaped like fans grew on the trees. The falls got louder and the stones turned to boulders. An offering to the gods was perched on a boulder—four small stones wrapped in a taro leaf. We came to a clearing where tiny rainbows arced in the mist. We hiked over a final cluster of boulders and stood before a black pool. Water cascaded down from a gorge two hundred feet above. The lava on either side of the waterfall was draped in a mesh of tuberoses, hyacinths, and orchids.

Ben climbed up on a boulder and pulled off his combat boots.

"That pool's deep," I said.

"How do you know?"

I walked to the edge. "No reflection."

He striped down to his trunks. "What do you think the General's doing right now?"

"Yelling at someone in the firm."

"They must hate him there."

"He says all the secretaries want his bod."

"Those wahines get paid to kiss his okole," he said. "But you know what?"

"What?"

"I'm going to beat 'im at his own game."

"What game?"

"The money game. He thinks I can't make it without college."

"How much do you make now?"

"Five-forty an hour. But I'll be supervisor next month."

"Do supervisors make kala?"

"Yeah, and I'll start my own company, just wait and see." He hung his toes off the edge of the boulder and dove in head first. He surfaced and swam to the far end of the pool. "Cold!" he said. The pool was fringed with white ginger and the green bulbs of night-blooming cereus.

"Can you touch bottom?" I asked.

Ben dove down. It seemed like minutes before he came up. "Couldn't find it," he said.

"It's bottomless."

"Don't look now, Peanut, but your momona girlfriend's right behind you."

I heard rustling and turned—a huge sow foraged near a tree fern. Six piglets battled for nipples. "Gramma wants a greased pig," I said.

"Careful she doesn't charge."

"She doesn't have tusks."

"Are you pupule? She'll rip off your balls with one bite."

I made the Sign of the Cross. "Go in peace," I told the pigs, "the Mass has ended."

"Thanks be to God," he said.

*   *   *

We returned to the stone beach at sunset. We were starving after swimming the falls and hiking Olokui. Ben had wanted to keep going until we found the source of the falls but I convinced him starting dinner was more practical.

He dug through our packs inside the tent and held up a can. "Cling peaches."

"For dinner?" I asked.

He held up a second can. "Vienna sausages."

"Let's catch prawns in the river."

"With what?" he asked. "Our bare hands?" He picked up a can of pork and beans, found his opener, and worked it around the can.

"Peachy keen," I said, "now we're Cub Scouts."

He popped the top and sauce leaked out. He licked the sauce off the side of the can. "Better than starving."

"Drop your line."

"I need prawns for bait."

"Use sand crabs."

"Where's the sand?"

The flap of our tent lifted. Kimmi peered in. She wore a red apron over a white top with spaghetti straps and paisley clam diggers. "Like join me fo' dinnah?" she asked. "Get planny kaukau."

"Sure," I said.

"Should we bring anything?" Ben asked.

"No need."

Kimmi fired up a Coleman stove next to her tent and put a pot of rice over the flame. A bag of prawns sat on a butcher block beside the stove. She flipped opened a cook book. "You folks like sweet an' sou-ah coconut fried prawns?" she asked.

"Love 'em," Ben said. "Mind if I use one of those prawns for bait?"

"Help yo'self."

He baited a hook and set up his pole for dunking. Ten minutes went by and the warning bell rang—he ran over the stones to check for a strike.

It was getting dark so Kimmi lit a propane lantern

perched on a driftwood table. She rubbed white coconut meat against a grater. "T'ink Ben catch?" she asked.

"The wind's making that bell ring," I said.

She finished grating and stir-fried the prawns with ginger and garlic in her wok. The aroma was intoxicating. She made her sweet and sour from plum sauce, brown sugar, pineapple juice, and rice wine vinegar. She turned off the stove and poured the sweet and sour over the crispy prawns. The sauce bubbled in the wok. She sprinkled grated coconut over everything.

"You're the Galloping Gourmet of Wailau," I told her.

She opened the rice pot and steam rose like a phantom above the tent. "Da rice stay perfec'," she said, "hot an' sticky."

"We go eat!" I called to Ben.

She served her sweet and sour prawns in koa bowls. I let the sweet and sour soak into the rice and scooped up mouthfuls with a plastic fork. The prawns were the freshest I'd ever had.

"You should be head chef at Hotel Moloka'i," Ben told Kimmi as she sprinkled coconut on his second helping.

"I no like," she said.

"Why not?" I asked.

"I only like cook fo' friends."

After dinner, she took off her apron and we exchanged ghost stories. I told her about the Squid Lady that Gramma saw in the road at Buchanan Fishpond. "Eight legs just goin' it," I said, "then the Squid Lady stops at the edge of the road, gives Gramma the evil eye, and jumps in the pond."

"Auwe," she said rubbing her bare shoulders, "you wen

geev me da kine chicken skin!"

"Gramma was probably drunk," Ben said.

Kimmi told us spirits lived in the black pool at the falls. The force of the falls prevented the spirits from surfacing.

"Were those your stones in the taro leaf?" I asked her.

"Why? You wen touch?"

"No."

"Dat's mah off'ring."

"Offering to who?" Ben asked.

"Pele, Lono dem."

He smirked. "I thought you were Catholic?"

"I is."

"Catholics can't worship Hawaiian gods."

"Can," she said, "free country." She told us about a boy whose auntie had hiked with him to the falls to go swimming. The auntie tied a small stone to the end of a ti leaf when they got to the pool. She placed it in the water to see if the mo'o, a spirit dragon, was hiding in the water. The ti leaf kept spinning in the pool. "No can go in," the auntie said. "Get mo'o." The boy dove in anyway. The auntie waited for him to surface but he never came up. She heard his cries as the water fell from the falls into the pool below.

"Try listen close," Kimmi said, "dat boy still cryin' fo' his auntie."

"That's funny," Ben said, "I didn't hear anything."

"He dove in without doing that ti leaf trick," I told Kimmi.

"Tomorrow," she said, "you make off'ring."

He laughed. "I made shishi in da waddah."

"You hewa," Kimmi warned.

*   *   *

The next morning, we borrowed Kimmi's 'opae sticks—
two bamboo sticks joined by a piece of small-eyed net.

"You catch," she said, "I cook."

"You shouldn't be cooking for us," Ben said.

"I like," she said. "Dat's mah t'erapy."

We found prawns hiding under submerged leaves and
in the hollows of sunken logs. We took turns inching the sticks
along the river bottom, cornering the prawns, and scooping them
up. We also gathered the clam-like hi'iwai clinging to stones.
Kimmi gave me a big aluminum pot and I simmered the hi'iwai
over a fire on the stone beach. I added limu kohu from the ocean
and rock salt I'd found on the lava near the tide pools. She
brought out a jar of Chinese black beans and spooned some in
the pot.

"Goin' broke da mout'," she said.

I stirred the mixture with a kiawe stick. "Think so?"

"Mo' bettah dan Pau Hana Inn."

*   *   *

Ben and I lived in our tank tops and trunks. Every
morning we'd wake in our tent to the aroma of prawn meat
pancakes and crispy fishcake rolls. We'd roll up our sleeping
bags and pick papayas and apple bananas off trees near the river
and join Kimmi for breakfast. At sunset, Ben would reach into
the burlap bag he kept submerged in the river and snatch a live
prawn. He'd just laugh if the prawn bit him. He'd thread a
hook through its body, swing his pole, and hurl the hooked
prawn into the ocean. But, despite our location, he hadn't caught
anything the first two nights.

"No more fish in the ocean," I said on our third night.

"Patience," he replied.

"Maybe they're sick of prawns."

"What would you use instead?"

"Vienna sausages."

He baited his hook. "I can't believe any university would take you."

I followed him to the shore and watched him drop his line. The waves were three feet but ten-foot swells smashed into a lava pinnacle at the edge of the bay. The salt air smelled good. He wound the reel until the line was taut and slipped the end of the pole into the plastic barrel of a sand spike. He wedged the spike between two stones and attached a copper bell to the tip of the pole.

The bell rang early that evening. I shined a flashlight as Ben ran along the stones. The pole flexed with life and the bell fell in the water. He pulled the pole out of the plastic barrel and tightened the drag. "Tell Kimmi bring the lantern," he said.

I hustled to the tent. "Kimmi!"

"Wot?"

"Ben needs more light!"

She snatched the lantern. We ran to the shore and watched him battle the fish—he stood on stones with his legs spread for balance. The light from the lantern turned the water to liquid glass and I spotted the silvery blue body of an ulua zigzagging as it tried throwing the hook. Its dorsal fin cut the water like the fin of a shark. The pole whipped up and down.

Kimmi ran to the water's edge with the lantern. "You wen catch!"

"Not yet," he said.

He pulled the ulua close to the stones and I thought the fight was over. But the ulua saw the stones and ran with the line. The pole flexed down and the reel whined as the ulua disappeared into the black water. He tightened the drag. His biceps bulged as he held the pole and guided the ulua to shore. It saw the stones but made a shorter run. He pulled hard—the fish came out of the water and flailed on the stones.

Kimmi placed the lantern beside the ulua. It was blue on top and silver at the sides. The red gills were like feathers and the tail flapped furiously. The hook was embedded in the side of its mouth.

"Nani!" she said.

Ben jiggled the hook.

"Looks like a forty-pounder," I said.

"Fifty!" said Kimmi.

He extracted the hook and the ulua made a sound like a porpoise. "I wanna mount that tail," he said.

"I cut fo' you," she said and picked up the lantern.

Ben held the ulua by the tail and I carried his pole. We headed back and Kimmi placed the lantern on her driftwood table and ducked inside her tent. She returned with a copy of *Cousin Popo's Island Cooking*. She sat beside the lantern and hunted through the pages. She stopped turning and checked out a recipe. "Hea," she said.

"What?" he asked.

"Fried ulua in da kine ginga shoyu sauce."

"Ono," he said and placed the fish on the driftwood table. I handed him his pole and he returned to the river to get another prawn for bait.

Later, when the smells of ginger and shoyu mixed in the twilight and we'd stuffed ourselves with fried ulua, something big hit. Half of the line on the reel was gone by the time Ben reached the pole. I aimed the flashlight as he examined the frayed catgut and hairline cracks in his fiberglass pole. Kimmi ran over the stones with her lantern.

"Musta been a shark," he said.

I nodded. "Now with a hook in its mouth."

"Pua t'ing," Kimmi said.

"Whatever it was," he answered, "that hook'll kill it."

*   *   *

On our final day, Kimmi painted her fingernails the same shade as the orange ginger lilies in her quilt. She took us up a hill thick with ilima bushes. She wore a green one piece and did a swan dive one hundred feet down into the bay. "Jump when da swell come!" she called from below.

Ben sat beside a tiny loulu palm. "You jumping?" he asked me.

I clung to an ilima bush. "Maybe a little lower."

"What's on the menu tonight?"

"Baked Ben in Buttah Sauce."

"She's still got ulua."

I squeezed my belly with both hands and shook the fat. "I'm gaining weight in Wailau."

"Me too."

"No sked 'um!" Kimmi said.

He slid his way to the edge and dangled his feet over. He pressed his palms to the lava and pushed off. "Bonzai!"

I heard him land in the water.

"Good kine!" Kimmi said.

I retreated to an outcropping of lava twenty feet lower. A swell moved in but I waited too long. A second swell came— I sprung feet first and fell behind it. I entered the ocean and my feet hit the lava bottom. I kicked off the lava and propelled myself up. "Ya-hoo!" I said when I surfaced.

Nobody was there.

Ben and Kimmi were deep in conversation on the beach.

*   *   *

At dusk, Ben dug through the canned goods in our tent. He wanted to give Kimmi a gift for all her cooking. He rummaged through my pack and two cans fell out. "How 'bout pear halves?" he asked.

"She's more of a pork and beans girl," I replied.

"Funny."

"You gave her the ulua, isn't that enough?"

"Pa'a the waha."

"Why?"

"She's right outside," he whispered.

Kimmi lifted the flap. She wore a white bikini top and a jade skirt. Her belly was muscled and tan. "You boys sick of prawns, seafoods, li'dat?"

"Why?" Ben asked.

"I get Spam."

"I could barbecue it," he offered.

She licked her lips. "I stay way ono fo' Spam."

Ben started a fire with kiawe branches he'd found at the high tide line. The kiawe made its own charcoal. He placed a mesh of chicken wire over the coals while Kimmi teased her hair with a koa Afrocomb. Her ehu hair sparkled as she ran the comb through it. Ben opened cans of Spam and cut the slabs into slices.

I stirred a pan of hi'iwai and Chinese black beans over a slow fire.

Kimmi lit the propane lantern. "You folks goin' hele in da mornin'?"

Ben flipped the Spam on the mesh. "Gotta get home for work," he said. "Gotta make kala."

"I need to trim coconut trees at Hale Kia," I told her.

She smiled. "Good to help Auntie Brownie."

Before our dinner of barbecued Spam and hi'iwai in black bean sauce, Kimmi took out a bottle of brandy and glass snifters.

"Jeez," Ben said, "you've got everything in that tent."

She handed us glasses and poured the brandy. "I get big kine confession."

"What?" I asked.

"I been to Sweden."

I raised my glass. "A toast to Kimmi," I said, "you're a woman now."

She giggled and our three glasses converged. After our first sips, she showed us how to drink brandy.

"Lif' 'um wit' da tongue," she said, "den push 'um agains' da gums, above da front teet'."

"Where'd you learn that?" Ben asked.

"Stockholms."

We did as she instructed and watched the moon rise over Makanalua Peninsula, where the lepers lived. Lights flickered on their coast. Ben finished grilling the Spam and I served the hi'iwai in coconut bowls.

"Unreal," he said after tasting the hi'iwai.

"Bettah dan sweets?" Kimmi asked.

"Almost."

"Get papaya cake fo' dessert."

He slurped and lowered the bowl. "I'll save some room."

We finished the hi'iwai and Spam. Then we polished off hunks of papaya cake. Ben asked Kimmi what she was doing in Wailau. She said the first half of her life had been a lie and she needed to come to Wailau to decide the best way to spend the second half. She held her diamond ring up to the lantern. "See dis?"

"That's a rock," he said.

"Stay one gif'." She told us she'd been a stripper in North Hollywood after her trip to Sweden. The ring was a present from a client, a celebrity who begged her to be his kept woman. She'd refused and he beat her. She tapped her front teeth with an orange fingernail. "Dese not fo' real."

"Did he know about Sweden?" I asked.

"Aftah I tell 'um, he like me mo'."

"Was it Burt Reynolds?" Ben asked.

"Mums da word," she said and held a finger over her lips.

A moth the size of a half-dollar landed on my forearm. It unfurled its tongue against my skin. The tongue was used for sucking nectar from flowers. Two splotches on its wings resembled eyes and pink stripes ran along its opu. I turned my arm so the moth was upside down.

"Careful," Kimmi warned.

"It won't bite," I replied.

"Go blind if get da dust from da wings in yo' eyes."

"I shoulda brought Raid," Ben said.

I held my forearm close to the light. The moth retracted its tongue and wiggled its antennae. "That dust thing's an old wives' tale," I said.

"I stay old," she replied, "but no stay one wife."

"How old are you anyway?" Ben asked.

"T'irty foah."

He shook his head. "That's not old."

The moth fluttered its wings and flew straight at the lantern. It hit the hood, looped back, and brushed Kimmi's leg.

"Owie!" she said and swung at the moth.

The moth flew off into the darkness.

"He go falls," she said. "Get da kine night-bloomin' cereus fo' eat."

"I'm going moemoe," I said. "Mahalo for the Spam, Kimmi."

She smiled. "You so welcome, Jeff."

Ben yawned and stretched. "I'll be along," he said.

*   *   *

Ben wasn't in the tent the next morning. His sleeping bag was still rolled up against the canvas wall. I didn't smell prawn meat pancakes or crispy fishcake rolls. I left the tent and hopped from stone to stone across the beach. The tide was high and half the beach was gone. Waves broke thirty feet out and rolled in white. Swells slammed the lava pinnacle. It was overcast and my head ached from drinking brandy. Ben's sand spike was wedged in the low stone wall and his pole leaned against Kimmi's tent. The line was reeled in and the hook looped through one of the pole's eyes. Fish scales gleamed like sequins on the sand beneath the driftwood table. I spotted Ben. He was sitting on a kiawe stump next to the river. I walked over and joined him. He seemed lost in thought and hurt somehow.

"You all right, Juicy?" I asked.

"You'll never believe it," he said.

"Believe what?"

"Guess who Kimmi likes."

"Who?"

He picked up a stone and hurled it at the river. "Spida."

*   *   *

After our boat ride back to Halawa Valley, Spida drove us to Hale Kia in his truck. I rode in the cab and Ben sat in the bed. Spida offered to drive him to the airport but he said he'd find his own way. We got out beside the pasture.

"Laydahs," Spida said and continued west on Kam Highway.

The roadside brush was powdered with red dust. We hung our backpacks on kiawe fence posts. Gramma's hand-painted KAPU NO TRESPASSING sign was nailed to a kukui nut tree and the black letters had faded to gray. This was the same spot we'd waited for the tsunami to hit.

Ben pulled something wrapped in ti leaves from his backpack—it was the tail of the ulua he'd caught in Wailau. He examined it for a second and tossed it over the fence.

"Wha'd you do that for?" I asked.

"Hauna," he said.

"How you getting to the airport?"

"Hitchin'."

"Let me take you in the Scout."

The bicep on his right arm flexed. "No," he said. He plucked his backpack off the post and slung it over his shoulder. The rifle's barrel and the tip of his pole poked out of the top. "You're the lucky one, Peanut."

"How am I lucky?"

"You get to go away."

"Go with me."

"And do what?" he asked. "Shovel snow for a living?"

I looked over the flatlands. The dogs jogged the dirt road and ran through the pasture. "Here come your pals," I said.

"Honays," he called. "Now you come hea, honays!"

The mares ambled toward the water trough and the dogs raced past them. Leo and Spotty scampered to the fence, squeezed under the bottom strand of wire, and jumped up on Ben. They rolled over on their backs and showed him their bellies. Both of their muzzles had turned gray and one of Leo's eyes had clouded over.

He drummed their bellies with his palms. "Momonas!" he said.

I spotted a blue station wagon heading west. It rumbled over the bridge at Kainalu Stream and the dogs got up and wagged their tails. Ben held out his thumb and the station wagon stopped. A faded Saint Joseph's statue was on the dash and fuzzy dice hung from the rearview mirror. The driver was Jesse, the man who sold painted coral at the roadside stand. He wore a Harvard T-shirt and polyester pants. Big Ruth sat in the passenger seat. Her hair was down and she smiled at Ben. I waved at her and she gave me a halfhearted wave back.

"Wheah to?" Jesse asked.

"Airport," Ben said.

"I go Maunaloa."

"Righteous," he replied opening the rear door. Jars of raw opihi took up half the rear seat. He placed his pack next to the jars and extended his hand. "See you, Peanut."

"Aloha, Juicy," I said and we shook.

He climbed in and sat beside the jars. The dogs yipped and I held them by their collars. The station wagon cruised west along the mauka fence and vanished in the kukui nut forest.

Epilogue

I let the dogs go and headed through the long blades of pili grass. Sandy, Sparkling Eyes, and Old Sissy took turns at the trough. Beyond the pasture was the beach house. My grandmother was like that house—strong and resilient, ready to stand up to whatever adversity rolled through the flatlands. I walked past the mango tree, slipped through the fence, and jogged to the front lawn. I guessed Gramma was watching the soaps in the big room. She wasn't there. A note on the table said to come down to the shack.

I left my pack on the lanai and walked toward the swamp. The dogs followed. Shadows from the trees spilled over the road and I remembered my summers on the Lonely Isle. Gramma was more of a mother than a grandmother to us. She'd been tough and direct but that was what helped her survive the challenges on Moloka'i. She had showed us a world of love and hate, generosity and greed, forgiveness and retribution. We'd learned to respect and defend the land. But I ached knowing she'd run out of summers to make things right with Ben.

The Scout was parked next to the jasmine in Chipper's yard. A painting was in the bed—the horses we'd sketched had become wild mustangs standing on a sunset ridge. The fence was gone and the meadow was now a pine forest. The sun bathed the mustangs in pink light.

The dogs reached the swamp. They lapped at the water and jogged the banks. The shack's corrugated roof had turned rust orange. New coconut trees were sprouting up around the shack and even in the dump. The coconut trees that had been burned in the house fire survived to become towering giants that formed a canopy of palms over the orange roof.

Gramma and Chipper sat at a picnic table under a kamani tree drinking iced tea from tall glasses. A coconut cake glistened on a crystal platter. He had on a short sleeve shirt, jeans, and a porkpie hat. His gold band was on his ring finger. I'd never seen the hat before and I guessed he'd bought it in Kaunakakai. The table they sat at had washed up on the beach earlier that summer and I'd dragged it over to his lawn. He'd replaced the two missing slats and gave the table a cherrywood finish. It looked brand new.

"Pehea 'oe?" Chipper greeted me.

"Maika'i," I replied. "Are we celebrating something today?"

"Life," Gramma said holding up her glass, "to a long, long life." She wore denims, cowboy boots, and a green blouse she'd ordered from Liberty House. Her bifocals were folded on the table and I noticed she had on her wedding band.

"Wailau no ka oi?" he asked picking up a yellow pitcher

and pouring iced tea into a fresh glass.

"Yeah," I said. "We dove off the cliffs and hiked to the falls. Ben caught an ulua."

Gramma lowered her eyes. "Mistah Ben's on Moloka'i?"

"He's on his way to the airport," I said. "He bummed a ride with Jesse."

"Fo' the luva Pete."

Chipper handed me the glass and I gulped the tea down. It was ice cold and had a lemon zip.

"I miss my Ben," Gramma said.

Chipper nodded. "Me too."

"Oh, Chip," she said, "I plumb forgot. Gotta paintin' fo' you in the Scout."

"Paintin'?"

"That's right."

"Wheah in the world do I hang that?"

"Wheah any ol' fool can see it," she replied and placed her hand over his.

That afternoon was my last visit with Chipper Daniels. I had never had better iced tea or coconut cake and the day seemed suspended in time. I had given up hope that I could ever bring Chipper and Gramma together but in a small way I had. I wasn't predicting wedding bells or anything. It was enough they were sharing the day and had learned to put enough of the bad things behind them to remember the good. Ben and I weren't going to be around anymore and it was great they had each other. Chipper told me about taking the steamer over from Oahu and how he prayed the whale they'd seen marooned on the lava pinnacle wasn't a bad omen. He admitted he'd made a lot of mistakes in life but that marrying my grandmother wasn't one of them. She told Chipper he was full of hot air. I knew he'd pleased her. It made me feel good to hear them talk about the early days at Hale Kia and all the years they'd shared as a couple.

That's when I realized love is a tough, ever hopeful thing, not easily destroyed.

Glossary

ae: yes

aholehole: small, silvery fish found in brackish water

ahupua'a: land division from shore to mountain

ai ya: damn

aina: land

aiwaiwa: mysterious

akamai: smart

akua: ghost

akulikuli: herb with long narrow leaves and white flowers

ali'i: chief

aloha: hello, goodbye, and love

a'ole: no

aumakua: family or personal god often represented as a fetish

auwe: my goodness

awa: root used to prepare a narcotic drink with healing powers

Aysoos: Jesus

balut: duck egg with fetus

beah: beer

beef: fight

bess: best

boddah: bother

bolohead: bald

broke da mout': delicious

bufo: toad

bumbye: soon enough

chicken skin: goosebumps

chy: try

da kine: meaning depends on context of conversation

dirty lickings: a beating

ehu: reddish tinge to dark hair

fut: fart

garans ballbarans: guaranteed

geev: give

geev 'um: give it one-hundred percent

hala: pandanus or screw pine

hale: home

Hale Kia: home of the deer

hana: work

hanabata: phlegm

hana hou: one more time

hanai: raised by extended family, typically the grandparents

haole: white person

hapa haole: part Hawaiian and part white

hapai: pregnant

hau: tree with impenetrable thickets found along the coast

hauna: stink

haupia: coconut pudding

heiau: altar

hele: go

hele mai 'ai: come eat

hemo: take off, remove

hewa: wicked, sinful

hi'iwai: freshwater clam

ho: wow

holoku: seamed dress with yoke

howzit: how's it going

huhu: mad

hui: hello

hukilau: encircling a bay with a net and dragging both ends

hukilau net: long net with rope attached to either side

ilima: shrub with strong whip-like branches but delicate flowers

imu: underground oven using steam to cook food

inamona: relish made from the kukui nut

kahuna: priest, sorcerer, wizard

kai make: super low tide

kaka: to fish for ulua with hook and line but no pole

kala: money

kalua: steamed underground in an imu

kama'aina: local

kamani: large shoreline tree with white flowers

kanaka: person with Hawaiian blood

kane: man

kapu: forbidden, sacred

kaukau: food

keiki: child

keiki manuahi: illegitimate child

keiki o ka aina: child of the land and the sea

kia: deer

kiawe: Algaroba tree known for its thorny branches

koa: strong lustrous wood used to make canoes

kolohe: rascal

Kona weather: humid and still

kua'aina: country bumpkin, idiot

kukae: excrement

kuku: weed with clumps of sharp burrs

kukui: Candlenut tree

kuleana: small homestead, half-acre or less

kulikuli: be quiet

kulolo: pudding made from steamed taro and coconut cream

kupuna: elder

ku'u ipo: sweetheart

lauhala: leaf of the hala tree used for weaving mats

laulau: pork or fish steamed with taro tops inside ti leaf package

lawe aku: take away

laydahs: see you later

lehua: flower or the tree itself

li'dat: like that

lilikoi: passion fruit

limu: seaweed

limu kohu: red seaweed found past the reef

loi: taro paddy

lolo: crazy

lomilomi: massage

Lono: Hawaiian god of war

loulu: indigenous Hawaiian palm

luau: party featuring a meal of poi and kalua pig

luau feet: big feet

luna: straw boss

mahalo: thank-you

mahimahi: delicious fish found in island waters

mahu: gay

mai nani i ka ulu i waho, a'ole nau ia ulu: the breadfruit is out of reach

maika: Hawaiian game similar to bowling

maika'i: good

maka piapia: grit that collects in the eyes during sleep

makai: ocean side

makas: eyes

make: dead or death

malasada: Portuguese donut

manini: surgeonfish with black and yellow stripes

manju: tightwad

manong: Filipino

manuahi: illegitimate

mauka: mountain side

mo': more

moemoe: sleep

mokihana: a green cube-shaped fruit

Moloka'i Nui Ahina: great mother of Moloka'i

momona: fat

mo'o: spirit dragon

Mo'o Ali'i: shark god

mo'opuna: grandchild

Naha Stone: lifted by Kamehameaha to prove his royal blood

nani: beautiful

nano no i ka ulu i ke alo, nau ia ulu: the breadfruit is right in front of you

naupaka: soft green bush fringing the Moloka'i coastline

nene: endangered Hawaiian goose

niho palaoa: ivory hook on necklace of human hair

no ack: don't act up

no ka oi: the best, finest

no sked 'um: don't be afraid

'o'io: bonefish

'O'io: Night Marching ghosts of Old Hawai'i

okole: ass

okolehao: liquor distilled from the ti root

okole kala: stingy

ono: delicious

ono fo': hungry for, have a thing for

'o'o: iron bar used for digging

'opae: freshwater shrimp

opihi: limpet attached to shoreline stones

opu: belly

owama: baby goatfish found schooling near shore

pa'a the waha: shut your mouth

paipo: belly board

pakalaki: bad, unlucky

pakalolo: marijuana

Pake: Chinese

pala'a fern: lace fern

palaka: checkered blue and white shirt of block-print cloth

paniolo: cowboy

papio: juvenile skipjack

pau: finished

pau hana: work's done

pehea 'oe: how are you

pehea 'oe i ke ea la kakahiaka: how are you this morning

Pele: Hawaiian goddess of fire

pikake: Arabian jasmine

pili: thick, pliable grass

pilikia: trouble

pipi kalua: beef cooked in an imu

poha: gooseberry

pohaku: rock or stone

Pohakumake: the Death Rock

poi: pudding made by pulverizing the taro root

poi dog: mutt of mixed blood

poke: hors d'oeuvre made with raw tuna

pololi: hungry

popolo: black

pua: poor

puhi'u: fart

puka: hole

pune'e: bed that doubles as a couch

pupu: hors d'oeuvre

pupule: crazy

Pu'u O Hoku: Star Hill

shishi: pee or in the act of peeing

shoots: okay

shuah: sure

skebbe: dirty old man

spahk: see

stay: is, are

talk story: chat, gossip

tapa: cloth made from the bark of trees

taro: root of this leafy green plant is pounded to make poi

ti: plant with narrow leaves that protects from bad spirits

uhaloa: root of this flowering weed makes a healing tea

'uhane: day ghosts with the power to kill

ulu: breadfruit

ulua: skipjack

ulu maika: stone used like bowling ball

'um: her, him, them

wahine: woman or girl

wana: black sea urchin with long, poisonous spines

weke: goatfish

wiliwili: spiny tree with a short, thick trunk

wot: what

yo': your, you're

About the Author

Kirby Wright was born and raised in Honolulu and graduated from Punahou School. He was an Arts Council Silicon Valley fellow and has degrees from the University of California at San Diego and San Francisco State University. He has been nominated for two Pushcart Prizes and is a past recipient of the Ann Fields Poetry Prize, the Academy of American Poets Award, a pair of Browning Society Awards for Dramatic Monologue, and three San Diego Book Awards. His writing has appeared in literary reviews, magazines, and anthologies around the world. This is his second novel.